UNFAITHFUL

BOOKS BY NATALIE BARELLI

NATALIE BARELLI

UNFAITHFUL

Bookouture

Published by Bookouture in 2020

An imprint of Storyfire Ltd.
Carmelite House
50 Victoria Embankment
London EC4Y 0DZ

www.bookouture.com

ISBN: 978-1-80019-095-5
eBook ISBN: 978-1-80019-094-8

CHAPTER 1

I wake up too early, too hot, my legs entangled in the sheet. I dreamt of something stressful, something to do with missing a flight or losing my passport. Then there was a ladder that didn't quite get up to a top floor and was swaying dangerously.

It's the phone ringing that pulls me out of the dream. I reach for it quickly so as not to wake Luis, my pulse still racing.

"Hello?"

"It's me."

I raise myself on one elbow. "Alex? What time is it?"

"I don't know. Five? Six? I need to see you."

Beside me Luis stirs.

"I'll have to call you back."

"When can you come?"

He has that urgent tone, the way he speaks when he wants my attention, immediately. It's not even six in the morning and I'm exhausted already. "I don't know, Alex. I have a meeting this morning. I'll come after."

"No! You have to come now!"

"Alex, I can't. I'll come later, as soon as I'm free, all right? What's going on, anyway?"

He sighs into the phone. Or maybe he's smoking. He says he doesn't but I've smelt it on him often enough. Dope, mostly. "I'll tell you when you get here. Bring the notebooks with you."

"All of them?"

"Yes. It's important, Anna. Bring them, okay?" He hangs up. I turn to look at Luis who is sleeping beside me, one arm flung above his head, calm as smiling Buddha. I bet he's not dreaming of swaying ladders and missed flights. I kiss his bare shoulder and he doesn't even stir. Nothing can wake up Luis, except Luis.

"Who was that?" he croaks.

"Sorry, I was hoping you were still asleep. That was Alex."

"Of course it was. Can you ask your students not to call in the middle of the night, please?"

He turns on his side and I push playfully against his back. "It's not the middle of the night, it's six a.m." I can hear the birds outside, and there's a sliver of dawn light slipping around the edge of the blinds.

"I was up late," he mumbles.

"I know." I rub my face with both hands. I may as well get up. "You want me to bring you a cup of coffee?"

"No, thank you."

Downstairs, Roxy greets me by dropping a chewed-up toy at my feet. We go through our usual routine where I stroke her head and she rolls on her back, exposing her pink belly for me to scratch. She's a French bulldog and technically she's Mateo's dog. I let her out the back door and into the yard, then turn on the coffee machine. While I wait for it to warm up I empty the dishwasher, change the water in Roxy's bowl, open a bag of dog food and scoop some into her food bowl.

All the time I am thinking about Alex, analyzing how he sounded just now, what it might mean. Alex is my best, brightest PhD student. He's a genius, really. I've never had a student like him before. He's on the cusp of publishing something extraordinary, and my job with him is to make sure he gets there in one piece.

Sipping my coffee, I open my laptop to go over my notes. First thing this morning is a faculty meeting. We're facing an uncertain future, and I suggested to Geoff about getting together a fundraising committee weeks ago. I did it to make a good impression, to show that I'm a team player and full of good ideas. Geoff agreed to my suggestion—he almost always does. Geoff is the chair of the mathematics department and what Geoff thinks matters. Especially as any day now I will find out if my full professorship application has been successful. I am pretty confident. Or I'm trying to be, anyway. Part of me feels that if I don't get it after all the extra work I've been doing, I may as well give up. Those of us who applied in the department expected to have heard by now, but this year there's only one full-time position because of our budget cuts and it's taken longer than usual. Nail-bitingly longer, you could say, but still, I'm cautiously optimistic.

I go back upstairs to shower and get dressed into my usual meeting attire: linen skirt and pearl-colored blouse. Professional but feminine. I clip on a pair of small diamond earrings—not real diamonds, we do all right but we're not that rich—and fasten a silver necklace with a small heart-shaped pendant around my neck, a gift from the children for Mother's Day.

In the mirror I catch Luis watching me from the bed, one arm bent behind his head. He's frowning.

"What's wrong?" I ask.

"You look… conservative. Like a school teacher."

"I am a school teacher."

"You know what I mean."

I smile and reach for my lipstick—*Desert Rose*—and stare back at my reflection. My mother's voice pops into my head, unbidden. *Look your best to do your best!*

I close my eyes. Why did I have to think of my mother now? Now she's going to be like an elephant around my neck all day—or is it an albatross? Whatever. A big cumbersome weight dragging me down, making me feel inadequate, reminding me that I'm not quite living up to my potential. Unless I don't let her. *Easier said than done*, I think, as I run a brush through my hair.

"Where are you off to, anyway?" Luis asks.

"Faculty meeting, remember?"

"Oh yeah," he says, but I know he doesn't. I pick up the bottle of perfume he bought me for my birthday, Lancôme's *La Vie est Belle*, and I spray a cloud at the base of my throat.

Geoff at work commented on the scent once: "Is it you who smells so delish?"

Delish. It seemed so suggestive. Sometimes I think if I were willing—which I'm not, at all—but if I were… I used to think he was kind of handsome for an academic, with his dark gray messy curly hair, swept back and reaching down his neck. He wears glasses, thin-rimmed ones, and has a graying beard that makes him look like Neil Gaiman.

Luis rubs his knuckles over his head and throws off the covers.

"Why don't you stay in bed?" I say.

"That's okay." He yawns. "I'm awake now. I'll be in the shower."

On the way downstairs I pass by Mateo's room. He's still fast asleep, his Batman-themed comforter thrown onto the floor, his arms and legs spread out like a starfish. I turn on the light, kiss his hair. "Come on, Matti, time to get up, honey." He stirs, yawns and his eyes pop open. I pick a sweatshirt up off the floor and put it on the back of his chair, then tell him to get ready and make sure to pack his gym bag.

In Carla's room, I find her at her desk doing some last-minute revision.

"Morning you, did you sleep well?" I ask, kissing the top of her head.

"Yes, thanks."

She barely moves, one elbow on the desk, her head propped up on her hand. I kiss her again, smell her long soft hair. At thirteen she's as tall as me already. "Come and have breakfast." She nods, mumbles that she'll be down in a minute.

In the kitchen, I'm preparing school lunches for my children when they bounce in arguing, jostling each other at the fridge, for the milk, over the box of cereal. They work around me, all of us anticipating each other's movements. Cupboard doors fly open and sometimes get closed again. Bowls are dropped on the kitchen table with a clatter and are filled with cereal and milk, fruit and yoghurt. I try to keep up, put things away as needed, scolding them half-heartedly for making a mess but secretly loving how noisy they are, the chaos they create, and the sense that I'm at the center of it, bringing order to their lives.

Luis joins us, dressed in jeans and a white shirt, his hair still damp from the shower. He grabs a yoghurt from the refrigerator and slowly spoons it into his mouth, leaning against the kitchen counter. Mateo has gone back upstairs and shouts down that he has lost a sneaker and it's *really bad!* because he has soccer practice today. I go up to his room and locate the shoe under his bed along with a bevy of dirty socks and underpants. I add them to a load of washing and turn the machine on.

"Will you please fix the tap today?" I ask Luis. Every day I bring up the dripping tap in the kitchen, and every day, Luis says he'll fix it. Every day I say something like, *If you don't have time, I can get the plumber in*, and every day he assures me that's a waste of money and he'll do it himself.

Today is no exception.

"And since you're up early, would you walk Roxy, please?"

He drops the yoghurt container in the trashcan and kisses the top of my head. "Sorry, I have to get back to the gallery. I'm under the gun."

I put my hands on his chest. "I know, I remember." Luis's upcoming exhibition is a very big deal. He's been stressed about it for months and my job is to support him when he's like that. It's my favorite job, actually, looking after my family. I run my hand through his dark hair, still as thick as ever and always falling over his forehead. Whenever I picture Luis in my mind's eye, it's with one hand pushing back a lock of hair between his thumb and forefinger.

"You'll be fine. Do what you have to," I say.

Carla reappears, dressed and ready for school.

"Will you put the washing out on the line when you get home?" I ask her.

"Why can't Matti do it?"

"Because he's got soccer practice and you'll be home way before him."

"Okay."

Luis hugs the kids, kisses me goodbye. I remind him to pick up Matti from soccer practice this afternoon. "And please don't be late," I plead. Mateo gets very anxious when people are late. One time Luis and I had a misunderstanding about who was where when and no one picked up Matti. He sat on a bench at a bus stop and waited for twenty-six minutes—that's what he said, twenty-six minutes, repeatedly—and by the time I got there he had wet himself. It took over an hour to console him. Luis and I had a huge fight afterwards about who was supposed to pick him up, and we never agreed on it, although to this day I know it was supposed to be Luis.

"And don't forget tonight."

"What about tonight?" he says.

"Ha ha, you're so funny you should have been on the stage."

"I tried. They wouldn't even let me audition."

I laugh. It's an accidental joke because tonight the kids are putting on a show. Carla has written a play for the Young Playwrights Competition and she is staging a special preview performance for us, having roped in her little brother to play various roles, all in our very own living room. I think I'm as excited as they are.

"Do I need to get anything for dinner?" Luis asks.

"No, all done."

It's pizza night tonight. One day, when my children are old enough to go to restaurants by themselves, they will realize that real pizza tastes like heaven, drips with oily, melted cheese, has very few vegetables on it and miles of pepperoni. Pizza, here, chez Sanchez, consists of homemade wholegrain sourdough spread with homemade low-salt tomato passata, truckloads of seasonal vegetables and low-fat cottage cheese. Sometimes I wonder how much of what I do to look after my family will end up as a discussion on a therapist's couch.

Luis gives me that lovely smile of his that still makes my heart flutter, then with another kiss he's gone.

I hug my children goodbye, tell them I love them to bits, accidentally mess up Carla's hair—"Mom!"—and, after they're gone, I grab the leash and the roll of dog poop bags from the hook behind the door of the laundry and let Roxy out for a quick walk around the block.

CHAPTER 2

"Good morning, everyone."

Geoff is standing at the white board. We don't use screens or projectors for small meetings like this, just good old-fashioned magnetic boards. He shoots me an annoyed look over his shoulder.

"Hey, there you are," he says.

"Yeah, sorry. Dog walking. Lost track of time."

There are five of us in this committee. Geoff of course, as the department chair, and the other two mathematics professors: Rohan and John. Then there's Mila, the youngest in the faculty—as she likes to remind everyone on a regular basis—and me.

We're here because our future funding is tenuous at best. Our generous endowment has been frittered away by our so-called investment advisors who managed to get a return at about a third the rate of everyone else, and now we have to come up with new sources of income. That, in a nutshell, is the meeting.

I nod at each of them and set my laptop on the table.

"So, where are we up to?" I wake up the laptop and open a new document while surreptitiously checking out Mila. She's wearing a loose top that droops over her bare shoulder in a *can't keep it up, it's too big* sort of way, revealing a thin silver bra strap—at least she's wearing a bra—over a fine collarbone. I look down at her skinny jeans, fashionably torn at the knees and cut off above her delicate ankles.

I don't know. She's obviously smart—after all, she's an associate professor at twenty-six—but she's also very pretty, with shiny black hair and olive skin, and eyelashes so long I suspect they're false. Being sexy shouldn't be a disadvantage in this job, but I think it is. I'd never dress like that for a business meeting. What was it Luis said this morning? *You look conservative.* I catch Mila looking at me looking at her and I quickly return to my laptop, my finger poised over the keyboard.

"Since you're here, will you take minutes, Anna?"

"Sure, happy to." I always take minutes. I may as well have it tattooed on my forehead. *Team player, no job too small or too menial.* Then Geoff adds, "I know I always ask you, but you're the only one I can trust to do it right."

I smile. Then I think I'm blushing. Am I blushing? I sure hope not. "It's no problem," I stress. Of course, it's not really my job to take minutes. He could have asked June, the department secretary, to sit in, but the truth is, I *am* the only one who can be trusted to do it right. That's one thing everyone always says about me: I am dependable. I will always step in and help, and often make things right. Which is probably why I'm always in meetings. When I'm not teaching, I mean. I seem to always put my hand up for things: committees, student support, fundraising, grant applications, acquittals. Sometimes I end up on committees I don't remember signing up for. But, if the work needs to be done, I am ready. I rally when the going gets tough. I'm a rallier.

"Ideas," Geoff says now. "Let's hear them. Anyone?"

At the top of my document, I type: "New Funding Opportunities—Staff Suggestions" and bold it.

Mila takes the pencil she's chewing out of her mouth. "We could contact our alumni? Organize a fundraising dinner?"

"Good. Thank you, Mila."

Geoff writes down Mila's suggestion on the board, like it's a very valid one and I'm thinking, *Really? Is that the best you can do?* Then he says, "Anna, will you organize it?"

I blink. I'm about to say, *Why doesn't Mila organize it? It's her idea.* But being a team player, a rallier, I just nod. Although I do ask: "Don't we do that already?"

"No, we don't. So let's."

"Okay." Anyway, as a member of the teaching staff, I don't think he actually means for *me* to organize it. I make a note to mention it to June.

"Let's not beat around the bush here, people," Geoff continues. "This faculty will not get bailed out again by the executive. At this rate, we'll be lucky if we make it to the end of next year. We are in early talks with a number of philanthropic institutions—June and I are handling that—but I'll be blunt, it doesn't look good. So if you have any bright ideas… What's going on, Anna?"

I look up.

"Nothing, why?"

"You're smiling."

I plaster on my most innocent face. Puzzled, sincere. If I could, I wouldn't just say it out loud, I would scream it from the top of my lungs. Because when I suggested this committee, I didn't know that Alex—*my* Alex, *my* PhD student—was about to prove one of mathematics' most important conjectures. And once Alex and I publish our paper, donors will be falling over themselves to throw money at us. That's how important this paper is. It's groundbreaking, and marvelous, and it's the best thing to come out of Locke Weidman University, ever. And while it's absolutely Alex's work, as Alex's advisor, I can say I am responsible, in my own small way, for that achievement. I imagine Geoff's face when he finds out that I am co-author of a groundbreaking paper that is going to bring googolplexes of dollars to our university. I mean, let's face it, the last time I published anything was a comment on a working moms' Facebook group about a one-pot recipe: *My whole family loved it! 5 stars!*

I shake my head. "Nope, all good, as you were."

He winks at me and turns back to the board. "Okay then."

*

Alex had come to study at this little university because of me, he said. He had stumbled upon a paper I had published a million years ago, back when I was a grad student myself, and had walked into my office brandishing a copy of a now-defunct mathematics journal. He wanted me to supervise his thesis which, at the time, was on theta and zeta functions. He'd had offers from other universities, some certainly more prestigious than ours, but: "I must do it here, with you," he'd argued.

My first impression, from the way he looked and the way he spoke, was that he would have been more at home at Princeton than at our humble institution. He's athletic, very handsome, with fair hair and when he smiles, which isn't that often anymore, I always find myself staring at his teeth, so perfect, so white.

Was I flattered that very first day? Absolutely. Did I want the extra work? No. But he wore me down, with his big, pleading blue eyes and his earnest face.

"Please, Dr. Sanchez! You're the only one that I want!"

I'd laughed, and he smiled in that seductive way of his, all teeth and charm, like he already knew he'd won. And he had, I guess, because I said yes, because he did spike my interest, and because it is nice to be wanted.

It was immediately obvious that he was bright. I mean, really bright. But, like a lot of geniuses, he's also obsessive. He can spend days poring over a minute and insignificant detail. It's as if he can't differentiate what's important from the trivial. He also gets distracted easily.

After he'd been working on his chosen topic for a few weeks, he came to my office, closed the door, sat down and said, "I have to tell you something."

We didn't have a meeting scheduled but that never bothered Alex. He just comes in whenever he likes and if I'm sitting with another student, he'll wait outside, tap his foot against the door jamb loud enough for us to hear, cough, make a nuisance of himself until we're done, or until we give up.

"What is it?" I asked.

"You have to promise to keep it secret."

I rubbed my forehead. "I can't promise that. What have you done?"

He looked sideways and sighed.

"Did you get drunk? Do something you regret? Did anyone get hurt? Do we need to speak to student services?"

"Anna! Are you for real? Is that the first thing that comes into your mind?"

"Just tell me, Alex."

He handed me an ordinary spiral notebook—Alex does all his preliminary work on paper, which is not that unusual.

I opened it. The writing was messy, full of crossed-out equations and shorthand notes, but I knew how to read it, and it made my stomach twist. I stared at it for a long time, and for a moment I wondered if he was playing a joke on me.

"Can you tell what this is?" he said.

I couldn't even look at him and I couldn't speak either. The Pentti-Stone conjecture. A famous problem, unsolved, first proposed in 1905 by mother and daughter mathematicians Claudia Pentti and Noemi Stone. Then the world forgot about them until an American billionaire and futurist called Leo Forrester resurrected them. His foundation awards prizes to innovative discoveries and he'd stumbled upon the Pentti-Stone and realized that if it were solved, it would revolutionize too many things to list, from computing power to aircraft design.

The reason I knew so much about the Pentti-Stone was because of my mother. She was a scientist and I was an only child who turned out to be a bit of a math prodigy, an aptitude I nurtured and generally worked very hard at because it felt like it was the only thing she liked about me. If I had to describe my mother,

I would say she was cool, strict to the point of austere, and not very motherly.

When I was fourteen years old, my mother assigned the Pentti-Stone problem to me as some kind of punishment for sneaking out one night and going to a party I hadn't been allowed to go to. That summer, when my friends were hanging out by the river, going to the mall, having sleepovers, I was at my little desk trying to solve a math problem that had grown men punching the wall in frustration. But that was the deal, she'd said. If I could solve it, I could go out and play. I didn't know it was some kind of trick and I spent the entire summer on it, poring over equations just like the ones I was staring at in Alex's notebook, until my eyes felt like I'd rubbed salt into them.

I didn't solve it—that should go without saying—and to this day the very name Pentti-Stone makes me want to bite someone.

I flicked through Alex's notebook, numbers blurring as I swiped the pages quickly back and forth, unable to fully absorb what I was looking at, feeling confused by the familiar, the aberrant, knowing I should feel excited by the possibility but feeling devastated instead. Finally, I looked up. He was grinning, and I wanted him to go away. I wanted to say I had work to do, that I had no time for this.

Then he said it.

"The Pentti-Stone conjecture. I think I have an angle."

He looked nervous, almost frightened.

"Really?"

"Yes."

There's a prize too: $500,000 to the first person to prove or disprove the Pentti-Stone. Not as much as mathematics' Millennium Prize—that's the big one, at $1,000,000—but not small change, either.

I stood up to close the door, even though the room felt airless. "You want to talk me through it?"

He did, animatedly, chaotically and yet beautifully. He hadn't come up with a complete solution yet, but the work he'd done on his thesis to date had accidentally nudged him in the right direction.

"I think I can do it," he said, breathless.

I paused, willing my heart to slow down. "It's harder than you think."

"I know. I need your help, Anna. Will you help me?"

Would I help him? My first thought was no. *Absolutely not.* But how could I say no? What if he found another supervisor? Someone at MIT maybe? Could I bear it? And if I said yes, I could think of it as closing a circle. The end of the work I'd started so very long ago.

"And I want to change my PhD topic to this," he continued. "Can I do that?"

I thought about it. The ramifications were negligible; people changed their topic all the time.

"And it has to remain secret," he added. "For obvious reasons."

"Obviously." If it became known at this point, even just within the university, that Alex was close to solving the Pentti-Stone, and especially what his approach was, there was no doubt someone else would jump on it and quite possibly snatch the prize before he did. Us academics might look mild-mannered and geeky on the surface, but underneath we're a bunch of hyenas who'd do anything for a scrap of recognition.

"Not even your husband," he said.

"Honestly, Alex, Luis wouldn't know the Pentti-Stone from the Rosetta Stone."

"I don't care. Nobody can know, you have to swear. Nobody."

I did. I swore. I'm good at keeping secrets, I said. I was already thinking of what it might mean for the university, the research funding we'd be able to attract. This would be a game changer for our faculty. We would join the ranks of the most prestigious academic institutions in America.

After that, the conjecture was all he could think about, but passion has its consequences: he lost weight, lost sleep, grew dark circles under his eyes.

We spent months on it, which is not very long in the scheme of things. People spend years, decades, trying to solve a conjecture. He went down rabbit holes a few times. He'd think he was so close, then one detail would make the whole thing crash and he'd have to start again.

Then he became paranoid that people were spying on his work. He wouldn't put anything at all in a computer in case we got hacked. He wrote everything by hand and kept it in a locked drawer in my desk, even though he had his own locked cabinet in an office he shared with other students.

"I don't trust them," he said.

"So, lock it in your cabinet then."

"Anna, they're on wheels!"

In the end we agreed he could work in my office, which I would lock whenever I was out. I also had a small desk brought in especially for him. It was kind of exhilarating because we made progress so quickly. But when his health deteriorated, when he couldn't cope with the pressure, he was awful to be around. I dreaded coming to work. He was always angry, sad, desperate. Manic. Then he became resentful of me because he thought I wasn't doing enough to help him. As if somehow it was my fault he hadn't solved it yet. Like it was simple multiplication and I hadn't explained to him how to do it.

Then he stopped coming altogether. I knew he wasn't working on it at home because all his notes were in my office. Then one night I woke up in the middle of a dream with an idea. I tiptoed downstairs and called him. I told him my theory. *What if…? What do you think? Would that work?* Two days later he'd cracked it.

A PhD thesis can only be authored by the student in question. But we agreed to write a paper together about the Pentti-Stone conjecture and its proof. We'd be co-authors, which was not that unusual between the student and his or her adviser, but to co-author a paper on such groundbreaking work is worth its weight in gold for any academic. His name would be first, there was no question about that. But we would have to be quick. Even though I wasn't paranoid like he was, ideas have been known to hop from head to head until they find a willing host.

Often they find more than one, and whoever gets there first, wins.

CHAPTER 3

"You look nice today," Geoff says. The others have gone and it's just him and me left. He's packing up his laptop and I'm tidying up the meeting room, making sure to leave it the way I'd like to find it.

"Do I?" I give a little laugh, turning to wipe the whiteboard so I don't have to look at him. "That's nice. Luis thought I looked conservative."

He comes up right next to me and takes the block eraser from my hand, puts it down in the tray.

"What?" I ask.

He takes my shoulders so that I'm facing him, then reaches for the top of my shirt and swiftly undoes the button.

"There." He smiles. "Fixed it."

I feel myself redden. The top edge of my plain white bra is visible now, and my first thought is, *I wish I'd worn a nicer one.*

Geoff walks away, stops at the door. "See you around," he says, with a wink.

I finish tidying the room, a little embarrassed, a little shocked even, yet unable to suppress the small smile playing on my lips.

Last year, when Geoff and I were away at some conference in Chicago, something almost happened between us. He'd been looking at me like a ravenous wolf all evening and I was flattered, probably more than I should have been. Somehow, I ended up drinking too much, certainly more than I'd intended, and next thing I knew, we were in his room and he'd gone down to his boxer shorts. But I checked out at the last minute. It was as if I'd woken up from a dream, and an image of Carla and Mateo's cute little faces looking up at me popped into my mind. I excused myself and ran out of the room, and I thank my lucky stars every day that I came to my senses before anything *actually* happened.

I was embarrassed the next day, my memory blurry from all the alcohol I'd consumed. I rushed to apologize, although for which part I'm not sure. The part where I almost went through with it? Or the part where I didn't?

He laughed. "Don't worry about it, Anna." Then he made a show of checking no one was around before leaning forward and in a low voice he said, "Next time."

And I laughed. "I don't think so," I said, even though I was kind of flattered he still wanted to.

He made a sad face and put both hands over his heart. "You're killing me!"

I chuckled, lightly punched his shoulder. I was so grateful we could laugh about it. I shudder to think what might have happened, but now it's like a secret joke between us: one time, someone mentioned Chicago in a meeting, and we immediately looked at each other and cracked up behind our hands.

I make a short detour to see June on the way back from the meeting so I can tell her about the alumni dinner. And I'll make sure to tell her that it was Mila's initiative, not mine. I don't want her to think I'm assigning extra work to her. I've almost reached her when Clyde, the associate dean of the college, slaps a sheaf of papers on her desk.

"For Christ's sake, June! Are you *completely* stupid? These are last year's figures! I asked for this year's intake! Can you get it right this time?" Then he turns around, mutters something about having to do everything twice around here and marches back down the corridor.

It was a shocking performance, and if I'd had time to turn away, I would have. But it's too late now. It would only add to June's embarrassment. So I stand there, inches from her desk, a smile plastered on my face like nothing's wrong, or if it is, I didn't notice.

She reaches for the bundle with a trembling hand and pulls it slowly towards her. She looks like she's going to cry with her head down and her black curls falling forward, almost hiding her face.

"He's a bully," I say simply. "He speaks like that to me all the time."

I don't know why I say that since it's not true. I just want to soften her humiliation. I certainly don't think Clyde should speak to anyone like that and I make a mental note to pull him up on it later.

June looks up, crimson patches blooming on her cheeks. She tries to smile, and fails. Her chin wobbles. "I doubt that very much."

"You'd be surprised."

"It's not even my job," she says. "His secretary is off sick and I've been asked to step in."

I lean forward and whisper, "I searched his desk for a stapler once, and I found a penis enlargement pump. Top left drawer, under that stupid little tray he keeps his paperclips and rubber bands in." I stand up. "Just think about *that* next time he talks to you like that."

We both know I just made that up. She drops her head and laughs silently, and it takes a moment for her to recover. When she looks up again, the smile is real.

"Thank you," she says, still trying, and failing, to stop grinning.

I wink at her. "My pleasure."

I tell her about the alumni dinner proposition, then head back in my office and type up the minutes so they're ready to email before I leave to meet Alex.

Then Mila comes in. There's a guffaw of student laughter outside and she closes the door.

"Anna, do you have a moment?"

"Of course, Mila. Please." I indicate the seat opposite. "How can I help you?"

She looks skyward, like she's thinking about it. I wait, my hands knotted together, a benign smile on my face. I'm going for the mentor-to-mentee look, even though I'm wondering if she's going to ask me to do something. Pick up one of her tasks. Find someone to mark her exams. Organize the alumni dinner.

"How can I help?" I repeat.

"I wanted to tell you myself, make sure you were okay."

"Oh?"

She looks sideways, takes in a small, sharp breath, closes her eyes briefly, and I know now it's going to be bad. For me.

"I got the professorship. I found out this morning."

I manage to stretch my lips thinly over my teeth and into a smile. My knuckles have turned white and I feel my chest rise and fall as my pulse races. I repeat the words in my head, in case I got them wrong the first time. *I got the professorship.* Nope, no change, stomach still clenched. I'm trying to think of something to say and we just stare at each other in silence for a while.

"I didn't know you'd applied."

"Yeah, it was on impulse, really—just a last-minute thing. Geoff suggested it."

"He did?" *A last-minute thing?* It takes weeks, months, to put an application like that together. Is she going to say she wrote the application twenty minutes before the deadline? I don't get it. Does she want me to feel even worse?

Then it occurs to me maybe there's more than one professorship this year after all. Maybe I too will find out today.

"So they announced it?"

"This morning. And Anna, let me say that I was completely surprised. Shocked, really. I was sure it would be you, and it *should* have been you. I don't know why they gave it to me. I keep expecting someone to tap me on the shoulder and say they've made a mistake." She gives a small, self-deprecating laugh.

There are probably things I should say, but I can't speak. It's like my throat has clammed up and nothing will squeeze by except maybe my last breath.

"I know you must be disappointed." She tilts her head at me, checking to see just how disappointed, presumably.

"Not at all," I manage, finally. "I'm very"—I was going to say 'happy' but it gets caught—"pleased, for you."

"Really?"

"Of course! Why wouldn't I be?"

She puts a hand on top of her chest, just below her throat. "Oh, thank god. I was really hoping you'd say that but I was a little bit nervous. Especially since you were one of the people who interviewed me when I first started."

"Yes, I remember."

"You'd think the more senior person would get it first—I would have thought anyway, so I'm glad you're being so good about it."

There's a lone paperclip on my desk, and I see myself in my mind's eye straightening it out and shoving it in her cheek just to shut her up. "Don't be silly! It's fabulous! I couldn't be happier. Well deserved. Congratulations." I get up, because I'm starting to shake and I'm afraid she'll see it, which would only add to my humiliation.

She gets to her feet. "Thank you for being so good about it," she says again.

I can't get to the women's toilets fast enough. I lock myself in a cubicle, close the seat and sit down. I'm breathing too fast, too loud. I drop my head in my hands and time my breaths, wait for my pulse to slow down. I press my fingers against my eyes. Of course I didn't get it. I haven't published anything in years. I just teach, work, sit on useless committees and take minutes. That's not a track to full professor. That's a track to full-blown idiot-moron-gofer-errand girl. And what was it she said? *A last-minute thing. Geoff suggested it.* Why would he do that when he'd already suggested to me that *I* apply, and there was only one position available?

Except he didn't suggest it, did he. But he sure didn't stop me when I brought it up. Quite the opposite, I would have thought, considering all the extra work I've been doing these last few months *which will make a good impression on the committee, Anna. They love a team player.*

At the sink I splash water on my face and dab at my eyes. I recover myself enough to go back to my office, only for Geoff to stick his head round the door a moment later.

"Ah. Anna, can I have a word?"

"Is this about Mila? Because I think it's great, really great. Wonderful news."

"Yes, good, so you know."

"Yes, couldn't be happier for her."

"Okay. Good. Oh, by the way, did you type those minutes?"

"In your inbox."

"Well done, good stuff."

I want to go home and curl up in my bed, go to sleep for a year or two, but I can't because I have a class. Maybe I could say I'm sick, ask June to get a replacement teacher for the afternoon. One of the post docs.

No. Mila will know it's because of her, and then she'll think I'm upset and she'll be making cooey noises at me: *Oh! You* are *upset, Anna. I'm so, so sorry.* I wonder if Mila will offload some of her classes on me now. Of course she will.

Then I remember I am supposed to go and see Alex. Good. This is what I need to focus on: Alex and the Pentti-Stone conjecture. It sounds like a children's book title: *Alex and the Pentti-Stone Conjecture.* I blow my nose, picturing Geoff's face—and Mila's—when they find out our paper got published. I imagine Geoff realizing he backed the wrong applicant. Mila's words echo in my mind: *It should have been you.*

Damn right it should.

I think back to the phone call from Alex. What is he up to? He sounded… upset? Not exactly. Intense? Yes. Definitely. Should I brace myself for more bad news? Has he found an error? Will he say we can't submit yet? It would be a setback, certainly, but we'd had those before. Maybe this one is much more serious. But I know the work and I know the paper, and I know it's ready. Unless I've missed something, and considering it was only this morning that I was quietly confident I'd find out any day now that I got the professorship, and I didn't even twig that Mila was in the running, let alone that she'd beat me to it, maybe I shouldn't trust my own judgment.

But I need this paper. This is my opportunity to prove them wrong, to laugh in their face, to quit the job and get a better one elsewhere—maybe move the family to Boston so I could teach at MIT.

I grab my bag and snatch my jacket from the back of my chair. I don't care what Alex's problem is right now, I'll sort it out. I don't care what it takes, either. I just want to see the look on Mila's face when our paper gets published. I want to get to tap her on the shoulder and say, *I think they* did *make a mistake after all, Mila.*

CHAPTER 4

I've been to Alex's apartment a few times before and I park around the corner, turn off the ignition and take a moment. I need to be calm and reassuring. Alex has a tendency to over-react and god knows he can get himself into a state of despair over the smallest thing. He's twenty-seven years old but sometimes he may as well be twelve. But, he is the genius behind our work and my future depends on how well I can manage him, as I remind myself as I make my way up the stairs.

His apartment is very nice, certainly not what you'd expect a student to live in. It's roomy, with a big flat screen on one wall of the living room and beige, glass and chrome furnishing that would look great in an office, or a showroom. He shares it with another student who from memory is studying journalism. But Alex doesn't need the rent his roommate brings in. His parents are paying, and he joked once he'd only got someone to move in so he'd have someone to talk to.

I knock and he opens the door immediately, shirtless, his pupils dilated, and it occurs to me suddenly that he could be on something, some kind of amphetamines. By the looks of him he must have been abusing them for a while and I chide myself for not checking in with him sooner.

"Where's your roommate?" I ask, taking my jacket off and laying it on the arm of the sofa. "What's his name again?"

"Vernon. He's out. Do you have the notebooks?"

"Oh, shit! Sorry."

"Anna! Did you forget?"

"Sorry, I did. Lots going on this morning."

He breathes out loudly through his nose, but then seems to relax again. "You want a coffee? I'm about to have one."

"Sure."

He does a double take. "You've been crying?"

"No."

"Your eyes are all puffy."

"I said no."

He shrugs and I follow him to the kitchen and watch him spoon ground coffee into the machine. I'm about to ask what the problem is when he blurts it out.

"I've changed my mind."

I wait for the rest but he's silent; just keeps making the coffee and won't meet my eye as he fusses with the cups and the sugar bowl.

"Okay, about what?" I'm already exhausted as I brace myself for his inevitable self-doubt, for the speech about how he thinks he has it wrong. The submission committee at the *Journal of Applied Number Theory* won't accept it if there is any doubt about the validity of the solution. He knows that. And I have friends at MIT who could take a look now if he doesn't want to wait that long. They'd sign a confidentiality agreement. This kind of thing happens all the time. He knows that, too.

"Talk to me, Alex. Don't you want to publish it yet? Is that it?"

He snaps his head around. "My thesis? Of course I'm publishing it. Are you nuts?"

"Okay, good to hear. So what are we talking about?"

He's smiling as he thinks about it, then his features harden until his mouth is so taut that when he speaks again, he can barely move his lips. "You're not gonna like it."

Jesus. He really looks bad. When did I see him last? Two weeks at least.

He pulls out a letter from his back pocket and hands it to me. I hesitate, then take the envelope from him between two fingers, trying not to stare at his filthy fingernails. "What's this?" I'm about to pull out the single sheet of paper from it when he speaks.

"I'm going to publish it alone. The thesis, of course, but also the research paper."

"I'm sorry?"

"I don't want you to co-author it anymore."

I almost laugh. "This is a joke, right?"

His hand shakes as he handles the coffee, and some of it spills onto the table. My first instinct is to grab a kitchen cloth and clean it up, but I don't.

"I've thought long and hard about it," he says. "It's mine."

A wave of outrage flares through me and I grip the envelope tighter in my fist but then tell myself to calm down. I take a breath and let it slip from my fingers. He doesn't mean it. He's panicking about something. There's no need for me to do the same.

He leans against the window ledge stirring his coffee with a spoon, a breeze from the partly open sash window behind him ruffling his hair.

"Come on, Alex, I helped you, you know that. You couldn't have done it without me."

He smirks, rudely. "Are you listening to yourself? I *did* do it without you, Anna. You were there, in the room, and that's about the extent of your contribution."

"You know that's not true." I think of all the hours I spent with him, poring over his work, trying to grab hold of the slimmest gossamer thread that we could tug and unspool into the light. I think of all the times he despaired and wanted me to hold him until it passed, the times he would sob on my shoulder like a child while I whispered soothing words to him. He told me once that I was much nicer than his own mother.

Thinking back on it in this moment, I realize something I didn't want to confront then, but I may have to now. Alex is unhinged.

I think of that night when I called him at almost midnight. I woke him up and he was annoyed because it was the first time in weeks that he'd had a few hours' uninterrupted sleep. Until I called, that is. But I'd had that sliver of an idea and it was enough for him to get unstuck. It was the final, missing piece of the puzzle. We had the solution.

I put all this to him now, through clenched teeth. "You don't remember that? Really, Alex?"

He smiles from one side of his mouth. The arrogance dripping from his sneer makes me want to slap him.

"Do you honestly believe you made that much difference? You're not that good, Anna. It's you who is trying to ride on my coattails here, not the other way around. And, anyway, I told you. I've thought long and hard about it over the last few weeks, and—"

"*Weeks?* You've been letting me do all this work on the paper for the last few *weeks?*"

He shrugs. "So? Give me an invoice."

"Alex! What are you saying? You can't do this!"

"Get over yourself. I'm the best thing that's ever happened to your career, even without your name as co-author. You were my advisor. You'll get lots of accolades from that. And your precious university will get its reward, just because I was your PhD student."

"Don't do this. You know it's not fair."

"Life isn't fair. Get used to it."

I laugh. "I'm finding that out." But then I see his face and I don't know whether to punch him or beg him. I take a closer look at him. His trembling hands. The spittle in the corners of his mouth. The dilated pupils. His skin so pale it's almost blue. "Have you been sleeping?" I ask, more gently.

He snorts. "I can sleep when this is done."

I cock my head at him. "What did you take, Alex?" I reach out to touch him and he jerks backwards. "I think I should call someone. We can discuss all that stuff later, but I think you need help. Have you seen your parents recently?"

"Shut up." He starts to rub his forehead over and over.

I move around the table toward him. I just want to hug him. Hold him tight until this passes. "I'm worried about you."

"No, you're not. Stay away from me!"

"It's okay." But his nose has started to bleed. "Honey, please. Look at me. I'm not moving. I'm right here, Alex. What's wrong? I'm not going to hurt you, you know that." But he's backing against the window behind him, his eyes darting around as if searching for escape.

"I've said my piece and I want you to leave! Now!"

I have to call someone. I have to do it now. He needs an ambulance, but my bag and my phone are in the living room, so I keep talking, holding his gaze as I walk slowly to him. "You can publish alone, I don't care. I really don't. Come on, Alex, come and sit down with me."

I extend my hand to him again but he just laughs.

I come closer. So close I can almost touch him.

He raises his arm over his face. "Leave me alone!"

For a horrible moment I think he's afraid of me. Then in one motion he turns, pushes up the sash window and swings one leg out so that he is sitting astride the window sill, looking down. I scream for him to stop but he's already slipped under the top sash and I am standing with my arms outstretched and a scream garbled in my throat.

"Alex!"

But Alex isn't there anymore.

CHAPTER 5

It's so strange, unreal, like a dream. He didn't scream, or shout, or make a noise. He just disappeared.

I want to run to the window, but I can't move. Black dots swirl in front of my eyes and I put one hand flat on the table to steady myself.

"Alex?"

After a moment I take a step, then another, until I've reached the window.

"Alex?" Slowly, I peer down, along the alley that borders the west side of the building. I can't see him. I'm looking, but I can't see him and for one beautiful moment I think maybe he's playing a joke on me, until I see his bare foot. His body is wedged between the brick wall of the building and a dumpster. A piece of metal has pierced his torso and anyone can see that he's dead. I clasp my hands over my mouth to stop myself from screaming and drop to the floor, my back against the wall.

I have to get help. I crawl to the living room, stumble upright and snatch up my bag from where I left it on the couch. It's a tanned soft leather bag with a single shoulder strap and Luis had once joked that searching for something in it was like shoving your hand inside a giant mushroom. I think about that now, the giant mushroom, and I don't know what's real anymore. Am I tripping? Did Alex give me something in that coffee and walk out of the apartment? Is this some kind of prank?

No. I didn't touch my coffee. I empty the bag on the floor because that's the quickest way to locate my phone. I snatch it with shaking hands, then stop.

Alex is dead. I'm sure of it. Should I ring the university first? Or should I ring his parents? What will I say to them? I should ring the ambulance. That's it. That's what I need to do. My finger hovers over the first digit, 9.

And tell them what, exactly?

He was going to leave my name off the paper and then he fell out the window.

I remember the letter he gave me earlier, lying on the kitchen table. I pick it up with shaking fingers. It's typed on thick, cream-colored stationery.

Dear Anna,

Firstly, I want to thank you for being my thesis advisor, and for everything you've done to make me feel welcome at Locke Weidman.

I've decided to publish my work alone. That includes the paper based on my thesis. I know that we had discussed you being cited as co-author, but upon further reflection I have come to the conclusion that there's no reason at all for your name to be included. To be honest, I'm concerned that having you as co-author will lend your contribution more weight than is warranted.
I trust you'll understand and respect my position.
Please forward any written material in your possession.

Below that he'd added in a handwritten scrawl, like an afterthought:

Sorry,
Alex

I put a hand over my eyes. They'll think I did it. Of course they will. They'll read the letter, then they'll say I pushed him in a fit of rage. They won't believe me when I explain that he just jumped. He was there, then he wasn't. Because that's what happened here, isn't it?

Will I go to jail? Yes, of course I'll go to jail. Our doctoral students die. We kill them. Or I kill them. That's what they'll say in the newspaper headlines, the blogs, the social media posts and talk-back radio.

Killer.

And for some insane reason I think of my mother and I can almost hear the soft click of her tongue, impatient and disappointed.

I return to the window, slowly, like a cat, listening the entire time. Every sound seems amplified, like I have bionic hearing. Distant traffic, a dog barking, the clanging of a distant hammer in a construction site. No sirens. Yet.

Okay. I need to breathe. Focus. I think of my children as I crumple the letter and shove it in my pocket. I wash the cup and wipe it dry with the tea towel before putting it back in its place on the shelf. Not that I'm concerned about prints or DNA but best not to raise questions about who was there this morning with Alex.

In the living room I'm on my knees as I frantically gather everything I dropped earlier, my heart bouncing around my chest: two tampons, a packet of tissues, a long-lost silver pen, make-up, sunglasses, wallet, keys, loose receipts. An unopened packet of mints. An ID pass on a lanyard for a panel I attended at UCLA last year. A throat soother stuck in its wrapper, the sight of which makes me want to burst into tears. I remembered Mateo doing that, sucking on it and changing his mind, putting it back in its wrapper and dropping it in my bag. I shove it all back into my purse and I'm almost hyperventilating as I dart around the room for anything else of mine. Then finally, softly, quietly, I open the front door.

I'm about to check the hallway when I hear footsteps coming up the stairs. I push the door closed again, my heart pounding as

I hold my breath, praying that it's not his roommate. In my head I'm already making excuses as to why I'm here, alone, when the footsteps continue past this floor, up another flight, and I let my breath out. On impulse I grab a light beige beanie from the coat rack and push it down over my ears, then I put my sunglasses on.

I slip out and almost run down the stairs. I only need a minute, less, thirty seconds, and I'll be outside. But just as I reach the last flight of stairs, someone comes into the building.

I hold my breath and keep my head down as I slip pass. I catch a flash of dark hair and the glimmer of a silver and purple ring on an index finger.

"Sorry," I mumble.

I step out onto the sidewalk and run to my car.

CHAPTER 6

I shove the beanie in the glove compartment and drive off. My heart is still pounding. Every sense is heightened. Every sound is a roar. Even the breeze on my skin feels like a hurricane.

Did anybody see me? I visualize the wall opposite Alex's window. It's a plain brick wall, the side of an old warehouse building. No windows that I can remember. The alley is narrow, empty except for trash cans and the dumpster. He didn't make a sound when he fell, which is possibly the strangest part. How long was I in the apartment after that? I don't know. Two minutes? Five maybe?

I try to remember if I told anyone I was going to see Alex, but no, I don't think so. Then I think *Don't think so* isn't good enough so I rack my brain, retrace my steps. There's the call, of course, from this morning, but that's not unusual.

In the parking lot back at the university, I pull out the letter, as if, somehow, that's going to tell me something. I smooth its creases against my thigh and begin to read it again just as a loud bang above me makes my heart somersault.

"You okay, ma'am?"

It's the attendant, or maybe a security guard: I can't tell, but he's wearing a uniform. I realize he tapped the roof of my car to get my attention. I wind my window down. "Yes, thank you."

"Okay, then."

How long have I been sitting here? I tear the letter in as many pieces as I can and grab the beanie from the glove compartment.

I shove the lot in the trashcan near the elevator, then make my way upstairs, drop my things off and go to teach my next class.

I am normally a very engaged teacher. I ask questions as I go, make sure I'm not losing anyone along the way. But today, I teach the class on autopilot. I don't even snap at Melanie—one of my brightest first years, but with an attitude problem—when she puts one leg up on the foldaway tablet arm of her chair. About a third of my class is young women, which is not unusual in the first year. They'll fall away, though, most of them anyway, over the next three years. At the beginning of term, I usually play a mental game where I try to guess which ones will stick it out. Melanie is one of them: she's so smart, and I really believe she loves the subjects, but she puts people off with her insolence. Especially me. She seems to have zeroed in on the fact that I'm a bit of a pushover and unconvincing in my admonitions. Whenever I tell her off—half-heartedly, as she scares me a little—she'll double down and pop a bubble of gum moments later.

At one stage I hear her scoff something like, *Hello?* and I realize I haven't said anything in a while. That's because I heard muffled voices out in the corridor and I thought, *This is it. They know. They're going to burst in the door and announce that Alex is dead.* Except it doesn't happen and the voices move on.

I get through the rest of the class and then walk quickly to the staff room. I grab my tuna and egg salad from the fridge so that I can pretend to eat it back at my desk. I say pretend, because I don't touch it. I can't eat anything, let alone tuna and egg, but I tell myself that that's what I would be doing normally. So that's what I'm doing. I pull the lid off the Tupperware, poke at the food with my fork, close it again and shove it in the trash, container and all.

I go through my tasks during the rest of the day like I'm in suspended animation—I almost have to physically jerk myself forward at regular intervals just to keep moving. At one stage Geoff pops his head in and I think, *This is* really *it*. He says the name, *Alex*, but he doesn't say, *dead*, and I blink in confusion.

"What did you say?"

"I was asking if Alex is doing a presentation next Tuesday for the panel...?"

I picture him lying behind the dumpster. Why hasn't he been found yet? How long is it going to take? Or maybe he has, but no one will tell us. Could that happen? Should I say something soon? Something like, *I was expecting to hear from Alex, he's not answering my calls. I wonder if he's all right?*

"Is he?" Geoff asks again.

Post-graduate students are asked to do a presentation every three months to evaluate their progress. They're not compulsory, but you'd have to have a good reason not to attend. Alex didn't do the last two because by then he'd decided to switch his topic and he wasn't ready to disclose that. We'd discussed this one, coming up, just last week.

"I can't get you another dispensation. It's getting awkward, but I'll think of something," I said at the time.

"No, let's do it."

"Really? Okay, but I'm surprised. I thought you didn't want to discuss it publicly?"

He'd grinned. "I'll present on the theta and zeta functions. That's what everyone thinks I'm working on, anyway."

"Oh." I'd nodded, not hugely comfortable about this. It's one thing to keep your work under wraps, it's quite another to deliberately mislead the entire department.

"Do you have something new to present?"

"No."

"So how's that going to work?"

He paused, then he turned to me, his face bright, like he'd just thought of something. "*You* could do it. You could write up something in no time! It's your field, right?"

He hadn't *just thought of it* obviously. He'd known he was going to ask me. But I told him, no. In no uncertain terms. Even worse than lying to the department, it's downright cheating. "Categorically out of the question," I said. "And you may not have noticed this, but I'm kinda busy, Alex."

"But don't you see? That way, they'll leave me alone! Otherwise they'll start to ask questions! They'll suspect something. Or maybe they'll drop me from the program!"

"No, they won't. I'm your supervisor. Only I get to drop you." Which wasn't strictly true. But saying no to Alex is like arguing with a particularly willful three year old. He begged, he sulked, he got angry, he pleaded, he threatened, he sulked again, and, in the end, I said yes because I just wanted the conversation to end. So I did the work. I stayed up until four in the morning to do it. I would have given myself an A+ for it, too.

Geoff clears his throat.

"Sorry. Yes. He's confirmed that to me. He'll be there."

He nods. "Good. I look forward to it." He's about to leave but stops, turns around. "You okay?"

"Sure, why?"

"You just seem a long way away."

"Sorry. Just tired."

"You look tired. You're not upset about the promotion, are you?" And it occurs to me then that he didn't even bother to tell me himself. Nobody told me, except for Mila, and that doesn't count. She was just gloating.

"No, I'm not upset about the promotion."

I wait until I am back in my car to have a cry. Then I drive home, and when I walk in the door, into the noise of my kids preparing Carla's play, there's a moment where I almost convince myself it never happened.

"Hello?" I say, as I move towards the living room.

"No!" they shout. "Don't come in!"

"Okay! Sorry! Where's your dad?"

"In the shed!" they shout.

I stride across the garden to the shed and stand in the doorway. Luis is bent over his bicycle and for a moment I'm almost tempted to blurt it out. *Something horrible happened today.*

"Hey, babe, how was your day?" he says, without looking up.

It occurs to me, not for the first time, that a certain distance has crept between us recently. It's the way he says, *How was your day?* like he's not actually interested, or he's too distracted to really listen. But maybe I'm over-thinking it. Maybe it's because he's been so busy. And yet, right now, as I stare at him in silence, I'd give anything for him to look up, to see me, to ask me what is wrong even though I can't tell him. Just so I know he sees me.

But he doesn't.

"Good," I say, finally. "I'll see you inside."

The laundry is still sitting in the washing machine. I could call out Carla on it, but I don't have the energy and I just shove it in the dryer, then proceed to make dinner.

Luis returns, opens a bottle of wine and gets plates out. Normally—a word that right now makes me want to hoot with laughter—we eat together at the table. I always insist on that. But because of the kids' play, which luckily is only twenty minutes or so, we're eating at the coffee table in the lounge.

I go through the motions. I laugh when Luis laughs, clap when Luis claps. I'm unable to comprehend what's happening but I do my darnedest to hide it, and I'm grateful that I have something to look at other than the images in my own mind. When the performance is over, we give feedback, which in my case consists of repeating everything Luis says, but with different words, and telling them how wonderful they both were. Afterwards, they go to their room to finish homework and Luis says he has to go back to the studio to work.

"I have so much to do," he says.

"I know," I say. "I understand." But deep down I wish he would stay. We could sit on the couch and he would put his arm around me, and we could talk of other things, simple things, family things, and I could forget about Alex and maybe even pretend it never happened.

Then it hits me, the enormity of what I've done, and for a moment I can't catch my breath. I mumble something about going to the bathroom and I sit there on the edge of the bathtub, my head in my hands. What have I done? What's the matter with me? I should never have bolted like this. I should have called an ambulance, explained what happened. I bet his system is full of drugs. I didn't need to tell them about the letter but I didn't think. I panicked, and now it's too late, because there's no way I can tell anyone now. What would I say? I forgot? I prevaricated? Then changed my mind?

When I get back to the living room, Luis is shrugging his jacket on.

"I'll be at the studio till late. Don't wait up," he says, then takes off on his bicycle. Later, after the kids go to bed, I watch an episode of *Martha's Vineyard Mysteries*. I can't concentrate on the plot—I just watch the scenery, the boats, the sea, the pretty houses—and by the time Luis comes home, I've worked myself into such a state of anxiety that I have to pretend to be asleep so he can't see the fear in my eyes.

CHAPTER 7

The next day, and I'm doing it all over again. Except that I have not slept, so my brain is frazzled. Sometimes it zaps, literally zaps, with a sharp noise like someone has cracked a whip inside my skull.

I've carefully made up my face, and put on my colorful Mona print shirtdress. I even made pancakes for breakfast. Matti shrieked with excitement and Carla gave me her brightest smile. I love seeing them happy. I love it so much I almost cried.

"Knock, knock! Ready for the staff meeting?"

Rohan stands in the doorway. I stare at him for a second too long and he lifts an eyebrow. Still no news about Alex. "Oh, staff meeting. Right." I'd completely forgotten. I make a show of checking my watch. "Wow, ten o'clock already. Be right there." I expect him to leave but he doesn't, so I get to my feet and I do what I always do, which is to reach for my laptop. But then I think, *You know what? Forget it. Let someone else take minutes for a change.* But I change my mind back because I need to act normal. I grab it and carry it under my arm.

"Sorry about the professorship," Rohan says. I turn to look at him, unexpected tears nipping at the back of my eyes; partly because I know he means it, partly because I've been holding back tears for hours now, and they're threatening to be set off at the smallest display of emotion. I rest my hand on his arm.

"Forget it. The extra work isn't worth the money, anyway."

He laughs. "You have a point."

"But, thank you, it's all good." Let's face it, the professorship is the least of my problems.

I get through the rest of the day with no news, and by this point I'm seriously considering calling the police myself. I'm marking papers with the overhead light on. It's raining outside and it's getting cool, so I have an old Locke Weidman sweatshirt on because my office has a thin, horizontal window below the ceiling—more like a vent, really, the type that you tilt open by turning a crank—but it's been stuck for ages now so I can't close it.

The door is open, as it usually is, and June appears. She holds on to the handle and something in her demeanor makes me sure that finally, this is it. I hope I am ready. I don't feel ready.

"Have you heard?" she asks softly.

"Heard what?"

A beat. "About Alex?"

She's unusually pale and when she purses her lips together the corners of her mouth pull down like she's going to cry. I sit back in my chair and put the pen down on the desk. "Is something wrong?"

She takes one step closer and quickly glances behind her down the corridor before closing the door.

"He… Alex… he's dead. I'm so sorry."

I flinch. "Alex? *My* Alex?" I ask this with a hand on my chest and my eyes opened wide. Carla did that last night as part of her scene and I made a mental note of it, then rehearsed it myself in front of the bathroom mirror this morning.

June nods. "Yes."

I cock my head at her. "No, he's not. I spoke to him just yesterday." This was true, of course. There would be a record of that and I have just put it on the record that I am probably the last person to speak to him and I'm not hiding anything.

"He's dead, Anna. They found him a few hours ago."

Her words conjure the image I've been trying to banish from my mind. I feel my chest compress the air out of my lungs, and there's a moment where I'm not sure I can get it back in. I sit there, looking at her, suddenly unable to speak. The room is airless in spite of the broken crank. Then I realize I'm not asking any questions. I find my voice again.

"Who told you? Who found him?"

"The police called. Val in student services told me just now."

I cover my face with my hands. "Oh my god."

June comes around my desk and touches my shoulder gently. "It's not your fault, Anna." I look up so quickly it hurts my head.

"He was not well. Everyone knows that. There was nothing you could have done."

I breathe out again, slowly. "You don't know that."

"Yes, I do."

"Maybe I pushed him too hard." I stare at her in shock: did I really just say that? I put my hands over my face and pretend to cry but suddenly I'm laughing and I can't stop. Luckily, tears are streaming down my face anyway.

June scans the room for a chair, then pulls the one from the other side of the desk around to my side. She sits so close to me our knees almost touch. I've never been this close to June before. I barely notice her, to be honest. I realize now how pretty she is, with her bouncy black curls and her curvy shape. She looks younger than me, but I think that's because she's in better shape than I am; we're both nudging forty.

"That has nothing to do with it," she says, and for a moment I forgot what we were talking about. "You know what Alex was like, how difficult it was for him. He was depressed…"

I stare at her for a moment. "How would you know that?"

"He told me. He was worried about how obsessive he had become. He didn't sleep for days at a time. I don't know how he managed, frankly." I stare at her in disbelief. Alex was *my* student, *my* protégé, and yet June who, as the faculty executive assistant, isn't even part of the teaching staff, knew so much about his inner demons.

What else did she know?

"He told you all this? When?"

"I don't know exactly. Over the last few weeks. You saw what it was like. Did you see how much weight he'd lost? Did you see how he changed? He would get over-excited, too much so, like he was on drugs. He'd say to me, 'June, one day you'll be able to say you knew me when!' Then the next day he wanted to quit and go sailing for a year. To be honest, I never thought he was cut out for academic research, not at this level anyway. He was too... unstable."

"How did he die?"

June's face looks full of pain when she says it: "I'm so sorry, Anna. He jumped. Out the window of his apartment."

Bile rises and for a moment I think I'm going to be sick, right there on the dark blue carpet. "I thought you were going to say he took an overdose or something."

"I know."

"But jumping out of a window?" I feel as pale as June looks. "He's really gone?" I ask, god knows why. Maybe because hearing it from someone else makes it real. Even more real than yesterday, when I looked down at his bleeding and broken body wedged behind a dumpster three floors below.

June says something else but I don't hear the words, only the sound of blood pulsing inside my ears. Her mouth is still moving when I step out of the room and almost run down the stairs and around the corner to the parking lot. I drop my keys before I can open the driver's door of my car, where I spend the next twenty minutes with my forehead resting on the steering wheel, hyperventilating, vaguely recognizing the symptoms of a panic attack. I can't even tell if it's because Alex is dead or because of the magnitude of what I've done.

CHAPTER 8

I have a longing to be with Luis, to rest my head on his shoulder and hear his soothing voice. I reach for my bag on the passenger seat and fish around for my cellphone, but the call goes straight to voicemail, which I half-expected. He always turns off his phone when he's working.

"Hi, it's me. Can you call me back?" Then I add in a smaller voice: "I know you're busy, but do you think you could come home early?" I pause, about to tell him about Alex—*Remember Alex? He's dead*—but instead I just say, "I miss you."

I start the car, but let it sit idle for a moment. I shouldn't go home to my kids in this state. I will Luis to call me back, then I think, *Why don't I go to him?* I could watch him work while I tell him about Alex and why it's all my fault. Not the real '*all my fault*', obviously. I mean the bit about pushing him too hard, having high expectations. No. Don't tell him about Alex. I will tell him later. Instead I will say, "Let's go away after the exhibition, just the two of us. The kids will be fine without us. They can stay with your dad for a week or two. They'd love that. I'll take time off work. We wouldn't tell anyone where we were. Let's remember *us*, the way we were. I miss you." That's what I'll tell him.

I text Carla.

Working late, eat without me, there's a lasagna in the fridge you can microwave. Make sure Matti does his homework, please. I'll see you later, honey. Love you xox

She replies immediately.

K x

I stop by the liquor store on the way, because one thing I need right now is a drink. I've been needing a drink for hours. I pick up the first bottle I see, a Napa Valley cabernet, when I catch sight of the box wine further along the shelf. A wave of nostalgia rolls over me and for a moment I am back at college. Luis and I, seated crossed-legged on the floor of his room, Cher or Celine Dion on the CD player. We'd drink Franzia wine out of jam jars and kiss till my lips hurt. We'd talk of our plans for our future, how many kids we wanted (two: a boy and a girl), we'd talk over each other, our hands flying around as we constructed a life where Luis was a famous artist and I would be a famous mathematician.

I put the bottle back on the shelf and grab the box wine instead. The guy at the till recoils slightly at the sight of me. I glance at my reflection in the mirror behind him and see that my cheeks are streaked with dried-up rivulets of tears stained with mascara. I find a scrunched-up Kleenex in the bottom of my purse and check it. It's stained with something vaguely oily, vaguely yellow. Chicken korma from the other night, I bet. I use the least stained corner of it to wipe my cheeks clean and add a small packet of tissues from the counter to my purchase.

Luis's studio is in an old industrial warehouse on the west side of the city. He occupies half of the third floor, which is huge. It's perfect for him, with massive windows, exposed red bricks and high ceilings.

I park outside and automatically look up, expecting the light to be on, but his windows are dark. Could I have missed him? I check the time on the dashboard—ten to six. I pull out my phone and try his number again but still get voicemail. I text Carla.

Hi honey, is Dad home?

No. When r u coming home?

I don't know. Late probably. Love you xox

I wait a moment for a reply but none comes, so I slip the phone back in my bag and grab the box wine from the passenger seat. I know where the key is kept, and with a bit of luck it will still be there. There's a code to get in downstairs which I have to look up in my notes on my phone. I punch in the numbers and the heavy door opens with a click. I take the elevator—one of those enormous cargo lifts—to Luis's studio.

I find the spare key in its usual place, between two bricks where the mortar has crumbled away. It's small and flat, round at the top, and looks completely wrong for the big metal door. It feels gritty in my hand, like it hasn't been used in a long time. It catches in the lock and looks like it might not work after all, and suddenly I feel desperate to get in, to wait for him. I give it one more twist and it gets past the snaggy bit, and suddenly, I am in.

I haven't been in Luis's studio in months, but the smell is the same: a mix of turpentine and glue, or something like that. I flick the switch by the door and the fluorescent tubes flicker into life, and I gasp.

In the center of the room is a giant bird's nest made of twigs and feathers and bits of hay, and suspended by cabling so thin as to be invisible. I run my fingertips over a small part of it and realize it's not twigs and feathers but bits of recycled plastic made to look like them. Inside are two small, strange creatures emerging from their giant eggshells, their eyes pleading, and I have to look away.

Other than bits of materials on a trestle table, the place is surprisingly tidy. But Luis is always tidy. Very organized.

I take my box wine to the kitchenette at the far end of the room. It's just a sink set into a white tiled bench, one cupboard hanging on the wall above, and a small one below. I put the box on the bench and reach up to get a glass, then notice two of them lying in the drying rack. Wine glasses, too. I don't remember Luis's studio being stocked up in wine glasses. I check the cupboards and find two pretty blue and white bowls, the kind you'd serve olives or nuts in. The chipped, mismatched china plates he used to use have been replaced by a set of six ceramic dishes, sand colored on the outside, and handmade by the looks of it. Next to them on the shelf sits a set of matching cups, shaped like goblets. What on earth is this stuff doing here? It sure doesn't look like the kind of thing Luis would buy for himself. He doesn't care what he drinks out of when he's working. I search around for the battered old campfire mug with the Cleveland Browns logo on it that he's always holding and spot it on top of a milk crate, along with empty pickle jars and old newspapers.

My skin feels clammy. It's too stuffy in here. The windows in this studio are sealed shut except for the ones at the top. Luis has welded a hook to one end of a long steel rod to open and close them, and I find it leaning against the wall. I manage to hook it around the latch and tug a top pane open. A light breeze makes the long white feathers on the sculpture flutter.

I pick up a wine glass, admire its elegant design and pour myself a generous serve of wine just as the goods lift rattles into life outside. The knowledge he is here is like a warm wave of relief and I immediately pour the second glass for him, lean back against the counter, already smiling at the thought of surprising him. But after a few moments, the elevator clanks to a stop one floor above, followed by the sound of a door closing, then footsteps somewhere above my head, then nothing. I gulp the wine down and start on the second glass.

There's a small round marble table next to the sofa, reminiscent of a Parisian café. On it is a fat candle in a saucer and a box of matches. I light the candle, the match almost burning down to my fingers, then turn off the harsh overhead lighting and sit on the sofa. The giant nest casts a strange shadow onto the wall opposite. I lean back and close my eyes, empty my mind. I pretend I am in a bubble where nothing can touch me, let the sounds of the city wash over me, and wait for Luis to return.

When I open my eyes again, I am shivering. My heart is beating too fast. I was dreaming of Alex and for a confused moment I thought he was here, too. I sit up, feeling groggy and disoriented. The candle has gone out and the room is dark except for the streetlight seeping in through the windows. I pad my way over to where I left my bag and scramble for my phone. No messages from Luis. And it's 9:23 p.m. I try him one more time, but again am directed to his voicemail so I don't bother leaving another message. I turn on the lights once more to tidy up. I've had three glasses of wine which probably put me over the limit, even though I've slept some of it off. I rinse the glasses and return them to the rack, wipe the tiled counter and pick up my box of wine.

Then I put the key back in its hiding place and go home.

The kids have left all the lights on, even though they've both gone to their rooms. I check in on Mateo first and find him at his desk, playing some kind of computer game, wearing a pair of headphones almost as big as his head. I put my hand on his shoulder. "Don't, Mom, please?" he whines.

"It's almost ten o'clock…" But obviously he doesn't hear me. I tug at the headphones and he pushes me away. I grab a pen and piece of paper and scribble, *15 minutes then bed!* I put it on the desk right under his nose. He nods and grunts something that might have been "Okay."

Carla is already asleep. She's like me in that way. She goes to bed early and wakes up early. She has the blanket all the way up to her chin but when I kiss her cheek softly, she stirs.

"What's wrong, Mom?"

"Nothing. Go to sleep."

I sit at the kitchen table waiting for Luis, my phone in front of me. I keep wondering, *What's the first thing that would happen if someone suspected I was there when Alex died?* The cops would call me, surely. But there are no calls like that yet. No messages, no emails. I know, I've checked.

I pour myself another full glass of red wine even though it's making my stomach lurch. Where the hell is Luis? Did something happen to him? And what the heck are those wine glasses doing there? I think about Mila, and Geoff, and work, and I drop my forehead on my forearms and start to cry because I am just so very, very tired.

Then Luis walks in. "What are you still doing up?" he says. I wipe my tears with the back of my hand and he comes to my side, pulls out a chair next to me. "What's wrong, Anna? The kids—"

"The kids are fine. They're in bed."

He puts his arm around my shoulders. "What's the matter?"

I lean against him, my head on his chest, feeling the cold of his leather jacket against my cheek. He must have ridden his bike. I tell him about Alex, I speak through snot and tears. I've had so much wine by now I'm crying drunk.

"You should have called me."

"I did, I left a bunch of messages," I wail.

He quickly pulls his phone out of his pocket. "I'm sorry. I forgot to turn it back on."

"Where were you?"

"Oh, honey! At the studio! Did you forget? We talked about this, remember?" He brings me close again. "No, of course you don't. No wonder, with everything that's happened."

My head is fuzzy with all the wine I've consumed. It's sloshing inside me and I think I'm going to be sick. I should have eaten something, that's my problem.

"I'll be right back," I manage to blurt before stumbling into the bathroom and vomiting into the toilet bowl. When it's over I lean on the sink with both hands and stare at my reflection. Did Luis really say he was at the studio all evening?

I can hear him moving about out there and when I come out he's in a T-shirt, his jacket thrown over the chair. He's rinsing my glass. The memory of the two elegant wineglasses on the drying rack in his studio flash into my mind.

"You look pale, babe. You okay?"

I move him out of the way to fill a glass of water from the tap and nod. "I think so," I say, wiping my mouth with my sleeve. But my heart is thumping and I feel tears sting at the back of my eyes again. I think I am more upset about where Luis has been than anything else. "Did you come from the studio just now?"

"Yes, I'm sorry it's so late. I have so much to do. I got completely lost in my own head."

"Did you go out to eat?" I ask, thinking that maybe he went to a diner somewhere and came from there. That we have our wires crossed, our timelines disjointed.

He has his back to me, but he shakes his head. "I got takeout delivered from the deli. Around seven, I think."

No, you didn't, I want to say. And it's not just because I was there around seven, it's the fact that he's included the time. *Around seven, I think.* Inconsequential, so why mention it? But I keep my mouth shut and the question pops into my head, fully formed. *Are you cheating on me?* Because that's sure what it sounds like. I realize the thought has been lurking inside my brain ever since I found the pretty dishes in his studio.

"Come to bed," he says, and starts up the stairs, then stops to wait for me, even putting his hand out to me.

I am so angry my ears are hot. I take his hand because I see myself in my mind's eye yanking it back hard enough to make him fall backwards. I wouldn't try and catch him—that would defeat the purpose. I'd stand there, my vision blurry with alcohol and watch him crack his head on the wooden steps. But then I remember my children and I disengage my hand from his and grab the banister instead.

CHAPTER 9

I wake up with a dry mouth and a feeling of doom. Luis's side of the bed is empty and I roll into it, my fingers pressing into my eyes, turning the lie over in my head. But my head doesn't work anymore, so I give up. The smell of coffee tugs at me, and I slowly swing my legs to the floor.

"How you feeling, babe? I thought I'd let you sleep."

"Good, thanks. Better." I take the steaming coffee mug Luis hands me and search his face, waiting for some kind of correction. A slap on the forehead followed by something like: *Wait! Did I say I was at the studio last night? What an idiot! I was playing squash with Toby. He can confirm.* Toby is our next-door neighbor and they do play squash sometimes, although not at night, I don't think.

But all I get is, "You okay? You don't look good. Is it because of Alex?" and my stomach flips.

There's a kind of a hush around the department when I arrive. I go straight to my office without meeting anyone's eyes, then June checks in on me, her face a picture of concern. She brings with her a chocolate chip cookie on a small white plate and a coffee, which she puts down in front of me.

"John is taking your class this morning. How you feeling?"

"I'm okay," I say, hoping she'll go away so I can curl up beneath the desk. I stare at the cookie. June has never brought me a coffee before, let alone a cookie. I pick up the chocolate chip cookie and look at it closely. "Are you my mother?" I ask. She chuckles. Then I worry she might think I implied she was old enough to be my mother, which is ridiculous, obviously, so I add, "Because believe it or not, she bakes them just like that." Which is a complete lie. Maybe I'm just saying things to fill the void. Or to stop myself from saying things like, *By the way, I was there when Alex died and I can't stop wondering if he would have jumped had I not been there. Oh, and my husband is probably cheating on me.*

She puts a hand on my shoulder. "You look tired."

"Thank you. That's what my mother says."

"Which goes to show you should listen to your mother. You should take a couple of days off if you need them, Anna. I'll talk to Geoff if you like, make sure your classes are covered."

"I'm good, really, but thanks." I take a sip of the coffee, playing for time. Finally, when she makes a move to leave, I take the plunge.

"Can I ask you?"

She turns around. "Yes?"

"I'm trying to understand why Alex told you, what you said yesterday, about how he felt, and his moods…"

"I asked him. I could see something wasn't right. He'd been quieter, I thought—he'd lost that boisterous energy."

"He was exhausted," I say, nodding.

"He was depressed, Anna." She hesitates. "Could you not see it?"

I nod quickly. "Of course I did." But I hadn't. Not really. What I saw was the obsession and the highs and the lows, but I didn't see that he needed proper help. Not like that.

"It's not your fault," she says. And I'm thinking that if she keeps saying it, she must believe it is.

"I know. Thank you," I reply. Even though it's a lie, obviously. It *is* my fault. I may not have killed him, I don't think so anyway, but he is dead because of me. Because I was there, and he lost the plot.

God. I so don't want to think about that right now. But I can't help wondering just how much he's confided in June, especially considering I had no inkling they were even speaking to each other.

"Did he ever talk to you about me?" I ask.

She smiles. "He said that you were the best and that was why he wanted to do the best possible work he could. Because of you. You deserved it."

I think about that, wait another beat, but she's lost in her own thoughts now. So she doesn't know, clearly, that Alex had changed his mind about me. That he didn't think I deserved much at all in the end.

"Let me know if you need anything," she says. "Also, his father called. He said to thank you, on behalf of him and his wife. He said they really appreciated how much you did for their son."

It's like someone has their thumb on my throat. I can't speak.

"I know." She sighs. Then as she leaves, she adds, "The police will be here in an hour. I know they'll want to speak to you."

I breathe in at last. "Me? Why?"

She frowns. "Because, out of everyone here, you were closest to him."

"Of course. Sorry. Yes, I'll be here."

CHAPTER 10

Talking to the police turns out to be the easy part. Almost perfunctory, I think. There are two of them, a man and a woman whose names don't register through the white noise of my anxiety. They want to know about Alex's state of mind. I tell them how very bad it was, how we were terribly worried about him. I echo June's words. *He'd lost so much weight lately. He'd changed so much. He would get over-excited, too much so, like he was on drugs.* It dawns on me that I never liked Alex very much. That maybe I knew that deep down, but I never put it into words before. I liked what he brought out in me, I liked myself as his savior, the only person who could comfort him, put him back together when he fell apart, help him find his true genius. But now that he is dead, I have no feelings for him other than the lingering resentment of what he was about to do to me.

The police and I agree on how very tragic the whole situation is and I tell them the university is reviewing how it assesses students' mental health, which is something that just popped into my head—I make a mental note to bring it up at the next staff meeting. They nod, write things down and thank me for my time. They speak to June, who no doubt tells them the same thing, and to Geoff, who wouldn't have known anything anyway.

I am so relieved when they leave it makes my head spin. After that I can't concentrate. At one point, during a meeting with Bernie, one of my post-docs, I ask if he's able to help with tutorials next week and he says, "You okay?"

"Sure, why?"

"Because I've just spent fifteen minutes telling you I'm away next week. You haven't been listening to a word I said."

In the afternoon I stare at the pile of papers I still have to mark and wonder if I could offload them to one of the teachers' assistants, except that would mean I could leave for the day, and I just don't want to go home yet.

When I'm done marking, I sit with my fingers pressing into my eyes. Maybe I should confront Luis. But what will I say? I keep thinking about that odd artisanal dinner set. I didn't think it was Luis's style. Did she buy it for him? Maybe she's another artist working in the same building. Maybe the whole time I was there he was on another floor, kissing some willowy young thing. A potter maybe.

In the end it's Geoff who puts me out of my misery. I'm sitting with my forehead propped against the heel of my hands when he walks in. He knocks twice on my desk to make me look up and perches himself on the corner.

"What a day, hey? I'm sorry about Alex. Feel like a beer?"

I cock my head at him. "You should have told me I missed out on the professorship yourself, you know. Shouldn't I receive a formal notification? Having Mila tell me was a bit… weird."

"I know, I'm sorry. I didn't know she would do that."

"Out of curiosity, why didn't I get it?"

I'm sure I catch the glimpse of a smile, but it disappears so quickly I think I might have imagined it.

"Who knows? It's up to the board. But my guess is, you haven't published enough. That's where the gap is. And look, maybe it's not your thing. Plenty of people are happy to remain associate professors for life. Have you considered that?"

And I think, *What is it with everyone?* First Alex fires me from being his supervisor and co-author conveniently at the moment when his research is ready and he no longer needs me, and now Geoff, having let me do all that extra work for months in support of my application, all this stuff to show what an indispensable and *brilliant team player* I am, now tells me that it wasn't my thing anyway. Some days it's hard not to feel used and spat out in this world.

"You know that's not what I want," I say. "Why would you even say something like that?"

He frowns. "Because I'm not sure you're ambitious enough, Anna. Not in that way. When was the last time you presented a paper at a conference? Or chaired a panel? Or attended a symposium? Mila is all over that stuff. You're not."

He has no idea how much his words hurt me. I've always felt that Geoff and I had a certain kinship. If he thought that way about me, why wouldn't he say something before? And what's this about Mila anyway? *Mila is all over this stuff.* It feels like a slap in the face. Suddenly I feel old, past my sell-by date. Like the scales have fallen from my eyes and I see now that I don't stand a chance against the Milas of this world. All this time I thought I was the star of the show, it turns out I was just the supporting act.

Geoff gets to his feet. "Come on, come and have a beer. We can discuss it."

I sigh. "I don't know. You're paying?"

"Nope, Law is. There's a birthday party or something happening over there right now. If we move fast, we might score two each."

I hesitate. But then, I'm feeling so strung out anyway, I may as well go for it. I check my watch. Five thirty.

"Is Mila going?"

He cocks his head at me. "No, she's left for the day."

I look up at him under my eyelids.

"Come on, Anna. Let's go hang out."

I sigh. "Okay." I shut down my computer, grab my bag and follow him out of the building. Normally I'd walk on the path that meanders around the flower beds and then backtracks towards the Law faculty, but today I follow Geoff as he strides across the lawn, even though you're not supposed to, and steps over the leafy hosta patch and what's left of the blue irises. Maybe that's what's wrong with me: I never break the rules. Maybe that's why I never get what I want.

It's not a birthday party: it's a retirement farewell and we missed the speeches, but not the alcohol. I'd never do something like this normally—crash a professor's retirement party. That's very Geoff, though. He's always looking for a way to get something for free.

We stand at the drinks table—plastic cups, carrot sticks and dips—and Geoff finds two beers at the bottom of a plastic bucket full of watery ice. He hands me one and we clink bottles.

"I'll be right back," he says, then disappears to talk to someone at the other end of the room.

I watch him go, confused, and shake my head. I don't know why he bothered asking me along. I should just leave, I think, as I lean against the table, holding the bottle of beer without a bottle opener, wondering what I'm even doing here.

"Is that your boyfriend?" A man in his mid-thirties with a short beard and green eyes has slid up next to me. "Sorry, is it okay if I join you? I should probably have asked that first."

I'm about to say no, I'm leaving anyway, but I clock Geoff glancing my way, then checking this good-looking man chatting me up, and I change my mind.

I lift my beer. "If you can open this, you can absolutely join me."

He takes the bottle and unscrews the cap with his hand before handing it back to me. I laugh.

"Easiest job I've had all day," he says. He leans against the table too so we are next to each other, sipping our beers. He points with his chin in Geoff's direction. "So, is he?"

"What? Oh, no, he's not my boyfriend." He glances at my left hand. "Your husband then?"

"No, not my husband either." At the word 'husband' I feel the sting of tears in my nose and take a swig to hide my discomfort.

"He's an asshole," I say, wiping my mouth with the back of my hand. I'm not even sure who I'm talking about anymore.

"Really? Wow, okay, what's the story?"

My eyes never leave Geoff as I turn my head slightly so I can whisper in this stranger's ear.

"He's having sex with one of the math lecturers, and just gave her a full professorship in return."

"Ha! So the whole hashtag MeToo thing, not really on his radar, amiright?"

"Please. He wouldn't know how to spell hashtag." He laughs.

"The professorship was actually meant for me," I continue. "But I refused to have sex with him. He tried, once. I said no."

I don't know why I say that. It's like I'm throwing pieces of history in the air and letting them fall wherever they land, just to see what this new, random version sounds like. "That's why she got the promotion and not me." I take another swig.

"That's a terrible story. What's she like?"

I think of smart, beautiful Mila, with her long shiny hair and perfect skin and her thin gold chain around her delicate ankle. "Ordinary," I say, and shrug. "But some people will do anything to get ahead."

"You could sue, you know. You'd win."

I shrug. "Hey, I just roll with the punches. My husband is having an affair, that's my biggest problem right now." I'm completely unstoppable now. Maybe it's the beer. Or maybe I'm just lonely and tired of being everyone else's support system.

I could have confided in Lori, which would make a lot more sense, on the surface at least. Except that Lori—who I don't see much anymore since she moved to Seattle, and who is on her third marriage, with a teenage son from the first—always comments on how lucky I am. "You have the perfect husband, the perfect children, the perfect career! How did you do it?" she'd say. And I'd joke back with something like, "You can have my kids if you like them so much. Scratch that. I'll throw in the husband, too. Take the lot. See how you like them after a week." But, deep down, I believed she was right. I did have the perfect family and the perfect life. So there was no way I was going to confide in Lori right now. Maybe one day, after it had all blown over. I imagine myself in ten years on one of our ski trips in Colorado, sitting side by side on the chair lift, Lori commenting on my wonderful life.

Don't kid yourself, Lori. There was a time, you know, many years ago, when I thought we might not make it...

Meanwhile, I find myself telling this complete stranger about my marital problems. At least it takes my mind off Alex. In fact, what happened with Alex is beginning to feel like a distant memory. Even the police didn't seem that troubled by his suicide—this is what I do now: I make myself think of Alex's *suicide* as opposed to Alex's *death*. Meanwhile, this man listens intently to my woes, standing very close, head slightly bowed in concentration.

"Would you leave him?" he asks, when I finish.

I recoil. "My husband? No! I mean, I've fantasized about it sometimes, when he's annoyed me particularly."

"But don't you ever wonder? What it would be like to be with someone else?"

"What would it be like for me? It depends. I mean, I have wondered what it'd be like to be married to someone successful, tangibly so. Someone busy, driven." I look back at Geoff, who catches my eye and winks at me. Maybe I should have done it that night in Chicago; it sure had never occurred to me that Luis would be the one to stray. Maybe this is my punishment for flirting too much. Then a thought occurs to me, a terrible, stomach-clenching, bile-rising thought: *Is Luis planning to leave me?*

"No," I reply finally. "I never considered being with anyone else."

"Then don't say anything to your husband. Don't confront him."

"Do you think?"

"I do. You don't have enough information yet. You said so yourself."

"Are you married?" I ask.

"No. But I was in a long term relationship. I found out she had an affair and I confronted her."

I raise my eyebrows. "Really?"

"Really. Things got very messy and I asked her to leave. I thought she'd choose me, you see. I thought she'd beg me to take her back. She didn't. She's with the other woman now."

"Oh wow, the other woman?"

"Correct."

"Good to know the grass isn't any greener on the other side, then."

He smiles. "Do you have children?"

"Two. A boy and a girl."

"Even more reason to keep your mouth shut. If I were in your position, I'd fight for what I have."

Oh, I'll fight for what I have. Don't worry about that.

"Thank you. That's very wise." I raise my beer and we clink.

We're leaning back, saying deep things about life, our hands cupped on the edge of the table behind us. I feel his little finger inch closer to mine and it sends a strange shiver down my spine. He doesn't move his hand away, and neither do I.

"And when you do find out who it is," he says, "you could boil her in a cauldron full of bats. That's what we do where I come from."

I snap my head around. "Where do you come from?" He does have the most beautiful eyes, green with specks of gold, and they're nicely offset by his dark hair.

"Ireland. I've never lived there, I was born here, but my grandmother tells me these stories. I should have done it to my ex."

My mind is too frazzled to compute that and I stare at him, vaguely wondering where I could get bats.

He bursts out laughing. "I was joking." Then he adds, "We don't use bats. We're not savages."

I chuckle, and my gaze falls to his chest. The top two buttons of his shirt are undone and I get a glimpse of black, coarse hair. I wonder what it would feel like, to touch someone other than Luis. Then I wonder if he thinks about me when he touches his floozy, and whether she has nice breasts. I bet she does. I bet they're perky and pert. Like mine used to be before I had his kids.

The Irishman reaches behind him and lifts a bottle of Prosecco. "Come with me." I do as I'm told and when we reach the corridor he takes my hand and leads me around a corner and into an empty office. I reach blindly for the light switch that I assume is near the door but he cups my hand and whispers, "No, don't."

My skin feels tingly and I shudder. His tongue is on my lips, slow and soft like velvet. I'm about to argue, apologize if I gave the wrong impression, but then I think of Luis and I part my lips slightly. He undoes the buttons of my shirt and slips his hands behind my back, unhooks the clasp of my bra.

"Take it off," he whispers.

I'm shaking. I slip my arms out of my sleeves and let my shirt and bra fall to the floor. He has pulled his own shirt off and we stand against each other, my breasts against his chest, then we are on the floor and his mouth is on mine and his hand slides under the belt of my skirt.

"Wait!"

"You okay?" he asks.

"Give me a moment." I fling my arm over my eyes and feel him pull away.

What on earth am I doing? My head is spinning and a flash of light bursts behind my eyelids. What's that sound? A digital shutter. *Photo?*

I open my eyes quickly and sit up. In the dim light I see him smiling at me, his phone in his hand. I spring upright and reach for it, panic making my voice shrill. "Did you just take a photo of me?" But before he answers there's a movement behind the door, and a shadow interrupts the sliver of light beneath it. I put one finger on my lips to indicate we should be quiet. I hold my breath, then I'm sure I see the doorknob turn slowly, even though it's dark.

I scramble for my shirt and bra. Irishman is giggling. "Shut up!" I hiss. I throw his shirt at him. "Get dressed." My heart is thumping in my ears. I will whoever it is to go away as I manage to hook my bra back on and put my shirt back on. There's silence on the other side and I picture someone listening, one hand cupped around their ear against the door.

Finally the shadow moves away and I bow my head in relief as I get my breath back.

"Let's get out of here," I whisper, suddenly furious with this man for having put me in this position. I open the door an inch, check that the coast is clear.

He puts his hand on my arm. "Wait."

I shrug him off. "I have to go." I march down the hall, back to the party. A few stragglers are convened in the corner near the cheese board. Geoff is nowhere to be seen. I snatch my bag that is still hanging off the back of a chair and leave quickly, almost running to the car park.

Only then do I remember the photograph he took. I'd meant to get him to delete it immediately, but in that moment of almost getting caught out, I forgot. I start the car, and I see him as I drive out. He is standing on the sidewalk, his arms out wide in disbelief. I want to stop, to get him to delete the photo, but the traffic is moving and it's too late.

I bite my lip so hard it bleeds as my stomach clenches into tight knots the whole way home. When I get back I turn off the ignition and sit in the dark with my forehead against the steering wheel. I can't believe what I did back there. What was I thinking? That being unfaithful was going to help me get my husband back? I don't give a shit about the promotion. Not when my marriage is at stake. My family is the most important thing to me and to think

I would risk it so foolishly makes me hit my head with a closed fist—like that's going to put some sense back into me.

I lean back against the seat. It's okay. It's not the end of the world. He seemed like a nice enough guy. Tomorrow, I will go and see him and ask him to delete the photo. Then I will concentrate my energy on my family. Maybe if I can figure out who Luis is having an affair with, I can warn her off. It's just a fling, surely. Luis loves me, I know he does. And he is the most devoted father, and the most devoted husband.

Isn't he?

CHAPTER 11

The following morning I walk straight into the Law building, through the tiled entrance, down the corridor and upstairs to the office where I was the night before. I am determined. I tell myself I have every right to demand he delete that photo. I am desperately trying to work out what I'll do if he refuses.

The door to the office is open but instead of him, I come face to face with a woman with short gray hair and a birth mark on her left cheek. She is sitting behind the only desk in the room. She looks up over her glasses, startled. "Can I help you?"

"I'm... I'm looking for—" I don't know who I am looking for. I don't even know his name. "This is your office?"

"Yes. And you are?"

"There was a..." I am stuttering. I can't put words together to form a coherent sentence anymore. I try again. "I was at Professor Bashki's retirement party last night."

"And?"

"I'm looking for a man. He has a beard and green eyes."

She frowns, giving a small impatient shake of the head, understandably. She makes me feel like a schoolgirl tracking down the boy she kissed last night. Except I am almost forty years old.

She returns to her task. "I have no idea who you're talking about, I'm sorry. Try Admin down the hall."

"Okay. Thank you. My mistake." I walk back out, surreptitiously scanning the floor on the way out in case I left anything behind last night. Like my bra. Or my self-respect. I walk briskly in the direction she pointed me to and after a couple of wrong turns, I spot the sign that says *Student Services – Administration.*

The door is open and immediately I see the back of him. He is bending slightly at the water cooler. He turns around at my approach, a cup of water in one hand, and a grin spreads over his face.

"Well, hello there," he says, with a slight sneer that makes a shudder run down my spine, and not in a good way. He runs a hand through his hair. "It's nice to see you. You ran off very quickly last night."

My eyes dart around the room to see who might be listening. "Can I talk to you for a moment?" Two women at opposite desks look up.

"Sure."

I motion for him to follow me out until we're safely out of earshot. I stop, put my hand out. "Do you have your phone with you?"

He cocks his head and gives me a small smile. "My phone?"

"You know…" We're alone but I check my surroundings anyway. Then I lean closer. "You took a photo of me last night," I whisper. My stomach churns just saying the words.

"I did."

"I need you to delete it please."

He lifts his chin and stares at me for a moment. "And what if I don't?"

My heart races. "You have to. I never gave you permission." As if that ever meant anything to anyone.

"Maybe I like to look at it." He winks. "Maybe I—"

But I'm very close to him now, so angry that my nostrils are flaring. "You'd better delete that photo *right* now. I wasn't kidding when I said I never gave you permission. There are laws. I'll have you arrested or fired or whatever it takes."

He raises both hands in surrender. "Okay! Wow! Hold your horses there, lady! I was just kidding!"

"And I can't take a joke, so give me your phone."

He turns around and walks back in the direction of the admin office. For a moment I think he's just left me there, abandoned the conversation. My heart is pounding as I try to figure out what my next move is. But as I get to the door, I see him rummaging through a backpack on a chair by his desk. He pulls out his phone, taps the screen and walks back to where I am standing. I am so relieved it makes my legs wobble.

"Ryan?"

He turns around. A woman standing at the photocopier makes a face. "It's stuck, can you take a look?"

"Sure, give me a sec."

When he returns he holds up the screen to show me. "Done."

I narrow my eyes at him and reach for the phone. He hands it over. I flick through the camera roll. The last few pictures are of a dog in a park, a golden retriever with a red bandanna tied loosely around its neck. I scroll down quickly, my hands shaking. There's a blur of people, an older couple in a restaurant, him with his arm around a woman, a red-haired girl, both of them grinning, more pictures of the dog, sun setting in a park that looks vaguely familiar. Him—Ryan—with his arm around an older man's shoulders. A family resemblance. His dad, I suspect. After I've scrolled all the way up to the beginning, photos dated from over a year ago, I hand it back to him.

"Thank you."

He smirks. "You want to catch up for a coffee sometime?"

"No." I turn around to walk away.

"Anna?"

I stop, spin around. "How do you know my name?"

He gives an exaggerated eyeball roll. "Jeez, paranoid much? You told me."

He sneers at me, like a cocky teenager. *Did I really almost have sex with this man? What on earth was I thinking? I have a family. I have children, for Christ's sake.* I blame Luis. Luis who can't keep his penis in his pants. Luis who lied to me about where he was at the time I needed him most. Luis who suddenly drinks out of tall-stemmed wine glasses and eats olives stuffed with yak cheese off handmade pottery.

Ryan puts his hand on my arm but I shrug it off while pretending to pull the strap of my bag farther up my shoulder.

"You don't need to be embarrassed. About last night," he says.

"I'm not," I blurt. I feel myself blush crimson. I'm not embarrassed, I am humiliated.

There are more people around now, students, staff, professors, and I wish he would shut up. My eyes dart around like ball bearings in a pinball machine, frantically checking to see if anyone is listening. "Let's just forget about it, okay?"

"If you say so. Want to be friends? I'd like to be friends."

"Sorry. I really don't have time for that." Then I add, "But if you mention… anything about last night, I'll deny it."

I march out and this time he doesn't call out to me or try to stop me. I can still feel his hand on my skin. Like a burn.

I have a class that morning. Calculus. First years. I teach it on autopilot, distracted by everything going on in my life. Alex, Geoff, Ryan. Luis. When it's over I walk out and run into Geoff. Again. I'm beginning to wonder if he's doing it on purpose. Maybe he prefers to have all our conversations in corridors.

"What happened to you last night? I went looking for you everywhere. I thought we could share a cab home."

I almost blurt that I left early, claim a headache, then remember my handbag hanging on the back of the chair.

"Yes, sorry, I got sidetracked in conversation."

"Yeah, I saw that. That guy, right?" He smiles. "You two seemed to have a lot to talk about. Then you both disappeared!"

I feel a blush creep up my neck. "Right. Anyway, Geoff, I really have to go."

"Sure, sure. You have time for a chat after work?"

"Why?"

"No particular reason. I just want to see how you are. I imagine Alex's death must have hit you pretty hard."

"Thanks, but I can't." I am already walking away when he speaks again.

"Okay, next time then. I'm worried about you!" he shouts to my receding back.

CHAPTER 12

One week later, and I barely think about Alex anymore. It's a terrible thing to say, I know that. And when I do think of him, it is with anger. It's the thought that he used me just so he wouldn't have to write the paper himself that makes my chest vibrate. His death? I don't know. Maybe it hasn't really sunk in. Maybe it never will.

At this point, all I think about is Luis. Like I'm stuck on a loop. Luis and me, Luis and I, Luis and some other woman. The idea that Luis is having an affair—by now I have convinced myself of this fact—is obsessing me. Whenever he's out of the house I rummage through his things, his pockets, the drawer of the small desk that is unofficially his in the corner of the living room. The family computer that also is unofficially his and on which he keeps his email account. Carla came up with the password to that computer, and it's scribbled on a Post-It note sticky-taped to the bottom of the screen: *chez-les-sanchez.*

I trawl through his emails, fingers in my mouth, other hand on the mouse, scrolling, reading, scrolling, reading, until my eyes bleed. Nothing. Nothing unusual in his appointment book either, not even a squiggle or a code word that I can detect among Luis's organized, neat, everything-spelt-out entries. I pore over his cellphone bills, looking for a repeated number, an unusual one. I call the ones I don't recognize—*Hello, is this the aquarium?*—but they're all legitimate numbers: art supplies stores, 3-D printing, packing and transport; Perry Cube Gallery, recycling plants. Although it's not to say he didn't meet her at one of those places, obviously.

One day I surprise him at the studio for lunch. Salt and pepper calamari with creamy horseradish, his favorite. I don't find him *in flagrante delicto,* which I take as evidence that it's all in my head. He seems pleased to see me, so that's even better. We eat lunch on the couch in front of the giant nest. And he serves it on those pretty plates.

"Where did you get those?" I ask.

He shrugs. "Can't remember. Probably for one of the open studio shows."

And really, the more I try to catch him out, the more innocent he seems, the more I tell myself I'm being paranoid. It's my imagination getting the better of me, and a thousand other clichés. I convince myself that the whole Alex thing got me rattled and that I'm not thinking straight. But then the suspicious voice inside me pipes up: *You know he didn't get takeout from the deli that night. He lied to you.*

And every time I think of that lie my blood boils all over again. I spend hours awake at night thinking of all the things I do for my family, and that I do them with joy and gratitude. I clean, I cook, I send the kids to private schools plus ballet and drama and coding camp for Carla and soccer and fencing for Mateo, date nights with my husband once a month—did we go last month? I can't remember—sex once a week at least. And yet, somehow, it's never enough. *I'm* never enough.

June has brought me coffee in a real cup and saucer, and a plate of cookies. She has done this every day this week bar one. The other day I finally asked, "What have I done to deserve this?"

"That day, when the associate dean shouted at me, you were very kind. I just wanted to say thanks."

"Oh, really? Well, if that's the case, I'm thrilled he snapped at you. I hope he snaps at you lots more," I said, which made her guffaw.

"So, how're you feeling this morning?" she asks now.

"I'm okay, June, thank you." I bite off the edge of a cookie. "Ginger?"

She nods, gives me a small satisfied smile. "With cinnamon."

"Wow, they're amazing," I mumble, mouth full, catching a stray crumb trying to escape.

She laughs. "You said that yesterday. And the day before."

"What can I say, you outdo yourself every day, June, and every day I love you a little more for it."

She claps happily. "Great! And it's a new recipe I wanted to try."

I nod, shoveling the rest of the cookie in my mouth. "It's a keeper."

"Fabulous! Well, I'd better get back to it." She's at the door when she stops, turns and says, "Alex's parents. His father, I mean. He called. I'm sorry, but he wants us to Fedex anything of Alex's that is still here. Would you... is it all right for you to bring me anything you might have?"

My skin prickles. "What things?" I ask.

"Any personal papers, I guess. Did he have some textbooks, maybe? In his drawer?"

She starts to walk towards it and I spring upright. "I'll do it," I blurt.

She stops, startled. "Only if you want to, otherwise I can."

"Thank you, June, that's very thoughtful. But it's fine. I'd like to. And, anyway, there isn't much."

"Whatever you have. I'll send it off this morning."

"Of course. Give me a minute. I'll bring them out."

She walks out and I go to his little desk and sit down. It's an old wooden desk that someone from resources found god knows where, in some dark basement by the looks of it, and had brought up. We're so broke now, we can't even afford new desks. I run my hand along the top of it and bits of dust stick to my palm.

I open the first drawer and lift out two textbooks. I shake out the pages, but nothing falls out. I riffle through an almost empty drawer and gather the tidbits, junk mostly, he left behind: a biro, an eraser, a ruler and a hole puncher, of all things. I put them in a large envelope and put that on top of the textbooks. In the other drawer I find a notebook filled with squiggles and dark drawings and daggers dripping with blood over names that make no sense to me. I shove it in the trash can. I can't see there's anything there to bring joy to anyone.

I'm actually relieved but I don't know why exactly. I don't know what I thought I might find. But whatever it was, it's not there. Then I go to my own desk, and unlock the bottom drawer. That's where we kept his special notebooks, the ones I was supposed to bring along the day he died, but forgot. I stare at them. Nine large black spiral notebooks. They were his favorite type, he said. He liked the paper. He wouldn't use anything else.

I rest them on my lap, run my fingers along their edges. I open one at random. The proof. The only copy. I hesitate, glance at the door to make sure no one is watching, then slip them back in the drawer and lock them up again. I don't know why I do that. Maybe because his parents won't know or appreciate what they contain, and I need to think carefully about what to do with them.

I give June the pile.

"That's it?"

"Yes."

"Thank you. You look tired. Can you go home early?"

"Actually, I have to go home early. Big day today—it's Luis's opening night at Perry Cube."

"Oh, good luck with it. I hope it goes well."

"Thank you, June. I sure hope so, he has been working so hard."

I am reapplying my lipstick in front of the mirror in the living room. Propped on the mantelpiece is the invitation for tonight's opening. One side displays a detail of *The Nest*, the largest work in the exhibition. On the other is the time and date and the usual blurb.

You are invited to the opening of Without Us—*An Exhibition by Luis Sanchez at Perry Cube Gallery.*

Luis has been at the gallery all day but he's returned to get changed. He comes downstairs now, dressed in black jeans and a black shirt and a gray tie. "You look very handsome," I say, straightening his tie.

"Thanks, babe. I'm nervous as hell. Look how sweaty my palms are." He shows them to me before rubbing them on his thighs.

"They're going to love you," I say.

"You think?"

"Yes, I do."

I've finally started to believe I really was paranoid, that there was a simple explanation for why he wasn't at the studio that night. But since I never mentioned I was there, I just haven't been able to bring it up. And now it's well and truly too late, too weird, and it would display my lack of trust. "You're so jealous sometimes, Anna. Why can't you trust me?" he'd say, like he has said every other time.

He puts his arms around me and hugs me close, but not the way I would have liked. I want his hug to be, like, let-me-rip-those-clothes-off-your-sexy-body; instead, I get a soft pat-pat-on-the-back before he pulls away. I stand there, one hand on my hip.

"Notice anything?"

He takes a moment. I sweep one arm over my body to show my outfit. He laughs. "Yes! You look beautiful."

I'm wearing wide pants and high heels and a yellow puff-sleeve shirt. I bought the outfit at Beachwood Place yesterday. I spent hours in there, choosing the right look. Now I catch sight of our reflection in the mirror and there's no doubt we still make a beautiful couple after all these years.

Carla stomps down the stairs and stops in her tracks at the sight of us. "Wow, you guys spruce up nice. Where you off to?"

For a moment I think she's forgotten this is her father's big night, and I'm about to tell her off but then I catch the grin on her face.

"Ha ha," I say. "Very funny."

She holds out a small package wrapped in pretty crêpe paper. "There you go, Dad. I just wanted to say congratulations. I love you." Luis takes the present and she puts her arms around his neck and briefly rests her head on his shoulder and I think to myself, *There's* no *way he's having an affair. He wouldn't jeopardize his family. He loves us too much.* Carla pulls away while he unwraps his present. "I'd say break a leg, Dad, but you don't have to because I know you're going to knock 'em dead."

He's holding a beautiful book bound in leather, adorned with colorful birds. He opens it and caresses its thick, cream-colored blank pages. A luxurious sketching book.

"It's beautiful. Thank you, sweetheart." He kisses the top of her head. "Maybe not dead, if that's okay. I need them to live long enough to write glowing reviews. Maybe even buy a piece or two."

She nods. "Not dead then, just their socks off."

I reach out to her and wrap my arms around her. "Has Matti finished his homework?"

"He's doing it now," she says.

"And don't let him play Xbox tonight please, okay?"

"Yes, mother."

"And don't go to bed too late. Both of you."

"Yes, mother."

"And I love you."

"Yes, mother."

"Okay, go away."

She giggles, quickly disentangles herself from me, plants a kiss on my cheek and runs back up the stairs.

I'm so happy tonight. For Luis, and for me. It's the kind of thing I live for, this feeling that we are joined at the hip, meeting the world together, showing it what we're capable of. Tonight feels like we're about to embark on a great journey together. Luis's first major exhibition at one of the most prestigious private art galleries in the country, and me by his side.

But then, as Isabelle, the pretty, millennial-type curator, keeps bringing people over to Luis who *absolutely have to meet you, Luis* and Perry, the gallery owner, a small, bald man with thick-rimmed glasses, gives a speech that tells of *the exceptionally beautiful works that have become Luis Sanchez's signature, never failing to bring to our attention the urgent issues we confront today*, something shifts in my world.

At first, it's not even a shift, more like a hairline crack quietly creeping up in my line of vision. Maybe it's because red dots begin to appear next to every artwork, too quickly to keep count. It dawns on me just how many people are here, and who they are: not just art buyers, but serious collectors. They represent institutions and private collections and they have traveled from all over the country to admire—and acquire—Luis's art works. This has never happened before, and I experience something so unexpected that it takes me a while to recognize it: fear.

Of being left behind.

I used to think that the reason I held the family together was because I was indispensable. I work, I pay the bills, I support my husband in his career. Not for the first time, it occurs to me that my own prospects of success have passed me by. Suddenly, I am just an ordinary math teacher and Luis has chiseled his way into a bigger future while I wasn't paying attention. Could that be because I work long hours in a small, airless office then come home and put on a load of laundry? I make lunches for the kids to take to school and keep everyone to a regimented schedule of ballet lessons and soccer practice. And now, Luis has met his destiny and he doesn't need me anymore. My husband doesn't. need. me. anymore.

If only I'd been better at forging a career, become someone he could be proud to be seen with in public. Suddenly I feel like I never reached my potential, and now it's too late. That I am a disappointment to everyone. *Don't be silly*, says absolutely no one, especially not my mother.

I was looking away, nowhere in particular, lost in that hairline crack that has turned into a chasm by now, when I hear his voice. He is giving his speech, delivering his lines with boyish charm and self-deprecating jokes. It's a brilliant speech: short and sweet, funny, very interesting and completely different from what I'd expected, had I bothered to think about it. And, most importantly, it holds everyone's attention. You could have heard a pin drop right until the end.

He's glowing, my husband, like there's a halo around him. His eyes are upon me, filled with pride and love and I smile back at him, my eyes similarly sparkling with joy, my cheeks flushed with pleasure in the glow of his love.

But then it dawns on me. It's not me they're looking at, those eyes filled with pride and love. I see now that they're focused on a point just to my left, and I slowly turn around to look over my shoulder, until I locate the object of his adoring gaze.

CHAPTER 13

Isabelle. Beautiful, ethereal Isabelle. Even her name rolls off the tongue like a promise. *Isabelle.* Young, Isabelle. Very young. I can't peel my eyes off her. I stare at her shiny blonde hair styled in an elaborate updo, her perfect, porcelain skin, her sparkly blue eyes, and all I can think is, *Give up now, Anna. It's over. Just pick up your bat and go home.*

I've been slowly edged towards the back of the crowd as people elbowed their way closer to Luis. My outfit, which I was convinced up until now was stylish and professional, suddenly seems all wrong. Like I've made an effort, but not the right one. I am dressed for an important meeting while every other woman in the room is elegant, wealthy, sexy. Isabelle is dazzling in a slate-gray flowing layered ensemble that cascades in ripples of silk down her front, showing off her perfect breasts—at least I was right about that part—whereas I look like a life-insurance salesperson on her way to a seminar.

You can feel the sexual tension between them even standing as they are at opposite ends of the room. My chest is rising and falling with the effort of breathing. Were they together that night, while I waited alone in Luis's studio? Of course they were. That's what he's been doing these past few weeks, when I thought he was working hard on his exhibition.

I'm under the gun, babe. An image of myself holding a shotgun to his head pops into my mind and I leave it there for a moment because it makes me feel better.

What about all the nights I worked late on my application so I could get a better job, better paid, work harder for my family? All the healthy meals I prepared while he made love to her? The instructions I left peppered with exclamation marks and tips when I couldn't be home?

Salmon Teriyaki. Just fry the salmon (already dusted with flour, in the fridge) in the wok with lemon juice—1 min or so each side, make sure the wok is super hot first! Then add the teriyaki sauce (in the little blue and white jug—also in the fridge) and when it's almost bubbling, serve it up! Vegetables are cut up, ready to steam, in the container with red lid, bottom shelf of the fridge. Sorry I have to work late again, love you all! x

Was he licking her toes while I washed dog poop off our porch? Was she on her knees, begging for more, while I scoured for recipes that would be delicious *and* nutritious? A wave of nausea rises up my throat as I watch him lapping up the attention, and all I want is to walk up to him, slap him and yell, *Remember me?* right into his face.

They're posing for photos now, Luis and Isabelle. The artist and the curator. I thought Luis and I made a nice couple, but these two together look spectacular. How long has it been going on? I try to remember when these late nights started, the evasive answers about where he went, but I can't pin it down. I was hardly there myself in the evenings. Those months of work with Alex took care of that.

Is she going to reap what I've sown and tenderly nurtured all these years while my time came and went with barely a ripple?

Suddenly Luis is by my side, a glass of champagne in his hand. None for me, I note.

"What do you think?" he asks.

I pause and gather myself. I search his face for evidence of his treachery, a twitch of guilt even, but all I find is the beaming grin of a winner.

He raises his eyebrows. "So?"

"It's wonderful. Really, Luis. Congratulations."

"Thank you." He smiles. "But I couldn't have done it without Isabelle."

For a moment there I thought he was going to say, *But I couldn't have done it without you.*

I pull my lips wide into an approximation of a smile.

"She's amazing," he continues, in the tone of someone talking to himself, shaking his head in awe at how wonderful she is. "It looks like she might have a shot at selling *The Nest* to the contemporary art museum for their permanent collection. Nothing concrete yet"—he holds crossed fingers—"but they're considering it in their current acquisition round." He closes his eyes and tilts his face to the ceiling. "God, that would be so amazing." Then he turns to me and I guess he realizes I am here because he says, "Hey, you should talk to her, you'd really like her. She's massively talented." And I stand there thinking, *Am I ever going to wake up from this nightmare? What if I jumped in front of a bus—would anyone even notice I was missing?*

That night, when Luis comes to bed, I pretend to be asleep. He settles in with his back to me and within minutes he's snoring. I lean close to his ear and whisper, "You snore, did you know that?" But he doesn't move. I push the covers off me very slowly, swing my legs out of the bed and tiptoe over to his side. His cellphone is on the side table and I carefully pick it up. I try a code—not for the first time, that should go without saying. I've tried them all. Kids' birthdays, wedding anniversary, the day we met—even though I'm pretty sure he has no idea when that was. I stare at it as Luis stirs and rolls onto his back, one arm flung over the edge of the bed.

Gently, softly, I lift his hand and press his thumb over the button, thanking my lucky stars he had refused to upgrade his iPhone. *The environment, Anna!* says the man who makes sculptures out of plastic. *Ah, but it's recycled! See?*

The screen lights up and shudders.

Try again

I press his thumb harder this time. His eyes blink open.

"What are you doing?"

"You were having a nightmare," I whisper. "Go back to sleep."

He groans, rolls over.

I'm in.

I miss you.

It's right there, in black and white. And he has a nickname for her. *Belle.*

I love you so much.

I can't do this anymore. I can't do this to my children.

Babe, please don't shut me out. We'll work it out, I promise.

I can't stop thinking about you.

And I can't stop crying. I'm sitting at the table in the kitchen, big snotty sobs erupting and dribbling down my chin, sobs so loud I have to keep my hand over my mouth so as not to wake up the neighborhood.

I scroll back quickly. The first one I find is dated April, three months ago.

I'm so sorry, it should never have happened.

I miss you so much.

I miss you too, Belle,

Do you love her?

Don't.

He's going to leave me. She's going to make him, you can see that a mile off, the way she's pulling at him like a drug. All I can think about are my children. How would they cope if we split up? And, immediately, the next logical thought pops into my head.

Who will they choose?

There was a time when they were little and I was working all the time, when they became bonded to Luis. He was caring for them just about full time so I could work. I missed my children so much it hurt, but it seemed the right thing to do while Luis got on with his art practice. I liked supporting him. I was proud of him. But I can still remember with a flash of pain when Mateo fell off his bike in the park and, clutching a bleeding knee, wailed from the top of his lungs, *Dadddddyyyyy!!!* And yet I was right there, mere feet away. But Luis had already scooped him up and sat him on his lap on a bench, in full view of the other parents. They looked at me with pitying faces while Luis pretended to operate (scalpel? electric saw?), carefully putting a plaster with a picture of a ninja turtle on it (where did they come from? Did he carry them in his back pocket?). He kissed it better and sent him on his way. I resolved right there and then to spend a lot more time with the children. And I did. They needed me, and I needed them. I think they were puzzled at first by my insistence that I'd soothe them even when they weren't that sad, and mop their brow when they weren't that sick. I read stories whether they were tired or not and cooked hot meals that would make a child nutritionist want to quit their job and join the circus.

I go back through the texts, wailing into my palm. Her last text from last night:

I love you so much I could burst. Congratulations, my love.

And all I can think is, *Do. Please burst. Please. Let your flesh rip open and bits of your organs fly out all over the walls because you just can't hold it in anymore. All this love for my husband, it made you burst!*

In reply he texted:

I couldn't have done it without you. You're incredible. I love how smart you are.

Seriously? What about me? What am I? Chopped liver? Am *I* not smart enough anymore? Considering it's what has defined me my whole life, it's a blow, I won't lie. It's my nightmare of a childhood, my career and my sacrifices, and it's stupid Alex and the professorship I didn't even get. Maybe I'm not that smart. Maybe that's my problem. Maybe I'm not smart and everybody knows it except me.

"Come back to bed, Anna."

My heart somersaults in my chest and I slap the phone down, screen to the table, so hard I think I might have cracked it. Luis puts his hands on my shoulders and squeezes.

Without looking up, I reach up and take his hand. "I will. I just need a minute."

He picks up an empty glass from the table and puts it next to the sink. I shove the phone into the pocket of my bathrobe.

"Is it Alex?" he asks, stooping down and wiping my tears with his thumb.

I kind of nod, kind of not; anything to stop myself from laughing hysterically into his face.

Back in bed, he spoons me, strokes my hair, and I am so afraid I could die. I feel this yawning void stretch out before me. A schism of loneliness. All the promise of my life vanished. Alex's death has robbed me of my professional future, Luis's success has robbed me of my family. I put the pillow against my face to muffle my sobs.

CHAPTER 14

This morning I stare at my reflection in the bathroom mirror, purple crescents beneath my eyes. Puffy eyelids. Frazzled brain. Despairing mood.

"Hey, babe, have you seen my cellphone?"

I spin around. Luis is leaning into the bathroom, holding onto the doorjamb.

"Um, no?"

"Okay. You okay?"

I nod quickly. "Absolutely. Great night last night by the way. I'm sorry I got…"

"No, I get it."

"It's his parents—I had to gather his things for them. That's what got to me."

"Oh, Anna, you should have said."

"Don't be silly. It was your night. And a wonderful night it was, too. I'm so proud of you."

He smiles, slides a lock of hair in that space between his thumb and forefinger and pushes it out of the way. I can hear myself asking, *Are you going to leave us?* But his face doesn't change so I know it's only in my head.

"I'll make coffee."

"Thank you. I'll be there in a sec."

The moment he is gone, I pat the pocket of my robe and pull out his phone. After I get dressed, I make the bed and yell out, "Found your phone!" and he bounds up the stairs while I brandish it.

"It was on the floor."

*

I have a quiet afternoon today so I decide to follow her. I tell myself I just want to see what I'm up against. What is so special about her that Luis would risk breaking up his family? He said last night that she can help him break into major collections, that the sale of *The Nest* is just the beginning, which surely can't be reason enough that he'd leave us. Maybe she's good in bed. Maybe she does things that every man dreams of but would never dare ask his wife. Maybe I need to update my repertoire. Maybe we have fallen into the classic married-couple trap, when making love is just a quick release because we're too tired to do anything else.

I borrowed a cap from Carla, dark blue with a wide brim at the front and a small white pineapple logo. I know the gallery closes at five, so I sit in my car, the cap over my ears and my oversized, unbranded, mirrored aviator sunglasses over my eyes.

She emerges at ten past five, waves to someone inside and takes off on foot down the street. I slip out of my car and follow her, past the Westside Market and into Church Avenue. She walks into a vivid blue house that looks like something out of a movie set, with a pretty garden at the front. I'm surprised. I expected her to live in one of those renovation projects, a building that would have been some kind of factory once but is now converted into lofts and oversized apartments with floor to ceiling windows.

I get myself a takeout coffee from the deli across the road and wait idly for a while. I'm not sure she'll come out again and I'm just starting to think, *Why am I here again? So, she lives in a pretty blue house. Okay, can I go home now?* when her front door opens. She's changed into shiny, dark gray leggings and white running shoes with a hot pink stripy pattern on the side. She walks briskly down the street and crosses the river via a small pedestrian bridge, then takes the path that I know loops around the park and along the riverfront.

I'm red-faced and out of breath by the time I sit down on a bench with my coffee and watch her run in circles. She doesn't even break a sweat, her ponytail swinging in time with each strong, bouncy stride. Whenever she loops past me I am tempted to extend my leg and watch her tumble into the geraniums. It's surprisingly difficult to quash the urge, so in the end I leave and go home.

The next day I spend half an hour before the staff meeting browsing online until I find the exact same running shoes. I make a note of the brand and at lunchtime I go down to Champs and get myself a pair, even though they cost $160. I also buy a pair of leggings, which is kind of scary because my thighs are not what they used to be, and a T-shirt with little holes in it, just like she was wearing.

"We should go running together," I tell Luis that night.

He frowns. "Why?"

"It would be fun. Don't they say that couples who run together stay together?"

He laughs, because he thinks I'm joking. I'm about to argue, insist, but then I think I should probably practice first.

And I do. Only because I want to follow her again, and it's easier to do that if I'm running. I get to the park and there are so many of us runners and for the first five minutes I'm enjoying myself. I feel like I'm part of a tribe as we smile at each other as we pass. It's nice. I'm tempted to go up to Isabelle and say *Hi! Remember me?* just to see the expression on her face. But then she might suggest we run together and that's just not an option. Compared to Isabelle I look like a sad middle-aged woman with saggy breasts and an expanding waistline desperately trying to hang on to her youth. Which is exactly what I am, so that makes sense. I don't even know what I'm trying to achieve here, other than check her out. Size up the competition. And it's done now: I've checked her out and she's as beautiful as the first day I met her, which was just the other day, and she runs like a gazelle and I run like a duck.

Back home I put the clothes away in the bottom of the closet.

Three days later and I'm having a beauty day, as I call it. I've made an appointment after work at Marcus Bond Salon because it's eye-wateringly expensive, so I figure that's good, he should be able to fix me up.

I'm about to leave when Geoff shows up. "Anna, can you type up this grant acquittal, please?" He hands me the paperwork.

"It's the form," I say.

"Yes, I know."

"But it's blank. It hasn't been filled in."

"Yes, I know, that's why I'm asking."

"But it's going to take hours, and I can't right now."

"What do you mean, you can't? Why not?"

I slip on my jacket and grab my bag. "I have a hair appointment if you must know."

"Oh? A hair appointment?" He smiles. "You know you're beautiful just as you are."

He's still holding out the form. I tap it with one finger. "Ask Mila," I say. "She's all over this stuff."

Two hundred and twenty dollars later, and I walk out with my hair dyed almost black. It was brown, but with strands of gray peeking through which I had said I wanted to get rid of. It's been straightened to an inch of its life—it was vaguely wavy—and with bangs cut bluntly in a horizontal line. It's in a kind of short bob, and when I say short, I mean cut-it-any-shorter-and-you've-gone-past-my-hairline short, and also cut real short above my ears, and whatever is not the bob is shaved, which is most of the back of my head.

"Short hair makes you look younger," says the woman cutting my hair, who is not Marcus Bond, because apparently Marcus Bond only cuts for his regular clients.

It's terrifying. And I don't look younger. I look about fifty now, which is ten more years, boom, just like that, and I don't know what to say, and my chin wobbles when I pay but I don't want to cry at the hairdresser because who cries at the hairdresser? Other than small children, I mean.

I don't go back to work; I just go straight home and Luis says, "Oh, wow, Anna, what happened?" and he says it like I had an accident and I've walked in on crutches.

"It just needs a wash," I say. "You know what it's like. They put too much product in it. I'll be right back."

I rinse it over the sink and it's still very bad and very scary, so I grab my nail scissors and start to hack at it, hoping to transform it into some kind of cute pixie cut.

"Oh, wow, Mom, what happened?" the children say later.

"Nothing. You like it?"

"No."

"Okay then. Can you set the table, Matti?"

And that was my beauty day, and I couldn't even get that right.

I love how smart you are.

I think about those words until my blood boils and I'm biting the inside of my cheek so hard I taste blood. I think about them until my chest rises and falls with anger and my pulse races and my lips pucker and I'm breathing hard through my nose.

I think about them, and then I get to work. I'd like to say what I'm about to do next is a spur of the moment thing, but that would be a lie. I've been thinking about doing it for days, maybe even ever since Alex died. Was I thinking about this when I locked the notebooks in my drawer instead of giving them to his parents? Yes. I've turned the idea over in my mind ever since, trying it on for size, weighing up the risks. But I haven't done anything about it.

I close my office door but don't lock it because that would be weird and invite questions. I find myself muttering positive affirmations, which makes me sound like a mad woman, even to my own ears. *It's going to be fine. You deserve it. It's better this way. Think of the university.*

I open the document on my computer and read it again. *The Pentti-Stone Conjecture—A Simple Proof.*

It's short, under twenty pages, and beautiful. Elegant in its simplicity and as perfect as a circle. Then I cup my hand over the mouse and select Alex's name. I take a breath, my finger hovering over the delete button. I can still change my mind. There's still time.

I'm concerned that having you as co-author will lend your contribution more weight than is warranted.

Then I think of Luis and I think about Isabelle, I think of Luis and Isabelle together, kissing, making love, and a ripple of anger travels through me, so savage it made my jaw lock.

I love how smart you are.

One small click, and just like that, Alex's name is gone, leaving only mine.

I may not be the most beautiful woman in the world and I may have a shitty haircut, but if my husband loves smart so much, he's about to get an orgasm of volcanic proportions that's guaranteed to blow his brains out.

I load up the webpage of the *Journal of Applied Number Theory* submission form.

How many authors does your article have?

One. This paper has one author only. There. Not so hard, is it? I'm doing it. It's happening. *Stop thinking, Anna.* I fill in the rest of the form, typing quickly so I won't have time to think. *Name, Email Address, Institution.*

Just wait until my colleagues hear that one of their own has solved the Pentti-Stone conjecture. I just hope I'm there to see Geoff's face when he finds out. Our future will be assured. This will put us on the map. We will attract the brightest students in the country. All because of me.

I wonder if he'll ask Mila to take minutes.

I have the cursor on the submit button, gripping the mouse so hard my knuckles turn white. This is it, now or never.

"Anna, there you are. Did your friend find you?"

My heart jumps into my throat. "June! Jesus, you scared me."

She laughs. "Sorry, I wasn't sure you were in here. Your friend was looking for you."

I breathe in, my heart still thumping. "Okay, what friend?"

She lifts her shoulders. "He didn't say. I told him where your office was—maybe he thought you weren't here. You don't usually have your door closed."

"A student?"

"No. He said he was a friend of yours. A young man with dark curly hair and nice green eyes. Doesn't matter. I guess he didn't find you."

Dark curly hair. Nice green eyes. "Was his name Ryan?"

"Sorry, Anna, I didn't ask."

She waits, like this is a concern for her too. Why would Ryan come here? And why on earth would he call himself my *friend*?

"Everything all right?"

"Yes, thank you. I'm kind of busy here, June, so…"

"Oh, of course. I wanted to see if you were ready for your coffee. I made som—"

"June, honestly, I'm in the middle of something here! I do not want a coffee, okay? You don't have to bring me coffee and cookies every day, okay?"

She blinks, reddens. "Well, sure. I meant well." She leaves without looking at me, closes the door. I drop my head into my hands. Well, there's a sign if I ever saw one. I don't usually snap at and insult my friends, and yet I just did. What the hell am I doing? I sigh, open the browser again, ready to close the window and cancel the whole thing. It was a stupid idea anyway. What's wrong with submitting it the way it was intended? With both authors? And showing Geoff Alex's thesis, too? He'll wonder why I took so long but I'll say I wanted to put in the finishing touches, make sure it was truly ready. I'll still be co-author on the paper, we'll still gain a reputation of excellence. I'll still be credited. Nothing's changed.

I actually feel relieved. I will go and see June immediately and apologize. Then I glance at the screen.

Thank you for your submission. We will be in touch as soon as possible.

I blink. It looks like I clicked the mouse anyway. Immediately, part of me wants to reach into the computer and snatch it back from the jaws of the internet. But another part of me whispers in a low voice: *It's done now, Anna. What you gonna do? Get in touch with this prestigious journal and say, "Sorry, I didn't mean to send it because it's not really mine?" Or are you going to stand up for yourself for once, and take what you deserve?*

I unlock my bottom drawer, retrieve Alex's notebooks, shove them in my bag.

I wish June hadn't told me about this mysterious friend because instead of feeling triumph that I submitted the proof, I have a knot in my stomach. Why would Ryan come here? It probably wasn't Ryan. Maybe June got it wrong and it was a student. Or a prospective student. Yes, that makes sense. Well, whoever it was they can come back later.

Poor June. Her face just now, when I snapped at her... I'll go and apologize immediately, then get on with the rest of my day. What will I do with Alex's notebooks? Get rid of them, that goes without saying. I was going to find a dumpster for them, somewhere—it seems kind of fitting in a way—then I change my mind. I don't want to take any risk. Instead I find a secure shredding service online and arrange to drop them off later.

Then I pull out a hairbrush and get myself presentable for the staff meeting. It doesn't really work. I still look like a porcupine.

CHAPTER 15

At first I spent entire nights awake, my unblinking eyes staring into the dark, wishing I hadn't done it. After all, I'd had so many other, better choices. I could have gone to Geoff with the notebooks and told him about Alex's research. We could have published it in his memory. Maybe his family would have let us keep the prize money—they're wealthy, they don't need it. We could have started a scholarship in Alex's name.

But it's too late now. That's what I tell myself when I wake up in the dead of night. *It's too late now*, I whisper, my heart hammering, Alex's ghost hovering over my bed.

It's too late.

I sleepwalk through my life waiting for some indistinct hammer to fall, for things to go wrong, for Luis to leave me. I picture the recipient of my submission at the journal reading my paper, then squinting with the look of someone who *has heard of this solution before*. Because what if Alex had already contacted them without telling me? That would make sense, right? That would be very much in character for Alex. Do I have an explanation for how this could happen? How could *my* student submit a work of genius, then die, then for the *exact same* work of genius to be submitted again, except this time authored by me? Do I have an explanation for that? No, Officer, I do not. Not readily.

But as days turn into weeks and nothing happens, I begin to think maybe, just maybe, it's going to be okay. Instead of dreading the call, I start to resent how long it's taking before they approve the paper. I feel like I've crossed a threshold: I am already on the other side, drumming my fingers, waiting for everyone else to catch up. Then I worry that it's taking *too* long, even though I know mathematical proofs can take months to be peer-reviewed and validated. But I also know this won't be the case here because this proof—? Its beauty lies in its simplicity. It's the kind of proof that someone might review and wonder why no one had thought of it before, because it's just *so obvious*.

But I don't spend these long weeks of waiting idly. Instead, I devote them to the other part of my plan: to make my husband fall in love with me again. Turns out there's no shortage of information on the internet about how to do exactly that, and I'm good at research. Over the next few weeks I become not someone *else* exactly, but someone *better*. More devoted, kinder, more patient. Happy. I make myself look deliriously happy every time he walks into a room. I ask him about his work, I laugh with delight at his success, I nuzzle his neck and tell him he's handsome, I cook his favorite meals, I rub my nails lightly over his back when he looks stressed. I put candles out on the back deck after the children go to bed and invite him to watch the stars with me over a glass of wine; I buy sexy underwear and make love to him every night.

And I watch him like a hawk, that goes without saying. I haven't been able to access his texts again, but I pay close attention to his moods and take the occasional peek at his emails.

I make notes of my progress. "I like this dress on you, it's nice," he said the other day, with a cheeky smile. Unprompted, he will bring me a glass of wine when I'm preparing dinner. He talks to me. And he listens. He's become more attentive, more relaxed and flirty. I call all these things successes in their own right. I'm winning. I'm no longer a team player, I'm a winner.

Then, this morning, five weeks after I submitted it, I receive the call from the journal to congratulate me. The solution has been reviewed and accepted and will be published next month. "Its publication will allow you to claim the Pentti-Stone prize from the Leo Forrester Foundation," they added.

It's official, I have solved the Pentti-Stone conjecture.

And just like that, everything changes. My doubts, my fears, vanish with that phone call. I don't care if it's Alex's proof—it's mine too. I put the phone down and stare at my hands, reminding myself that I came up with the final piece of the puzzle. I banish the voices in my head for good and after a few minutes of silence, I go to Geoff's office with a grin on my face and butterflies in my stomach. June raises an eyebrow at me and I put one finger to my lips and wink at her. Then I walk in, close the door after me and lean against it.

"You'll never guess what happened," I say. Then I tell him. He doesn't believe me at first, understandably. Little old me, minute-taker-gofer-errand-loser with no ambition whatsoever suddenly solves a major math problem out of thin air.

I pull out the chair opposite his desk. "They're publishing it next month. I just got the call from the journal. Then an email from the Leo Forrester Foundation who want to come here, to the university I mean, and formally present the prize."

He looks at me sideways, squinting. "Is it the first of April today?"

I smile. "Nope."

He picks up the phone and speaks to someone at the journal. He actually had to do that, assert that it was true, that I wasn't just spinning it. Once he's checked the facts he doesn't speak for a long time, just stares at me.

I was really expecting more, and I feel a stab of disappointment. "You're happy?" I ask. "It'll be good for the university."

"This is incredible."

"I know," I say, relieved. I grin.

"But you never said…"

"I wanted to make sure. And then I didn't get the professorship so, you know…" There. I'm a winner now, I get to indulge in these little digs.

He sits back in his chair and plays with a pen, waves it in the air. He narrows his eyes at me. "Something isn't right."

I wait, tilt my head, but his expression doesn't change. It's dark and suspicious and suddenly I know, and it's like the entire edifice that is my new, winning life collapses around me. I screwed up. It's over. I just did a very, very foolish thing, because I'm an idiot. He knows—of course he knows. How could I have been so stupid? He must know about Alex and the proof. Alex always swore I was the only one he ever told, he made me swear not to tell anyone, especially not Geoff. He convinced me he was paranoid about his work being stolen. I took him at his word and now it's too late. I've made it official that I'm a thief and a fraud. I open my mouth to say something, formulate an apology, say there was a mistake and I always meant to submit it in his name when Geoff bursts out laughing.

"What?" I ask, blinking.

"We should be celebrating! There should be champagne!" He calls June and asks her to get everyone in here immediately, and to bring champagne and glasses. Yes, right now, he says. Yes, I know it's not even lunchtime, he says. Then he gets up and comes round and gives me a big hug. Suddenly everyone is here and everyone is hugging me, even Mila, and everyone is poking and pulling at me and they want to know why I never said anything and how I did it and I'm laughing because they're all talking over each other and if I'd known there'd be such a fuss I would have fixed my make-up. But I am so happy I could burst. I am happier than I've been in years, and this is just the beginning. And I tell them I'll be right back and with my glass of champagne in my hand I return to my office and close the door and call Luis.

I did it, I say. Did what? he asks, and I can hear a smile in his voice. I drop mine to a whisper, like this is too special to be said out loud. It's a surprise, I say. But remember last year, all those nights I worked late, and this year, too? Of course he remembers. Well, I didn't want to say anything, but I was working on an incredibly important project. I solved a major math problem. There's going to be a prize. Half a million dollars, Luis! And it's going to be published in the most prestigious journal in the country. *Do you love me now?* I almost add.

Then June comes in holding her own glass and the bottle of champagne. "Come on, you. We're all waiting for you."

"I have to go," I say to Luis.

"No, wait! This is wonderful news, Anna. I'm so proud of you, babe. You should have told me!"

"I couldn't tell you. I didn't want to jinx it."

"Well, I think you're incredible."

"Thank you, darling."

"Let's go out and celebrate—you, me and the kids," he says quickly. Then he drops his voice to a suggestive whisper. "Or maybe just you and me, what do you say?"

I laugh. "No, bring the kids. I'd like that."

"I'll make a reservation at the Confit d'Oie."

"Oh, yes! Do that! I've been dreaming of that place!"

He laughs. June has refilled my glass and I tell Luis I really should go.

"I love you, babe. I'm so proud of you," he says, and my heart runneth over.

June clinks her glass with mine and takes my arm as we walk back to Geoff's office. "Congratulations, Anna. I don't understand what any of this means, but I'm really happy for you."

"Oh, thank you, June."

Back in Geoff's office, he immediately elbows June out of the way, puts one arm around my shoulders and squeezes. "Let's get drunk after work, you and me. What do you say?"

"I can't—"

"Oh, come on. Sure you can."

"Luis is taking me and the children out to celebrate."

"How lovely. Where is he taking you?" June asks.

I move to extricate myself from Geoff's grip. "We're going to that new French restaurant over on Fulton Road."

"Oooh, very chic," she says.

"Yeah, very chick," Geoff quips. "I was thinking the sports bar across the road. June, you want to join me? Since we're not good enough anymore?"

She rolls her eyes at me. "I don't think so, Geoff."

"Another time, then. Meanwhile let's have a toast. To Anna!"

I leave at the end of the afternoon with a feeling of having reached the pinnacle of happiness. I savor every second as I walk out onto the street because I want to remember it all. I want to relive it any time I like. I want to be able to say, *Remember the day I won the Pentti-Stone? It was in the fall and the tupelos had turned bright red and the air had that smell of wet leaves, remember?*

I'm laughing to myself as I swing my satchel back and forth like a child but, as I approach my car, my key already pointed at it, I freeze, the grin still plastered on my face, my hand suspended in mid-air, my finger poised over the unlock button. At first I think someone threw dirt on it. Then as I get closer I see it's graffiti. But no. It's not graffiti.

Across the driver side, in big sharp letters, someone has scratched the word *WHORE.*

I stand there, jaw slack, mouth open, my satchel banging against my legs, then slowly walk around the rest of the car looking for any more vandalism, but there's none. Just that one word. I glance at the other cars on the street, walk up and down a few lengths, but the vandals picked mine, and mine only.

"Anna?" I spin around. June is walking towards me, smiling. "Where're you off to? Oh, wait, of course, you're celebrating."

"I thought you left ages ago," I say. "Didn't you leave ages ago?"

"I did, then I decided to do some shopping around here. Everything all right? You look worried." Then her gaze leaves my face and her hand flies to her mouth. "Is this your car?"

I had been trying to stand in front of the word so she wouldn't see it. Now I turn with a sigh to inspect the damage. "Yes, it's my car. I can't believe this happened. I knew I should have parked in the parking lot."

She bends down to take a closer look and I see the word in its entirety again instead of as a series of angry score marks. My high from moments ago has crashed like a bad trip. Now I feel like I'm going to cry. I bite the side of my thumb, expecting her to say something like, *Whore? Why? What did you do?* But she stands up straight and says, "Kids. Unfortunately it's a bit of a problem around here."

"It is?"

She sighs. "They're bored. There really should be more youth facilities for them. We really need it in this neighborhood. But look, it's just the surface. There's a good auto body place on Bellaire; I'm sure they'll fix that easily."

"Do you think?"

"Yes, I'm sure."

We both stare at the car for a moment.

"Don't worry," she says finally. "They'll have it as good as new, you'll see. Go to your dinner, and have fun. It's nothing."

"I know, it's just that I'm supposed to meet my family now and I just don't want to do it with *that*!" I point at it. "My son is only ten," I add.

She makes a face. "No, you probably shouldn't."

The sky turns gray, suddenly, and a gust of wind sends dust into my eyes and I screw them shut, rub my fingers over them.

"I'll have to leave it here. I'll call an Uber." I take out my cellphone and start tapping.

"Would you like me to take your car to the auto body place? It might be a good idea not to leave it here too long, and you can probably pick it up from them tomorrow."

"Oh my god, June, would you? I mean, I wouldn't be putting you out?"

"No. It's no problem, really. Go on, you've had such a great day. Don't let this thing get in the way."

I put my hand on her arm. "Thank you. That is so good of you."

"It's no problem at all. Hey, there you are." She turns to point at a black car that has stopped beside us. The driver is leaning to signal to us through the passenger window.

I motion to him to wait and hand her my car keys. "Thank you, June. I'm so grateful to you. I really am."

"Hey, it's no trouble, really. I'll ask them to call you when it's ready. See you tomorrow, Anna. Have a great time!"

I step into the back of the Uber, waving at her. June is right, of course, I think, as I click my seatbelt in. It's nothing, just kids. A prank. Then I close my eyes and remind myself that I'm a winner, and a little bit of vandalism is nothing, and I would be stupid to let it ruin my evening.

CHAPTER 16

It always fills me with pride when I go out with my family. I imagine the other diners glancing at us and thinking, *What a lovely family. Look at those children, so well-mannered, and so sweet. And what a handsome couple they make.*

Luis says we were lucky to get a table, that they were full, even though this is mid-week, but he explained his wife had just won a mathematics prize for work that's going to change the world, and they shuffled a couple of reservations around to make room for us.

"You're kidding," I say.

He smiles, his lovely, sexy smile and a lock of dark hair falls over his forehead. He pushes it back with two fingers. "You got me."

I laugh.

Then Carla hands me a small package. "Oh, honey, what's this?"

"It's not just from me, it's from all of us."

Luis is watching me with a twinkle in his eye. "Open it!" Matti says.

I rip the paper off quickly and open a small purple box. Inside is a pair of heart-shaped earrings in delicate silver filigree with small diamonds. Luis and I were waiting outside a jewelry store recently—I don't remember why anymore—and I pointed them out, because they were heart-shaped. This is what the new, improved me does now. Reacts to heart-shaped jewelry when my husband is within earshot, because everybody knows heart-shaped jewelry is cute and sweet and equals love and I want to remind him that we're in love and we're cute and sweet. But this is even better. Buying your wife heart-shaped jewelry is a message, it's loud and clear and I'm so touched he remembered that my eyes swim.

He kisses me on the lips. "Congratulations, babe. I knew you were incredible, and I didn't think you could surprise me anymore, but I was wrong. You are something else."

You're incredible. I remember those words too, imprinted as they are on my retina, and sent to someone else. If I was smiling before, now I'm positively grinning.

"Can we eat now?" Matti asks, and we all laugh. Everyone gets their favorite and we agree we will eat here as a family at least once a month from now on, which sends Mateo's eyes rolling back in his head.

Carla is telling us about some coding camp she wants to go to when Matti stops eating, fork up in the air, eyes firmly on the window.

"What is it, sweetie?" I ask.

"There's someone watching us."

I turn around to follow his gaze, but all I see is a guy looking at the restaurant, the way you might when you're wondering if it's a nice place to eat at.

"Who're you talking about?" Luis says.

"Outside," Matti says.

Then I get it. That young man is not gazing at the restaurant, or the menu that is displayed outside: he's staring at me. But I have no idea who he is, except all of a sudden, I do. I know those eyes.

My stomach rolls. It's Ryan. Ryan without a beard. Clean-shaven Ryan. Definitely Ryan, but he looks so young. His cheeks are flushed from the cold and the corners of his mouth are turned down, like he's upset about something.

"One of your fans?" Luis says, turning back to his food without looking at me.

Hardly, I think. But I laugh. "Probably."

"He doesn't look like a fan," Matti says. "He looks angry."

I don't think he looks angry, I think he looks confused. Luis squeezes my knee under the table and looks at me questioningly. I give him a quick shake of the head and go back to eating my food, wishing Ryan would go away, except he just stands there, still as a statue. I push pieces of duck around my plate and try to make light conversation. But my heart is beating too fast, too hard, and it's making the silk fabric of my dress visibly shudder with every beat. What if Ryan walks in and... what? Confronts me in front of my family? Tells everyone I rolled around on the carpet with him?

"I'll go and find out," Luis says, throwing down his napkin.

I quickly put one hand on his arm. "That's okay," I say, trying to sound cheery, and failing. "It's someone from work." I stand up so fast the table scrapes and shudders against my thighs, almost tipping our glasses over. I walk quickly outside into the cold air, unsure what I'm going to do or say, my stomach twisting a little more with every step. But Ryan isn't there anymore. I look around, but he's gone.

"You work with some weird people," Matti says under his breath as I return to my seat.

I laugh, embarrassed. "Someone from work?" Luis asks, one eyebrow at a sharp angle.

"Yes, that's what I said. I hadn't recognized him at first. He works in the law department. He must have seen me and hesitated about coming in. I don't know. He was gone when I got outside."

I pretend to laugh again, but I feel my mouth tremble with the effort of it. All I can think of is the word *WHORE* scratched on my car.

The following Monday I go straight to June's desk with a small potted green plant.

"For you," I say.

She beams as she takes it from me, reddens a little. "What for?"

"For helping me out with my car, of course. It's called a ZZ plant, and the florist assures me they're unkillable. Not that I doubt your nurturing skills, obviously, but you know, in this place, between the Fluro lighting and the unreliable aircon…"

"Thank you! And you're very welcome, Anna! There was no need for that."

"There was, and I wanted to. You've been so nice to me." For some reason as I say this, I feel my lips tremble. It's the stress of everything, it's the car, the vandalism, Ryan. Obviously I don't think it was kids anymore, but I don't tell her that.

She tilts her head at me. "Everything all right?"

"Yes, everything is great. I just need to…" I wave my hand vaguely in the direction of the elevator. "Anyway, I'll see you later, all right?"

I leave her to find the right spot for her plant and march right out of the building and over to the law faculty, up the stairs and down the corridor to the admin office where I last saw Ryan. I walk in with clenched fists, a thumping heart and a determined chin. The door to the admin office is opened and I see him immediately, his back to me, sitting at his desk in the corner. I'm nervous, even shaking a little, but deep down I am seething with anger. *What do you think you're doing? Did you do that to my car? Are you trying to intimidate me? Why?*

"How dare you?" I bark when I reach him, but the man who snaps his head around is not Ryan. He just looks a little bit like him from the back.

He startles. "Excuse me?"

I begin to stutter. "I'm—I'm looking for Ryan."

"Ryan?"

"He works here."

"Oh. Sorry. I don't work here. I mean I don't work on this floor. I'm only using the scanner."

"He's left," says someone. I turn around. A woman with short brown hair, older, is taking her glasses off and wiping them with a small piece of cloth. "Ryan the IT guy, right?"

"I think so, I mean his name is Ryan and he was working in this office a few weeks ago."

She nods. "The IT guy. He left a couple weeks ago. He doesn't work here anymore."

"Where did he go?"

The woman shrugs. "Search me."

I nod, try to think of what to do next. "Do you know where I can get an address for him?"

"No idea. Try HR."

Back at my desk, I pull out the university directory that lives in my bottom drawer and find a number for HR. I put my query forward. I am looking for a contact address for someone called Ryan.

"But you don't have a last name?"

"Unfortunately, I don't. He was an IT guy. That's all I know." I should have asked, of course. I was over there, in his old office, talking to someone who clearly knew him. But I barely slept last night and I am not thinking straight. "I could get a last name, if I must. But do you have many Ryans in IT who left the university recently?"

"What was his position exactly?"

"I don't know. IT."

"I know, but more precisely. Support desk? Network specialist? Hardware acquisitions?"

"He worked in the law building, does that help?"

"No. There are no IT people who work directly in the law building. He must have been there on a specific job. And you're in the math building, is that right?"

I rub a hand hard across my forehead. "Yes, that's right."

There's a pause. "The thing is, Dr. Sanchez, even if I did track the employee's home address, I'm not sure I'm at liberty to give it to you without his express permission. We have very strict privacy guidelines here, and I don't—"

There's a rap at my door. It's June.

"Right, thank you, you've been very helpful." I hang up. "Yes? What is it?"

She taps her watch. "They're waiting for you. In 16B. Your class?"

"Oh, shit. I'll be right there."

She narrows her eyes at me. "You sure you're okay?"

"Yes, I'm fine, thank you. Actually, June…"

"Yes?"

"Maybe you could help me with something?"

"Of course, what can I do?"

"I need to track down someone called Ryan, who was working in IT but he's left."

She waits for more, one hand on the door handle. I'm busy gathering my things for the class so I don't have to look at her.

"I don't understand," she says. "Do you need someone from IT to fix something?"

"No, I need to find this Ryan person." I look at her now, gnawing at my fingernail. "I don't have a last name. I called HR but they can't help me. I was thinking, maybe…"

"I'm sorry, Anna. I don't know anyone called Ryan who was in IT, if that's your question."

"I was hoping *you* could talk to HR. There can't be thousands of Ryans who worked in IT and were assigned to do a job at the law faculty recently, right?"

"But you said you already asked them."

"Yes, but if you ask they might tell you because you're admin too—maybe admin people help other admin people, I don't know. Look, you know what? Don't worry about it. It's fine. I'll figure it out. I was just thinking out loud."

I slip past her and out the door.

"I'm happy to help if—"

I raise a hand. "No, it's fine. Thank you!" Then I stop, turn around and say, "Forget I said anything, okay. I'd be grateful if you didn't mention it to anyone."

"Mention what?"

I sigh. "The Ryan thing. Just forget it, okay?"

I don't track down Ryan in the end, but I am on the alert, and it's only after a few days during which nothing happens that I begin to relax. He would have contacted me if he wanted to speak to me. He knows where I am. The ball is in his court, and there's not much I can do.

Tonight, the university hosts a dinner in my honor. And I mean, a real dinner. Not the cheese plate and dips version; this is a linen and flowers and crystal glasses and silverware affair, all hired for the occasion and set up on long tables in the main hall. The dean, who is retiring at the end of term, gives a warm speech where he thanks me for making the last year of his career the proudest and most memorable.

Luis is looking very handsome in his tuxedo. He's chatting to Rohan about art and mathematics, I think. I'm chatting to Bernie, one of my post-doctoral students. He's telling me about a robot who can make an omelet.

"Shouldn't that be a robot *that* can make an omelet?" I say.

Bernie pulls his hair back and ties it into a ponytail with a rubber band that was around his wrist. "People are more likely to trust robots that exhibit human traits, like gazing and nodding and shrugging. I like to think about robots as people. It makes me care more."

Then June walks up to us, holding a flower arrangement in both hands, like an offering. She's smiling. "These just came for you," she says.

She puts the arrangement down on the table and Bernie stands up, brandishing an empty bottle of wine. "I'll get us a refill."

"I'm sure the waiters will fix you up," I say, but he's already gone and June sits down in his place.

I pull the arrangement closer and unfasten the clear cellophane. Purple lisianthus and daisies set in a white cube.

Luis turns around and peers over my shoulder as I open the card. "Who's it from?" he asks.

I roll my eyes. "Who do you think? My mother."

Congratulations, Anna. I'm very proud of you.

"That's nice," June says.

I raise an eyebrow at her. "Not really. She could have come. I invited her, you know. It wouldn't kill her to make the trip once in a while." I point at the flowers with my chin. "She always sends the same whenever there's a birthday in the family. When she remembers them, anyway."

June helps herself to the jug of water. "You're not close?"

"You could say that. I never see her. She doesn't even come to visit her grandchildren."

"No!"

I shrug. "She's not a caring person, not in that way. And she's become a recluse of sorts in her old age." I fan myself with the card. "That's beside the point anyway, as we were never close. I know this is going to sound strange, but my mother didn't like me very much."

June scoffs, shocked I think. "I doubt that."

"Please. You don't know her." But I can tell she doesn't believe me. Maybe she thinks I'm exaggerating, or that I'm put out because my mother hasn't shown up for me.

I bring my chair closer to hers. "The thing is, both my parents were scientists. Physicists, to be exact. That's all they thought about. Science. And they had ambitions for me, because they believed—unscientifically, I might add—that all of their talents would be funneled into me. That I would be *Their Best Work*. My mother especially. I think my father just went along with her because it was easier for him. She, on the other hand, had this idea that I would be some kind of Marie Curie or Rosalind Franklin. She was obsessed with turning me into the perfect scientist. When I was eleven, she told me not to have children. I'm not kidding, June. She said 'They only interfere with The Work.' She always talked about *The Work* like she was devoting her life to humanity or something. 'Children serve no purpose,' she said, 'other than the survival of the family tree.' And just to reiterate here, my mother said this to me, her only child."

June is watching me, mouth open. "Oh, Anna. That's awful!"

I shake my head. "I could never be like that to my own children. I smother them in hugs and kisses every day just to balance her out."

June takes the card from me. "You are their best work, Anna." She points to the words. "And she is proud of you."

"Oh, yeah." I take the card from her and throw it on the table. "Imagine waiting your whole life for *this* crumb." But I feel a prick of tears and pinch my nose. I want to tell June about my mother forcing the Pentti-Stone on me at such a young age, all the pain she put me through with her hare-brained ideas, but I don't. "You'd think she would have come, for this," I say.

June is silent for a moment. "What does Luis think?"

I check over my shoulder to make sure he's not listening, then lean closer to her. "He's so angry with her. She didn't even come to our wedding, can you believe that? He says I should just drop contact altogether. Not that we have much of that." I laugh.

"I'm very sorry Anna. That's—"

But we're interrupted by Mila. "You are a bit of a dark horse, Anna!" she slurs. She grabs my arm to drag me off. June laughs and waves me away and I get up, glass in hand.

"I just wanted to say congratulations!"

"Thank you. I appreciate that." We clink our glasses. Her gestures are a little exaggerated.

"I wish you'd said something. I would have loved to help!" she says.

"I just wanted to wait until I was sure," I say.

She wags a finger at me. "You are a bit of a dark horse!" and I say, "Yes, you said that," and she laughs, congratulates me again. There's been a lot of congratulations lately but there's something in her eyes that doesn't match the smile. For a terrifying moment I think that she suspects something, and my heart leaps into my throat. I try to picture Alex and Mila together, confiding, chatting, plotting, but no, it doesn't resonate. I don't think Alex even liked Mila much, anyway. Then I tell myself that I have to stop this second-guessing of everything everyone says to me or I'll really go crazy.

Mila lifts her glass of champagne in my direction and says, "You kept it secret so I wouldn't try to worm it out of you. You think I would have stolen it for myself." She leans forward again. "You're right. I would have. Well done, you!"

Then Geoff appears and puts his arms around both of us.

"I told Mila to write up a story on you for the website," Geoff says. "We want a big splash page thing. Photos, quotes, the lot. Did she tell you?"

"Not yet."

"Yes," she says, dully. "What's a good day for you?" and I see then she doesn't like that one bit, that Geoff has asked her to do something probably quite mundane in her eyes, and that she thinks it's a subordinate task. And I want to laugh, because suddenly I see she has lost some of her glow. Geoff has backed the wrong horse—he should have promoted the dark horse, I guess, not the pretty, shiny one. I bet he asks her to take minutes from now on.

And if I were unkind, I'd say this is one of the best moments of the night.

I'm asked to make a speech even though we've had many of them already. I rise to the occasion, and I thank my colleagues, the university, my students. Then I thank Luis. I look right at him when I tell the room that the most important thing in my life isn't mathematics, it's my family. That I have done this for my husband and especially for my children so that they'd look up to their mom some day, which makes everyone laugh, even though it's the truth.

CHAPTER 17

Word has spread about the Pentti-Stone and I stand in a packed lecture hall staring at faces I'm sure I've never seen before. I don't know if they simply never showed up for class or if they don't belong here in the first place. Thorn-in-my-side Melanie still managed to stake her place at the front and when our eyes meet, she takes the gum out of her mouth and sticks it on a piece of paper in front of her. That's a first. Perhaps some of the infinite advantages in winning prizes includes respect.

I lose some of these first-time attendees though, somewhere between complex analysis and Reimann surfaces. By the time the class ends the sloping lecture hall is dotted with empty seats. It's actually hard not to feel slighted, that I wasn't as riveting as all that.

When the class ends and I return to my office, I run into June in the corridor.

"Geoff said you asked for extra support."

"Yes, I'm a bit overwhelmed with everything since the win."

"Well, from now on I'm to assist you with any admin work." She does a little captain's call, tipping her hand to her head. I laugh.

"That's nice. I'm glad. I've actually got a bunch of things for you to do. Let me put it together. You have time this afternoon to go over it with me?"

She seems pleased. "I certainly do. Name your time."

"Okay!"

"Also, would you like to go for a quick drink after work? Maybe even something to eat?"

I give her a confused tilt of the head. We've never done that before, socialize outside work. She registers my hesitation and gives me a quick, apologetic smile. "But I understand completely if you're busy at home. It's just a thought, a spur of the moment—"

I hesitate for a moment because Luis said last night that his sale fell through. Turns out *The Nest* is *not* going to a prestigious institution, and Isabelle was talking out of her proverbial. Part of me thinks I should be there for him. The other part thinks, *Screw it.* "You know what? I'm not busy, and I would really like that. I'll call Luis and tell him."

"He won't mind?"

"No. Trust me, there's truckloads of dinners ready to be reheated in my freezer. They'll be fine."

She suggests the tapas bar on Jefferson Avenue. It's close, the food is excellent.

"Perfect," I say, and suddenly I'm really looking forward to a night out with a friend. I haven't had a friend in a long time. I've forgotten how nice it feels. Then Mila appears beside us like something that's sprung out of a box.

"Ready?" she asks chirpily. Then turns to June. "I'm interviewing Anna for the website." June and I make a time to catch up later and Mila and I continue on into my office.

It's a brand new office, four times the size of my old one, with lovely windows overlooking the landscaped lawns. Mila makes all the right noises about how nice it is and sits right on the edge of the armchair. I drop loosely into the other one. "Okay, let's go." I say. I'm not concerned. I'm lining up lots of these interviews. I even have one coming up with the *New York Times* for their 'Profiles in Science' series. That's the big one. In comparison, this chat with Mila feels like a walk in the park.

"Sure. Okay," she says, pulling out her iPhone and setting it down on the table. "I'm recording this—you don't mind?"

"Of course not."

"Okay, good. So, I'd love to know about your process. How long have you been working on the proof?"

And just like that, my confidence evaporates. I feel ridiculously unprepared and now I want more time. I've been so cocky, I think I just assumed this would be a gushing session about how fabulous I am.

"A year?" I say finally.

Her eyebrows shoot up. "Wow, is that all?"

"Oh, okay, I meant, probably three years then?"

She tilts her head at me. "So what is it? One year or three?"

"Um. Three, I think." I could have said, *my whole life*, and that would be almost true. I think the reason I don't is because I hate to talk about that time of my childhood, when the Pentti-Stone conjecture represented nothing less than an instrument of torture.

"Okay." She writes it down. Then she wants to know why I kept the research secret for so long. I hesitate.

"Is it because as a woman you were worried you wouldn't be taken seriously?" she asks.

"Yes." I nod, slowly. "That's very perceptive of you."

Then she asks: "Have you some supporting documentation, anything we can upload to the website to accompany your article, and that isn't in the journal's paper? Something you held back from Forrester."

I cock my head at her. "Supporting documentation?"

"You know, your notebooks, work in progress, scribbles, doodles, anything you have that would be good visual material for the project. Visuals are great for this sort of thing. It doesn't matter if it's messy. The messier the better!"

I rub a finger on my forehead. "Okay, let me think. Um... I don't actually have much."

She chuckles. "But you must have notes. You didn't publish a pre-print, right?"

"A pre-print. No." It's unusual to publish a proof directly like I did. Normally you'd have a draft version made freely available for others to provide feedback on. I don't have a pre-print. Obviously. I didn't need one.

"I… I threw a lot of things away when I moved office. You know how it is. I might have thrown my notes, too."

She waits for me to say more, a cloud of confusion in her eyes. "But you submitted them to the Forrester Foundation."

Something tugs at the edge of my brain when she says that. "What do you mean?"

She tilts her head at me. "It's part of the rules. You know that, right? The Forrester Foundation will only award the prize if you submit *all* the notebooks. You have to show how you came to the solution."

"Oh, right!" I blink, breathe a sigh of relief. For a moment I thought she meant… I don't know what I thought. All I know is, I've already done that. I did that when I submitted the paper. "It's all in the published paper."

"Well, not really. Without supporting documentation, notebooks, workings, all that, they won't give you the prize. I mean, these are the rules, you know that, right?"

I wish she'd stop asking me that. I laugh. "Of course I know that!" I raise my hand. "You know what, it doesn't matter. I'll dig up any relevant notebooks I have and bring them along."

But I remember now. An email that came shortly after the Foundation confirmed my solution was accepted, something about sending them documentation. I ignored it, I don't know why. I thought it was for their records or something. Now I wait until she's gone to pore over the fine print on the Foundation's website. And there it is. *The submission must include the preliminary work that led to the discovery.* Then a paragraph detailing what's acceptable in terms of documentation.

I sit back. Push the palm of my hand between my eyes. I have a vague memory of knowing about this requirement, but I didn't think it was *compulsory*. Did Alex and I ever discuss this? Of course one requirement was that a paper be published about the solution in a reputable journal, and I've done that, and that's enough, surely. Who cares how I got there?

It was stupid of me to destroy the notebooks. I should have copied them first, so I'd have the workings in my own handwriting. I could have added rings from overflowing coffee cups, spilled red wine. Make it look like I'd been working late at night.

I wasn't thinking straight back then. Never mind. It will be fine. Of course it will be. They wouldn't have said I'd won the Pentti-Stone otherwise. I'm sure this so-called requirement is not absolute. I mean, I solved it, didn't I? The whole world knows I solved it. They could hardly *not* give me the prize! And if they ask, I'll just say… something. I'll think of something. It'll be fine.

The tapas bar isn't very far and June and I decide to walk. We're almost there when the weather changes abruptly and we wrap our coats tighter, raise our collars and squint against the icy wind. I take her hand to hurry her along and we almost fall into the restaurant, laughing, our cheeks red and our coats sparkling with melting crystals.

It's early enough to score a good table near the window. We drop ourselves on the hard wooden bench, rub our hands together and immediately order margaritas with lime juice and dry orange Curaçao. They arrive in jam jars while we scan the menu. Conversation flows, we find ourselves on a new level of friendship. I've asked her before about her personal life but she's always been cagey. "I'm not in relationship, not anymore anyway," she said. "Trevor. That's his name. We were together for years, and eighteen months ago I found out he was seeing my best friend behind my back. That's why I moved away and ended up here. New beginnings and all that. And the rent is cheap here."

"I'm sorry, June. That really sucks."

"Yeah, I'm getting over it. Tell me about your mother." She rests her elbows on the table, hands knotted together.

I cock my head at her. "You want to know about my mother?" I rub my eye, unwind the scarf I'm still wearing around my neck and fold it on the bench beside me. "Okay, I'll tell you about her." I cross my arms on the table. "The best way to explain my mother is to tell you about my friend Hope."

I take a sip of my drink. "I grew up in Youngstown and it was there, in middle school, that Hope arrived one morning, in the middle of term. As soon as I saw her sitting at her desk that day, I wanted to get to know her. It was like, friendship at first sight. She looked sweet, kind, with curly blonde hair, almost red, and she had chipped pink nail polish.

"Our teacher, Mrs. Johnson, asked for a volunteer to look after our new classmate, show her around, that sort of thing. I couldn't raise my hand fast enough. I'd do it, absolutely. 'You can count on me Mrs. Johnson,' I said.

"I'd never had a real friend until Hope. Her parents were hippies who made clothes out of ethically grown cotton and sold them at markets and in local stores. I loved to hang out at her house, so much so that I was there all the time. It was warm and comfortable and even the furniture was welcoming, with its soft shapes you could sink into and its bright, happy colors. My parents didn't care about making a home, let alone a welcoming one. They were too busy, and probably in some weird way thought it was beneath them, anyway. They worked, like, all the time. Even when they weren't working, they were working. As a result, my house was spartan and neglected. Sometimes when they went out I would pull out the vacuum cleaner from under the stairs and clean the living room to within an inch of its life. I'd squeeze lemons into a cup of water and dip my fingers in, flicking droplets over the carpet so that my house would smell like Hope's house—which it never did. I even made cushions once, with some fabric Hope's mother gave me, red with big blue and green flowers. My parents didn't notice. When I pointed this out to them, my parents looked around mildly bewildered and muttered something like, 'very nice'.

"At Hope's house, we'd sit on bean bags in her room and listen to Michael Jackson. She showed me her parents' stash of pot once. 'Smell that,' she said. I thought it smelt like rotting mushrooms, which possibly wasn't far from the truth. We'd talk about what we would do when we grew up, kind of like what Luis and I would do years later in college.

"But there was my mother. She disapproved, obviously, eventually, once she took the time to notice. Sometimes I think she simply didn't like seeing me happy. That it went against her grain. I should be studying instead, or something.

"'It's okay, you're rebelling. It's what most girls your age do,' she'd said. And I remember thinking, *I'm thirteen years old. I have no idea what you're talking about, Mother.*"

"So what happened?" June asks.

"It was almost summer. Hope had her fourteenth birthday party at her house. It was a Saturday afternoon, and my mother forbade me to go, but Hope helped me sneak out through my bedroom window. I was probably there for only an hour before my mother came to get me." I bury my face in my hands and groan. "You should have seen her. It was the most embarrassing day of my life. Hope's mother tried to coax her to stay—there were other parents there enjoying the party—and she offered her a glass of something that she'd poured from a large glass pitcher that had floating bits of fruit in it. But my mother stood there, her face white with fury, her lips pressed together into a thin line. She saw me, marched over and yanked me away. And that was it. I was grounded for the rest of the year."

June jerks back in shock. "The *year*?"

I nod. "She found a project for me. A mathematics project."

"What?"

"The Pentti-Stone conjecture." I take a swig of my drink.

"I don't really know what that means, Anna."

"It was to punish me for disobeying her. Although I'm sure she'd argue it was for my own education. But after that party, my mother declared that I was too possessive in my friendships and it was unhealthy. I wasn't, by the way, June. I really believe I was just a normal child, but she insisted I needed a distraction from my distractions. Next thing I know, she announced that we would solve the Pentti-Stone conjecture. I say 'we' because she was going to do it with me. She thought it would be... I don't know. Fun, I guess. Her idea of mother–daughter bonding. Except that I did all the work. Her only contribution was to check on my progress. She'd come into my bedroom and pick up my work, go over it, maybe ask me a question or two. Sometimes I thought I was on the right track and I'd say to her, 'Is it right? Would that work?' But she'd just shake her head. 'No. That's not going to work,' she'd say. Then she'd take my pen from me, put a diagonal line through the page and give me the notebook back. 'Try again,' she'd say, and I would cry myself to sleep. It felt so hopeless. I was never going to get it. I was locked up all summer. Every day. I missed Hope so much, I used to dream about her. I fantasized that she was trying to find ways to get me out, that we'd run away! Even after we went back to school the following term, I was locked up every weekend—metaphorically speaking of course, but still—in my room poring over it, trying to come up with a proof just so I could get out and play. Until then, no movies for me, no dances, no hanging out after school playing by the lake with my friends. Not that I had many of those to begin with." I poke at an anchovy with my fork. "I was thirteen years old. Grown men and women had spent years trying to solve that thing. My dad just pretended it wasn't happening. He deferred to my mother in every way anyway, a life-long habit he was not going to break, not even for his daughter's welfare." I feel a prickle of tears. I grab a napkin and press it against my eyes. "I don't know why I'm getting upset," I say. "It's a long time ago." The restaurant suddenly feels uncomfortably hot. I scrunch up the napkin into a ball. "It should go without saying I grew to loathe the Pentti-Stone conjecture. I still do. So you can imagine when Alex came to me with—"

I stop, leave the words hanging in the air. I want them to float away but they're still there, between us. I can't think of anything to say, and I look at June pleadingly, my mouth opening and closing like a fish.

"When Alex what?" June prompts. But she doesn't frown or narrow her eyes and there's no suspicion or shock in her tone, or anything to indicate I said the wrong thing. I feel my insides loosen and I shake my head. "Nothing," I finally reply. "Ignore me. I don't know what I'm saying anymore. Hey, shall we get another margarita?"

"Sure, why not?" She flags the waitress while I stare at my hands and will my heart to slow down. I can't believe I almost blurted it: *When Alex came to me with the proof.*

June pats my arm. "And you did it, you did solve it."

I smile. We sit there in silence for a while, staring into our glasses. "So what happened to Hope?" she asks.

I shrug. "The party was just before the end of term and I only saw her once after that, in class, and then her family moved away, so that was that. We drifted apart. I don't where she is now. I don't really like to think about those years, to tell you the truth. It's in the past now." I run my finger along my glass, leaving a trace in the condensation. "My mother used to say, back when she still talked to me, that I was an over-attached child. I would cling to her, she said; then I met Hope and I clung to Hope until they moved away. And maybe she was right, because now I cling to Luis, and my children of course, but especially Luis. Luis is the only friend I ever had after Hope, the only friend that is truly mine. I haven't even seen my mother in years, as she refuses to visit us. I told you she didn't come to our wedding, didn't I?"

June nods, biting into a small mushroom.

"This is how horrible she is." Are my words sounding a little slurred? "Before we got married, she called me. She said not to marry him. Something was 'wrong' with him. 'What do you mean?' I asked. But I knew what she meant. She saw I was happy. She was going to do it again, try to ruin it for me." I scoff. "I mean, really? I'm about to get married to the love of my life, and she tells me there's something wrong with him?" I make air quotes around *something*. "I laughed at her. I said, 'Yeah, he loves me, Mother. That's what's wrong with him.' Seriously, that woman will stop at nothing to ruin any chance of happiness for me. It's like it's embedded in her DNA. I told her, 'Honestly, Mother, enough. I'm a grown woman, I can do what I like. Save it.' She didn't come to my wedding after that. And then she moved away."

"Where to?"

"Some small town in California called Clearlake. I've emailed her that we'll come and visit, take the kids on vacation—most grandparents would love that, wouldn't they? You'd think so, wouldn't you? But no, not this one."

"But did you find out what she meant? About Luis?" June asks.

I give her a look. "Please. These were just the games she liked to play. There was nothing wrong with Luis. He loves me and she couldn't stand that because she's a sick woman. He is the only person left in my life who truly loves me. Sometimes, in my darkest hour, I believe that I will meet so few people in my life who will truly love me that when I find one, I have to hold on to them with everything I have."

CHAPTER 18

We're talking about relationships and I want to know more about Trevor, but June's not saying much, and I get a sense that she's still too sad to talk about it.

I lift a greasy finger. "Okay, so final question. How would you describe him, in one word?"

She thinks about it, and smiles. "Funny," she says. "He was really funny. He used to make me laugh a lot." I try to ask more but she waves my questions away with a flap of the hand.

"What about Luis, in one word?"

I peel a prawn and sink my teeth into its flesh. "Unfaithful," I say, sucking on the tail. She gasps and I look up abruptly. It's like the word escaped from me without my realizing it was even there. I start to laugh, but she's looking at me, her head tilted, her eyebrows drawn together. I want to say something but I'm stuck, and my eyes start to swim.

"Luis is having an affair?" Her eyes grow wide with understanding, but disbelief also, which makes sense considering I've just waxed lyrical about what a great husband and father he is for the last twenty minutes.

Hearing it like that, without adornments, is like having the carpet pulled from under my carefully constructed house of cards. I immediately regret saying anything, but it's too late.

"It's fine, June, he's not having an affair anymore. It's over."

"Oh, Anna! How did you find out?"

I tell her about my suspicions, then seeing him with Isabelle, and finally the coup de grâce, finding the texts. Especially the texts.

"How do you know it's over?"

"I just know."

"Have you checked his texts again?"

I shake my head. "His cell isn't always on his bedside table and, to be honest, I feel like I got away with it once, I'm not game to try it again."

"So, how do you know?"

I tell her what it's been like, how sweet he's been. I show her my silver earrings which I happen to be wearing. "He remembered I liked them," I say. "And they're heart-shaped. You know what that means? That we're in love again, that's what. Not that we ever stopped, but you know, it's gone back to the way it used to be. In a way." I smile at her, but the words sound hollow and I wonder if I ever really believed them. "And his show is over so he has no reason to go to the gallery anymore."

"Right," she says, staring intently at her plate.

"What does that mean?"

She shrugs. "Nothing, what do I know? I'm an idiot."

"Hey, that's my line! Come on, tell me."

"Just that…" She sighs, puts her fork down. "Listen to yourself, Anna. Why would Luis stop seeing Isabelle, just because you're trying so hard to be perfect? He can have his cake and eat it too, as far as I can see."

She registers the shock on my face and raises her hand. "Look, I'm only saying this because I've been there, and I did all the things you did. I was the perfect girlfriend and he still left me for her. Of course, it's very possible the affair is over, but you don't know that. You should be in control of this situation, Anna. Not try and second-guess it. If he's going to stop seeing… what's her name again?"

"Isabelle."

"If he's going to stop seeing Isabelle, it should be because you made it happen."

I laugh. "I thought I was. Believe me, I've turned up the seduction dial to stratospheric. What else are you suggesting?"

"Confront him! Give him an ultimatum! Make him take responsibility for his actions!"

I'm such a loser. Of course she's right. And yet… "What if he picks her?" I say in a small voice.

"He won't." Then she thinks about it and shrugs. "And if he does, well, he would have left sooner or later. But he won't," she says again. "Have you checked his toiletries bag for condoms?"

"What? No! Why his toiletries bag? I'm not even sure he has one."

"That's where Trevor kept them. Alternatively, you could always confront her. Have you considered that?"

"How do I do that? March up to her at her work and make a public spectacle of myself?"

"Of course not." She pauses. "You know what would be helpful here, I think, is if you could see them together? You could probably gauge a lot from how they interact. Like, are they trying too hard not to interact? You know what I'm saying?"

"I don't know how to do that, either," I say sullenly.

"Look, Anna, it's up to you. Don't listen to me. I'm the one who couldn't keep my own boyfriend, so what do I know? I'm sure you're right, it's over."

The first thing I think of when I wake up the next day, my head heavy and blurry, my tongue thick, my heart beating too hard, is that I wish I hadn't told June about Luis and Isabelle.

But as the fog clears, I decide that she's right. Winning the Pentti-Stone prize has made me complacent, if not a little smug. I've been walking around my own life as if I was more than enough. When have I ever been enough?

I have to wait another two days before I am alone in the house. It's Saturday morning and Luis has taken the children to the ice rink while I plead a headache. The moment they're gone I go through his things. It's almost a ritual by now: I go through his pockets, his shoes, his drawers, under his drawers, his emails, cellphone bills, especially cellphone bills. Nothing.

I check his toiletries bag for condoms—there are none—and I stand there, knowing that finding nothing doesn't prove he's not still seeing Isabelle. It just means I found nothing.

I don't even know what I'm looking for, and I really do get a headache. I press my fingers on my temples as I gaze out to the back garden and the shed. I should go to his studio and search there. That's what I should do. If there's anything to find, that's where it will be.

Then I focus my eyes. *The shed.*

The shed is completely Luis's domain. I hardly ever go in there, and why would I? It's where he tinkers with his bikes. There's nothing for me there. Which makes it the perfect hiding place.

I unlock the door and catch a whiff of chain oil. His red bicycle is resting upside down in the center, tools carefully laid out on the bench, ready to perform some intricate operation. Sometimes I think there's nothing wrong with his bicycle, but men are like children and they need toys to tinker with, and so Luis goes to his man-shed, takes his bicycle apart, rebuilds it, takes it apart again.

It doesn't take long to figure out I'm wasting my time here. I've looked under every tin of paint, shaken out every oily rag, searched drawers forensically. The only remotely incriminating thing I've found is a half-empty packet of Marlboros behind the antique wooden toolbox I gave him years ago.

It's only when I'm about to give up that I spot his canvas bag in the corner. The kind that you strap diagonally across your torso, like bicycle couriers use.

I open the flap and there's nothing there, except for a packet of Listerine strips, which is certainly interesting in itself and I wonder what they're for. Kissing, perhaps? There's a pocket at the front with its own flap and inside, carefully folded in half, is a receipt from Mol Creations. I smile. It's the receipt for the earrings Luis bought me to celebrate the Pentti-Stone win.

Except it's not.

It's the right jewelry store, Mol Creations, but the date is wrong. The receipt is from three months ago. Luis gave me the earrings only ten days ago. Could he have bought this for me? Something for my birthday, maybe? But that's in another four months, and our wedding anniversary is another month after that. It doesn't seem like Luis to plan a gift so far in advance.

I'm biting down on my teeth so hard I'm going to crack them if I don't unlock my jaw soon. I hold the receipt in my fist and crush it slowly. Because the worst part is, the receipt is not for the pair of heart-shaped earrings, it's for a necklace—14 karat gold. And it cost $510, which is three times as much as my earrings.

Necklace—14 karat gold does not tell me much and I absolutely have to know what it looks like. Is it pretty? Is it sexy? Does it spell her name between two interlocking hearts? Luis has taken the car, so I take an Uber to the jewelry store. In the back seat I stare out the window, fingernails digging into my palms. The driver is chatting idly, about the weather, what else, and checking me out occasionally in the rearview mirror. I ignore him. I don't trust myself to speak without yelling furiously. *Yes! It's cold, isn't it?!*

Instead I close my eyes and make myself breathe through my nose because I can't go in there with this out-of-control anger barreling through me. I'll end up smashing something—not a good look in a jewelry store, I don't think.

By the time I walk in I've regained some control. I hand my receipt over to a pretty blonde woman with a very elaborate hairdo, lots of make-up and a bright smile that doesn't reach her eyes. If they ever did a remake of *Stepford Wives*, she'd be perfect.

"My husband bought this for me," I say.

"Lucky you," she replies, and I nod. Lucky me.

"I was wondering if I could have it resized." Desperate, obviously. Lame even. I don't know what size it is to begin with. What if it's one of those long loopy necklaces that drops down to the navel?

"Oh? Well, let's take a look. Did you bring it with you?"

"No, I just wanted to know if it was possible first. Do you have another one here? I laugh for no reason whatsoever, waving the crumpled receipt in front of her. She raises her eyebrows and looks towards the door, as if to gauge her escape route. This is going completely wrong. She's going to have me arrested if I don't come down soon.

"May I?"

I nod, and she takes the receipt from me carefully, using the very tip of her fingers, and smoothes out the receipt on the glass counter. "I don't need to look it up. The design is listed right here, see?"

I squint, then I see it. *LILII* it says, right above her long red fingernail. "That's the model of the necklace."

"Oh, I thought it was…" I don't know what I thought. Some kind of inventory naming convention I guess.

"Unfortunately, I don't have another one here…" she says.

I bite a fingernail. "Do you have a picture of it I could look at? I'd really like to discuss with you how resizing it would work."

"Certainly." She pulls out a catalogue from under the counter, flicks it open, and turns it around so I can see it.

"Here we are. It sits above the collarbone. Is that not the case for you?" She tilts her head and looks at my neck, which is of normal size and certainly not so big that this necklace won't wrap around it.

But I'm not listening to her anymore. I pull the catalogue closer and stare at it. The necklace is shown in a full page, color photograph, and the only word for it is *exquisite*. Of course, the artist and the curator—what else could it possibly be? It's a fine gold chain, as fine as a gossamer thread, with two narrow baguette diamonds on one side, just above the collarbone. I'm going to be sick. My silver heart-shaped earrings suddenly feel trite, the kind of gift you give your wife to show you appreciate her but without the investment. A gift for the giver's benefit, just one step up from a KitchenAid.

I snatch up the receipt from the glass counter and walk out.

CHAPTER 19

It's been two days and I've been ruminating incessantly about the necklace. I did another forensic search that afternoon, in case there is a pretty gift box with my name on it hidden somewhere. It goes without saying that I didn't find one. I was almost tempted to confront him about it, but then I thought, the gift isn't recent, what if it was given in the heat of lust? What if it *is* over between them? Luis has been attentive to me lately. We are happier, aren't we? And what if the gift really *is* for me? How will it look if I've been snooping around, checking his receipts? *You're so jealous sometimes, Anna. Why can't you trust me?*

No. I made the decision: I absolutely have to pretend everything is fine until I figure out what's really going on here.

And now, it's Sunday morning, and Luis and I are strolling around the flea market, holding each other's gloved hand. I have a thing for winter outdoor markets. I love them. I love the icy air on my cheeks, the vendors with their fingerless gloves, the white sky, the promise of snow. I'm warm in my duffel coat, a blue and white woolen scarf that Carla knitted for me a few weeks ago around my neck. It's a new hobby for her and we're all wearing beanies that are too small and scarves that are strangely misshapen, and I love them all to bits.

Luis stops to look at a Bakelite clock and I turn around, scanning for the source of that roasted chestnut smell.

I nudge Luis. "Do you want some?" He looks up.

"Sure."

The vendor is roasting them on a hot plate and selling them in paper cones. I'm digging up the right change, fingers like blocks of ice, when a voice behind us calls out. "Luis?"

We both turn around.

Isabelle.

"Hello," she says, smiling at my husband. She's stunning with her bright smile and her blonde hair cascading out of an elegant black fur hat. She looks like she's just stepped out of a Disney movie.

I am not an angry person. I am a happy person. I am calm and dependable. Everyone says that about me. But right now I am livid as I watch my husband kiss her quickly on the cheek with a fake, desultory *Hey-how-are-you?* All very chaste, that goes without saying—I am here, after all. But my lips are trembling as I say hello through gritted teeth because is this meeting really accidental? They're standing too close to each other and it's making me boil. I imagine myself pushing her away with both hands, palms slapped hard against her long black leather coat. I picture her stumbling backwards and hitting her pretty head on the asphalt. I imagine her mouth making a perfect 'O' of surprise and her blue eyes wide in shock, and fear too, until her eyelids close like the eyes of a vintage doll. Then I imagine the blood. A tiny rivulet at first, seeping from the back of her head so slowly we don't notice it until it grows into a pool and we have to step away so as not to get it on our shoes. I imagine everyone agreeing it was an accident. The heels of her tall leather boots were too high, too thin, too unstable. Silly girl, she couldn't keep her balance.

I sigh. As tempting as it is, I don't push her. Because I am a happy person. And a rallier, which is why I make myself smile. It takes some effort, but after a few tries, I get there. Then I realize they're waiting for me to say something.

"Hello," I say, with as much fake cheer as I can muster. She asks after the family, we tell her we've been well, the family is well, thank you for asking.

"Anna just won a prize for her research," Luis says.

"Congratulations," she says to me.

"Thank you," I reply, then immediately ruin it by smirking and lifting one eyebrow in involuntary gleeful triumph.

Luis has put his arm around my shoulders and is giving me a kind of one-arm hug.

"I'm very happy for you," she says, and I don't know if she means about the prize or about Luis. I keep thinking about what June said, about how I should see them together and gauge their reaction. Now is the moment. I am looking for any evidence that they are still in touch, still screwing behind my back, and I can't find one exactly. I search Luis's face for any tell-tale sign: a tightening around the mouth, a quivering of the nostrils... and I find it.

It's when she says, "It's nice to see you." He turns bright red. Then he rubs his hand over his chin and I bite the inside of my cheek until I taste blood.

They are trying to appear relaxed, casual even, as they chat about the art world: have you seen so-and-so's show, what are you working on at the moment. What would I do if they were still cheating behind my back, I wonder? I don't know. I'd drag him away, move the family to Martha's Vineyard and add a moat around our house for good measure. I'd expose her, shame her. I'm not one to shame women when there's adultery involved, but now that I'm the wronged party, screw it. I'd personally carve the letter 'A' on her smooth-as-an-egg forehead.

Then something completely unexpected happens. A man, good looking, athletic build, nice square jaw, joins us. He puts one arm around Isabelle's waist and shakes Luis's hand.

"Hey, buddy, long time. How are you?"

"I'm great, Patrick. This is my wife, Anna."

I manage to close my jaw and say hello, and my gaze darts from Luis to Isabelle to Patrick. Luis seems to know a lot about Patrick:

he asks him about some deep sea diving trip he took last summer, and how their vacation plans are coming along.

Everything shifts in an instant and suddenly I am sure of nothing. Is it possible that it was never Isabelle? Maybe I had my wires crossed and there really was another woman called Belle who's been screwing my husband. Have I been so wrong? Do I see desire between every woman and my husband as a matter of course? Am I so insecure that I can't tell anymore?

"Hey, you guys want to come over for dinner?" I blurt, interrupting everyone. I suddenly really want to see them together, up close over an evening: Luis and Isabelle, Patrick and Isabelle, Luis and Patrick. I want to *know*.

There's a chorus of, "Oh sure, why not, sounds like fun, when?" and everyone pulls out their phone but it's harder than it looks because everyone is *so very* busy.

"Yeah, sorry, not going to happen until after Christmas for me," Patrick says, explaining he has to travel to Colorado for a conference and then somewhere else for something else. We all make noises about what busy lives we lead, then Patrick turns to Isabelle. "But you can go." And we laugh, because we're not joined at the hip, are we? The way some couples are? Don't we all hate that when one can't make it then the other is automatically also out of action?

"Great! Come next Friday night! It'll be fun!" I say very brightly. Too brightly. She smiles sweetly and taps the date into her calendar.

We say goodbye like old friends, she kisses me, one on each cheek. The collar of her coat is tall and folded back over itself. It gapes slightly as she leans to kiss me, and when I pull back I catch a glint of something. Just between the tip her collarbone and the hollow of her throat.

Two thin diamond baguettes on a gossamer thread of gold.

CHAPTER 20

After that I had to get as far away from Luis as I could without leaving the market. I didn't trust myself not to have some kind of breakdown. Just the effort of pretending nothing was wrong as I idly fingered a collection of old tobacco tins was making my chest hurt.

But he followed me, stood next to me and picked up a green tin, I think. I couldn't see properly: my vision had become blurry.

"I didn't know Isabelle had a boyfriend," I said. The only mildly good news in this whole screwed-up scenario.

He made a sound like "Mmm?" and slipped his arm into mine. I pulled away. I had to. I reached for something else on the display table but I didn't move away this time. I wanted to ask more, like, did they live together and were they engaged to be married, when he said, "Why did you do that?"

I waited a beat, confused. "You mean, invite her for dinner?"

"Yes."

"Oh. I don't know. It just came out."

"Okay," he said.

"Why? Is there a problem?"

"No, there's no problem. I would have preferred it if you checked with me first, that's all."

"Oh, I see." Then for some unknown reason other than a deep-seated habitual response, I add, "Sorry."

"That's okay. It's no problem. Just saying."

*

I said I had a headache after that and lay on my bed all afternoon, one arm flung over my eyes. I couldn't stop picturing that necklace around her thin white neck.

I got up eventually, and I was sitting at my dresser, my face buried in my hands, when Carla came into my room. I didn't hear her until she put her hand on my shoulder and said, "I love you, Mommy." I raised my head and ran both hands over my eyes before turning to face her.

"That's so sweet, baby. Thank you. I love you too, baby girl." I haven't called her that in years. I snatched a tissue from the box and blew my nose. "Hay fever. In winter. I really need to get some antihistamines." She put her arms around me and lay her head on my shoulder. "Hey, I'm okay, sweetie. Just trying to get rid of this runny nose! Whose turn is it to pick a movie tonight?" I hated myself for letting her see me like this. After she left, I washed my face and stared at my reflection in the mirror. I tried to see myself the way Isabelle might see me: Old. Boring. Ordinary. Unworthy. But I have children. *His* children. And I will do anything to protect my family. I sat tall and pulled myself together; I thought of my mother, for some reason. Probably because she would find all this display of emotion *weak*. I gave myself a pep talk. I held my head high and pushed my shoulders back. I told myself to stop being so pathetic.

I'll deal with Isabelle, I told myself in the mirror, close enough for my breath to leave a cloud of mist. *I'll deal with Isabelle*. Then I wiped it with my hand and went downstairs to be with my family.

At work the next day, I'm walking down the corridor, coffee in a styrofoam cup in my hand. I have my sunglasses on because my eyes look red and tired.

"You look awful, you all right?" June asks. I give a quick shake of my head. I spot Melanie walking towards me with another girl I don't recognize. When Melanie comes level with me she blows a small bubble of gum and pushes it out with her tongue. "You don't look very happy, Mrs. S."

"I'd be happier if you could submit your test on time, Melanie," I say to her. "There won't be another extension. You get that? I'll fail you if you don't deliver." She scoffs as I walk right past and I stop her in her tracks with one hand on her shoulder.

She jerks back. "Jeez, Okay Mrs S! Keep your pants on!"

"Hey!" I snap, pointing an angry finger right into her face. "Don't talk to me like that! Is that clear? I'm not one of your friends! I said, is that clear?"

The corners of her mouth drop. "Y-yes, I'm sorry."

I turn back, walk around the corner and into my office. I drop my bag on my desk and set down my coffee next to it. Some of it has spilled on my fingers and I dig out a crumpled tissue from my pocket to wipe them. Then I drop it on the floor without looking where it lands.

I sit down heavily. My eyes are burning with the gallons of tears I've been holding back all the way here.

"What's going on?" June asks. I didn't hear her come in. I press my fingers into my eyes.

"I'm scared," I wail.

"Why?"

"I think he's going to leave me."

"What?" She closes the door and sits opposite me. "What happened?"

I tell her about finding the receipt in Luis's bag, about my visit to the jeweler. Then I tell her about running into Isabelle at the market. I tell her about Patrick. I describe the scene linearly, frame by frame, all the way to its shocking conclusion. It's not that I want to relive it so much as I want June to know every little detail, so we can dissect and analyze and go over every moment with a fine-tooth comb until she points a way forward. A solution. A cupcake ending.

"Up till then, I honestly thought maybe the necklace was for me."

She rests her chin in her hands. "Tell me again, how was Luis during this whole exchange?"

I take a moment to find the right word. "Edgy, I think. Ill at ease. He was put out that I invited her. He actually said I should have checked with him first."

"Ooh, that's interesting."

"Is it?" I pop the lid off my cup of coffee. "Tell me! Why? What am I missing?"

"Think about it. You said so yourself, you two have been really good lately, isn't that right?"

I take a sip. "And?"

"Maybe she's hanging on, maybe he made a mistake and fixed it, broke it off. And now you invite her for dinner?"

She looks at me sideways and I laugh. "Oops."

Then my door opens wide and Geoff appears. He looks at me, then at June. He crosses his arms over his chest. "Well, isn't this cozy. Am I interrupting something?" He points to June. "Who are you again? Oh, yeah, *my* assistant!"

"Sorry, Geoff," I say. "I'll return her in a sec."

He narrows his eyes at me. "What's the matter?"

"Nothing, why?"

"You look upset."

I shake my head. "Just tired. Give us a moment, will you?"

"Sure, sure. Take all the time you need."

"Thank you," June and I say in unison.

"So, what are you going to do?" she asks, after he's gone.

"I don't know." My coffee is getting cold by now and I take a bigger gulp. "What do you think I should do?"

She doesn't reply, just thinks about it for a moment. "See how dinner goes. You're still having her over for dinner, right?"

"I wasn't going to."

"Oh, but you must. This is the only opportunity you'll have to judge the situation." She stands up and pats my shoulder. "By the end of it, you'll know. And if it's really bad and they're still together…"

"Then what?"

She lifts her shoulders in a half-shrug. "You'll think of something."

Later, on the way back from the tutorial room, I spot Geoff at the end of the hallway leaning against the pale green wall talking to a student. He sees me and raises his arm in my direction. "Anna! Come over here." When I reach him he puts his hand on my forearm and turns back to the student.

"I'll talk to you later, Ivan." Then he puts his arm around my shoulders and leads me away. "I just want to show you something—it's for the Forrester lecture. It'll only take a minute."

For some reason we end up standing outside the store cupboard. It's where we get our stationery supplies, which are kept under lock and key. It's also a storage room, filled mostly with cardboard archive boxes piled high against one wall. On the opposite wall are metal shelves filled with cleaning supplies. He glances both ways before pulling out a set of keys from his pocket and unlocking the door.

"What are you doing?" I ask.

"Just wait." He's talking to my breasts. He pulls me inside and closes the door. "What are you—?" but he pushes me against the metal shelves and an aerosol can clatters to the floor.

Oh god.

"No, sorry, Geoff." I press my palms against his chest to push him away, give a small embarrassed laugh. "I don't think so."

He presses harder against me. "Come on, Anna," he growls. "Tell me, what've you been doing with June, anyway?" He rubs his groin against me. "You two are always together, whispering to each other like school girls. Then this morning, the two of you were in your office, with the door closed, and you were crying. I saw you. What are the two of you up to, hey?"

A wave of panic engulfs me. I'm too far from the door to get out easily; he's too heavy, pressed against me like that. The shelves start to wobble behind me and something cuts into the small of my back.

"Enough, Geoff! What are you doing?" I push harder, start to shout, but he puts his hand on my face, extended so that his fingers are over my eyes and the palm of his hand is over my mouth. The taste of his skin makes me gag.

He licks the side of my neck. "What does your husband say? Does he know? About you and June?"

"Stop!" But my words are muffled. I can't breathe. My fingers frantically search behind me for something I can use against him but there's nothing. I wedge my knee between his thighs and he laughs softly, like I'm doing it on purpose, like I'm enjoying this. He moves his hand to hold my chin. Fingers like a vice on either side of my jaw.

I take a desperate breath.

"Get off me!" I shout as loudly as I can, my voice shrill with fear, my mouth distorted by his grip. I grab his wrist just as he brings his mouth close to mine. His breath is hot and reeks of stale alcohol.

"Come on," he groans into my face. "I know you want to. Don't tell me you're just a tease. You've been wanting me to do this to you ever since you first laid eyes on me." He brings his free hand up my skirt, his fingers sliding up my thigh. "How does that feel? Is that nice?"

His mouth is against mine, hot and wet, making me heave. I let out a wail, twist my head away, then grab his hand and bite it.

He jerks away suddenly. "Hey! What did you do that for?" He stares at his finger where my teeth have left a reddening crescent. He massages it, an astonished look on his face. "What the hell is wrong with you? That really hurt!"

I wipe snot off my face with my sleeve. I'm shaking with fury and humiliation. "You're out of your mind! I'll report you for this!"

He jerks his head back, an angry look of scorn and surprise on his face. "You're a bitch, you know that? You're just a tease. You've been at me like a bitch in heat since forever. And what about Chicago, hey? You played the tease then and I let you get away with it. But you never stopped coming on to me, did you? You want to play it that way again? Then you better watch yourself, Anna. Nothing good happens to women like you."

Does he actually believe I ever wanted this? I straighten my skirt, my entire body vibrating with anger while he straightens his clothes. He opens the door and light floods in from the corridor. Students walk past, their heads swinging towards me in unison. A burst of laughter.

"I won't let you get away with this," I say, between my teeth.

"Oh, really? What are you going to do, Anna? Report me? Who do you think you are? You want to tell them about Chicago? Or shall I? Because there's bound to be a whole lot of people who saw you get drunk and come on to me like you couldn't get enough of me. Plenty of people who saw us leave together that night. And I don't think your behavior was leaving much to the imagination, but hey, your call." He snorts. "And by the way." He rests one hand on the door handle. "Mila says you're avoiding her. That you refuse to talk about how you came up with the solution. What's that about?" He waits, chin forward, but I don't reply. I wipe my cheeks with trembling fingers and he shakes his head in disgust, steps into the corridor then changes his mind and turns around again. "And one more thing, you know why you didn't get the professorship?"

My chest is rising with every loud breath. I run my trembling fingers through my hair.

"I never submitted your application to the board. That's why. I never even nominated you." He smirks.

I search his face, looking for the lie, for the joke, for the punch line. I think of all the extra work I did, the many conversations I had with him about the best way to approach my application. All the proposals I devised, wrote and submitted: funding proposals, asset refurbishment proposals, how to attract more young women to study mathematics proposals. All to show I am a team player, a rallier.

He answers his own question. "I wasn't going to waste my time. I knew you wouldn't get it, so I didn't bother submitting it."

"You're an asshole," I say, my voice low and shaky.

He shrugs. "Maybe. And maybe I was wrong. You certainly surprised us all cracking the Pentti-Stone. But maybe I was right. Maybe you're hiding something. Maybe you're just a fraud. But hey…" He taps the door twice with the palm of his hand. "We'll find out one way or another, won't we?"

CHAPTER 21

I've washed my hands, my face, rinsed my mouth. Popped mints to fend off the impending nausea. I stare at my own reflection. Did I really bring this upon myself? Was I so taken by his attentions that I misunderstood what was going on? *I know you want to. You've been at me like a bitch in heat since forever.* And a part of me thinks it's true, that it's my fault. I sent the wrong signals. Even in the face of such violence I can't help but think it's me. Because in the end it's always me. Even when it's other people, it's me.

I already know I won't do anything about him. Nothing at all. For all my bluster about my family and what I'm prepared to do for them, I am a coward. I couldn't bear for Luis to find out about Chicago, and I have no doubt Geoff would make sure he does. For all I know, that's all Luis needs to run into Isabelle's arms for good.

I bring my hand over my eyes, Geoff's parting words still ringing in my ears: *Maybe you're hiding something. Maybe you're just a fraud.* For a terrifying moment I think he knows, has always known. But I make myself breathe, tell myself he doesn't know, because if he did, he would have said something by now. Wouldn't he?

It'll keep. That's what I tell myself as I wipe mascara off my cheeks in the staff bathroom. I can deal with it later. It's better for everyone if I wait until after the Forrester lecture. My word will have more weight then. I come up with so many ways to rationalize my own cowardice the words stop having any meaning. *I'm okay, it's okay. It's all okay. I can deal with it. Where's the rush? He's not going anywhere.*

I avoid him as the week goes on, plead too much work and avoid meetings. He throws me a look of contempt whenever he passes me, and I pretend I don't notice. After a few days I think it's not so bad; soon, I'll forget it ever happened. Everything will return to normal. Meanwhile, Mila is still at me, like an over-enthusiastic puppy, nipping relentlessly at my ankles. "Did you remember to bring your notes, Anna? I'm holding off publishing our interview until I get that material. I can't wait to see them! I'd love to know how you did it, how your brain works! Oh, no? What a shame. Where do you think they might be? I mean, you must have *something*, right? You didn't pop this work out of thin air, did you? You'll be in trouble if you did! Ha ha!"

Is that a coincidence, this fixation she has about my notes? Did Geoff speak to her about his doubts? I can't stand it anymore, this paranoia that's twisting my insides all the time, like no matter which way I turn, someone is out to get me.

"Mila, please. Why don't we leave it for now? I have The Forrester Foundation lecture to prepare for."

"Okay, I get it, you're a perfectionist like me. But it would be great if I could have your notebooks before the lecture. After all, we *are* your university. It would be nice to have this information before you present it. Like a scoop." She chuckles at her own wit.

"Of course. I'm on it."

She gives me a small nod, like she doesn't really believe me. "So how about Friday then?"

I can't think of anything so I tell her Friday is good. I'll have to think of something before then. I'm already exhausted thinking of all the excuses I'll need to drum up before she leaves me alone.

"All sorted then," I lie.

Over lunch June and I dissect the Isabelle situation. "I think it's an excellent idea to have her over for dinner. Make sure she sees how happy you and Luis are."

Friday comes around, and I'm walking out of a class trying to avoid the students piling out into the corridor as I turn my phone back on. There's a message from Isabelle and for a moment I think she's going to cancel on me, that she's got cold feet, and I'm already annoyed because I spent all week designing the menu: baked oysters and cheese puffs for entrées; venison Wellington with scalloped potatoes and cremini mushrooms in a cream and rosemary sauce; chocolate brownies which I stayed up until midnight last night to bake, to be served with mascarpone cream plus a dash of Grand Marnier for the adults; and I left work early yesterday so I could shop for it all and still have time to cook dinner for my family.

I call her back, the phone wedged in the crook of my neck, one hand holding my satchel open, the other shoving a bunch of papers inside.

"We're still on for dinner tonight?" she asks. She sounds so sweet, so eager.

A bell rings and students pour into the corridor from various directions, out of one class and into another. *Sorry Mrs. S,* they mutter as they bump into me.

I picture the necklace and feel my pulse quicken. I decide to sound forgetful, because I can't help myself. "Dinner. Tonight."

"You don't remember?"

"Oh, yes. Of course I do."

There's a pause. "Anna, it's okay if you want to change plans…" Suddenly I think maybe I was too convincing, while another part of me—I am made of many parts—is thinking, *Yes, please. I'm so tired. How about we do it another day and I'll just go home and put everything in the freezer and curl up in bed and tell Luis I'm sick, and can he please deal with the kids and empty the dishwasher.*

But I rally.

"No, of course not! There's a lot going on here and my brain is like a sieve. I'm really looking forward to it." I reel off the address and she says Luis already gave it to her, and can she bring something?

"Nothing at all, just you," I say.

"Okay, I'll bring some wine then. I'll see you tonight."

The upside of this, is that when Mila turns up to my office, tapping her watch, telling me she's been waiting for me and did I bring my notes? I get to apologize profusely and tell her I'd completely forgotten.

"Brain like a sieve, I swear."

I buy flowers on the way home, a bunch of cellophane-wrapped white lilies to cheer myself up. I'm so tired my feet are shuffling instead of walking. It's going to be a long night.

CHAPTER 22

I've put the flowers in a vase and I'm running an eye over the living room, checking every detail like a forensic scientist at a murder scene. I want everything to look perfect. I want everything to look *happy*. This is a happy home, I tell myself as I plump up cushions and wipe a wine stain from the glass coffee table. In the kitchen the surfaces are gleaming and still I run a cloth over them. Sometimes I go to other people's houses and the first thing I see is the dirt crusted in the corners of the window frames or spots of tomato sauce on the splash-back behind the stove, and I have to fight the urge to pick up a sponge and scrub the place.

I've already made the cheese puffs, so they just need to be warmed up. The venison is cooking gently on one shelf in the oven, and I'm getting the potatoes and mushroom dish ready to put on the other oven shelf when the doorbell rings. Isabelle isn't due for another forty minutes so it can't be her, which is just as well because I am not ready. I've done my hair but I still have to do my make-up. I bought a contouring kit—completely unlike me, my make-up kit consists of one tube of mascara and one tube of lipstick. It goes without saying I've never used a kit before, but I checked out a couple YouTube videos on how to make your cheekbones higher and your eyes wider and your chin more defined, and your face more desirable, generally speaking.

I wipe my hands on the tea-towel, and for a crazy moment I think maybe it's Geoff, that he has come to my house to... no. I'm going insane. Of course it's not Geoff. Still, when Carla bounds down the stairs I put my arm out to stop her while I peer around the blinds.

But it is Isabelle after all, and I'm strangely disappointed. I would almost have preferred if it was Geoff, or Ryan even; anyone but Isabelle, because I am absolutely not ready for her.

"Hello!"

She stands there, a bottle of wine in one hand and a white box with a pretty pink ribbon in the other.

"I know I'm early," she says, biting her bottom lip daintily. She looks stunning in her white coat and light blue woolen dress—even the snow crystals scattered throughout her thick blonde hair look magical, like she's just glided over from the set of *Frozen*. Now I'm really nervous. I wish Luis was home but he chose this very day to help his dad trim a tree that was in the way of the TV aerial. When I pointed out there was a lot to prepare for this evening, he insisted—conveniently, I thought—that it had to be today. He won't be back for a while, maybe even another hour. And I've already drunk half a bottle of wine, which was possibly a mistake.

"I slightly underestimated how far you live. Is that okay? I could wait in the car if you prefer and come back later. I was going to do that but I then I thought the wine should be in the refrigerator, so I here I am. And this is pecan caramel cheesecake, by the way. And I didn't make it, in case you're wondering."

I take the box from her. "I wasn't," I say, recognizing Mario's Patisserie's sticker on the cake box, thinking I wish she'd told me, I wouldn't have made the brownies if I'd known, but then I tell myself it's sweet and that it's going to be a long night if I'm already over-thinking things, so I should just stop right now.

"Hello," Carla says.

"Sweetheart, this is a friend of mine, Isabelle."

Carla tilts her head at me as if to say, *Friend? Don't be silly! You don't have any friends.*

"She's a friend of Daddy's too," I say. *A very good friend of Daddy's.*

"It's nice to meet you, Carla. You look just like your mom. How old are you?"

"Fourteen," Carla says, pulling her sleeves over her hands and standing with one socked foot over the other.

"Fourteen is a great age, isn't it, Anna?" And I'm thinking, *Is it? Not where I came from.*

"Very. Come in, Isabelle. I've only just started cooking but you can sit and fill me in on what you've been up to since, well, since you were born, I guess." I laugh. Carla stares at me sideways, trying to understand why I'm being weird. Isabelle is too polite to do so.

I take her coat and immediately scan her throat for the necklace, but her dress has a collar and I can't see it. I consider saying something like, *Oh wait, you have a leaf stuck there, let me get it for you,* just so I can tug at it, but I don't.

I touch my hair self-consciously as I lead her through to the kitchen. She looks so fresh and well put together, whereas I look like the local drug dealer with my messy hair and my gaunt, unmade face. Maybe once Luis finally gets home I could sneak upstairs and slap gallons of whatever is in that contouring kit on my face.

"I'd better finish dinner!" I laugh for no reason whatsoever. "Would you like something to drink, Isabelle?"

"Yes, how about this?" She brandishes the bottle of Chardonnay and I wonder if she caught me looking at it greedily moments earlier.

I pull out a glass for her, which makes me think of the elegant tall stem glasses in Luis's studio, which makes my hand twitch and I spill some of the wine on the table. I tear off a paper towel, laugh again, this time in a way that threatens to reach maniacal proportions, and wipe it off. It really is going to be a very long night. I check on the venison to steady myself, then finally I ask, "Where do you live, Isabelle?"

She takes an olive and drops the stone into her palm. I quickly put a small plate in front of her.

"Ohio City," she says.

"Oh, that's nice. I go running there sometimes."

I don't know what's the matter with me. I just seem to blurt out things for no reason whatsoever. Now of course she says, predictably, "Oh, that's so funny! So do I! We should go running together sometimes!"

"Well, that's a coincidence!" I say, one hand on my hip. I smile, sort of: it's hard to smile when your whole face is so tense it feels like rigor mortis setting in. But I'm just pleased the kids have disappeared right now. Because they would absolutely exclaim, *What's wrong with you, Mom? Why are you lying?*

Then, mercifully, I am alerted to Luis's arrival by the excited barks of Roxy.

"God, it's cold outside." He pats Roxy then rubs his hands together and suddenly I feel like I'm in a play, and my kitchen is just a set and we are all very bad actors delivering our wooden lines.

"Well, it's warm in here, come on in," I chirp.

We all laugh and they say a friendly hello which I can't help but keep a check on, but so far so very peck on the cheek. He comes over to me and kisses me on the lips, so that's nice. Then Carla and Mateo erupt into the room to greet their dad, as they do, and suddenly the atmosphere feels warm and festive. Luis opens another bottle of wine and the kids settle at the kitchen table, fascinated by this new guest who is a friend of their parents.

Isabelle asks them lots of questions, none of which are *How do you like school?* or *What do you want to do when you grow up?* which in their eyes is a definite tick. Then Luis says, *why don't we sit down at the dining table?* and I'm thinking, *Maybe because I'm here cooking?* but everyone else seems to think it's a good idea and they disappear, leaving me in the kitchen with a stained apron, sweating over a three-course gourmet meal for my husband and his floozy. Only then does it occur to me that maybe I didn't think this through.

I knock back the rest of the wine.

"This is nice," I say, pointing over baked oysters and cheese puffs at a silver ring on her index finger, even though it's not, not really, but I'm hoping it's from Patrick. I just want to hear her say it.

"Isn't it?" She slips it off to show me.

"It's interesting," I say, handing it back to her. "Kind of like a wonky bagel."

"I don't know about that!" she says, although I note she purses her lips as she slips it back on, so that's nice.

"He's a very interesting metal artist," Luis interjects. "French."

"Well, ooh la la!" I quip, then laugh, but they don't and I wonder, *How does he know, anyway? Did he give it to her too?*

"Are you and Patrick married, Isabelle?" Though she doesn't wear a wedding ring.

"No, we're not, but we're talking about it," she says coyly.

"Really?" Luis asks.

"That is such wonderful news," I say, only just restraining myself from clapping. "What a shame Patrick couldn't make it this evening."

"He travels all the time, that's the downside of his work, to me I mean, not to him. He's an athletics recruiter." The whole time I'm staring at Luis, searching for clues and finding none.

"How interesting!" I say. "And how did you two meet?"

She says something about being introduced through friends of friends, then Mateo pipes up.

"Mom and Dad met at school."

"At college, sweetie," I say.

"And Mom fell in love with my dad"—he punctuates this with a mini eye roll, something about the word *love*—"but he was going with another girl, then *she* died from eating a peanut, so Mom could be with Dad!"

He smiles, like it's a fairy tale with a happy ending. No one says anything except for Isabelle, who gives a little gasp. Luis stares at me accusingly. I should never have told that story to Matti.

I laugh. "What an imagination you have, Matti! It wasn't quite like that, sweetie." I turn to Isabelle. "It was awful. What was her name, Luis?"

"Monica."

"That's right." I turn back to Isabelle. "Monica had a peanut allergy, and she was usually very careful about what she ate, wasn't she, Luis?"

"Yes, very."

"So why did she die?" Carla asks. I desperately want to get off the subject, but I know my children. It's better to tackle things head on and move on.

"She used to bring back cake and sweet things to her room after dinner—we all did—but that one time she got it wrong." I sigh.

"Didn't she have an Epipen?" Carla asks. "At school there are two girls with a peanut allergy. They have to carry an Epipen with them all the time around their neck. There's even a spare one in the school infirmary."

"I should hope so!" I say.

"She did have an Epipen but it got misplaced that day," Luis, who has barely spoken throughout this exchange, replies. And it's my turn to shoot him an accusatory stare. It might be the truth, but I don't think it's right to say it in front of the children. It's the kind of tale nightmares are made of.

He catches my eye and smiles. "And then I married your mother, and you two monsters came along. How lucky was that!" He gets to his feet and starts piling up the plates. "Okay, who's for dessert?"

Matti screams "*Me!*" and Luis pretends to cut him into pieces to serve on plates. It's a standard joke in our house. So, of course,

Carla screams, "*Me! I'm for dessert!*" And Isabelle is laughing so much she's holding her stomach. I don't know if she really thinks it's *that* funny, or she's just playing it up for the kids. Then Luis asks again, "*Who's* for dessert?" and the kids scream, "*Isabelle!*" But Luis says, "What about Mommy?" Which is nice because *Mommy* never gets to play this game. *Mommy* is never for dessert. Maybe he tried once but I wriggled out of it, I suppose that's why. I laugh, extend my arms ready to be cut up to pieces but they're insistent. "Noooo!!! Isabelle's for dessert!" And I can see Luis doesn't want to do it. He steals sideways glances at her, probably hoping she'll saying something like, "*No, not me, please cut up Mommy instead.*" But she doesn't and the kids are over-excited and they won't let up so he relents, does his thing, cuts up Isabelle in pieces and serves her up on a plate. And I have to say, she's a natural, completely comfortable with my husband's hands on her and my kids pulling her limbs apart.

"I'll get the cheesecake," I say.

CHAPTER 23

The first time I ever saw Luis was at the college library. I was scanning the shelves for something and he appeared beside me. He smelt of something warm and sweet, like the whiff you catch as you walk past a bakery.

"Sorry," he whispered, reaching across me.

I fell in love with him the moment I saw him. Later, I found out he was going out with a girl from my dorm. Monica. I hadn't forgotten her name earlier, I just pretended to. He told me once that she was the first girl he loved. I rolled my eyes when he said that. I mean, every guy was in love with Monica, and it also betrayed a striking lack of imagination. She was the quintessential pretty girl next door. Perfect white teeth, bouncy blonde hair held back with barrettes. *Barrettes*. I couldn't see what she and Luis had in common, although she liked to draw, I remember that. I don't think she was any good though. She used to do portraits of some of the other girls and they all looked the same, with long heart-shaped faces and wide almond-shaped eyes, like a cross between Barbie and Bambi. A gaggle of Barmbies.

We didn't hang out, just passed each other in corridors on the way to the bathroom, her in cute animal slippers, tying the belt on her powder blue bathrobe, me in nylon pajamas and flips flops.

Somehow, Luis and I became friends. I say somehow as if it was random, but really, I sought him out, bumped into him on multiple occasions until he recognized me enough to say *Hi!* I remember what his smile did to me back then. Made me weak at the knees. We hung out sometimes, at the library mostly. I studied a heck of a lot more than he did, and we were not in the same classes, but we would still end up at the library at the same time, and we'd sit together at the big table downstairs, me revising physics, him reading about philosophy. He'd raise his head and catch me watching him, I'd blush furiously and he'd smile, that gorgeous sexy smile. This only happened whenever Monica was in class, obviously. I asked him once, long after we became a couple, if he knew then how deeply in love I was with him and he just smiled that same smile and didn't say anything.

There was a party one night and I knew Monica and Luis would be there. As it happened earlier that day I saw her get herself a treat from the cafeteria. She brought it back to her room, she did that sometimes—I know, because I did watch her a lot. The last time I saw her, I was in the bathroom washing my face, getting ready for the party, when Monica walked in. She barely acknowledged me, stepped into one of the shower cubicles with her pink plastic bathroom bag and her fluffy slippers.

I went to the party but Monica didn't. Luis was there, alone, looking forlorn. I stayed close to him all night. I plied him with Sangria in which I'd poured generous slugs of rum—isn't that what we were supposed to do, us crazy college kids?—then I tried to kiss him but he gently pushed me away and slurred in my face, his eyebrows knotted together.

"I'm sorry, Anna. I just really love Monica."

I giggled, slapped him on the chest playfully, said I hadn't meant to kiss him anyway. He pretended to believe me, but the rejection left me feeling worse than I'd anticipated.

By the time I returned to my dorm there were ambulances outside and chaos in the corridor. Monica had eaten the wrong cake. Her Epipen was nowhere to be found. She'd lost it somewhere—was the conclusion—and hadn't noticed until it was too late.

Luis was devastated, but I was right there. I comforted him, consoled him, talked to him softly late into the night, every night. I wrapped my arms around him and I never let go.

I was in love with Luis but he was with Monica. Then Monica ate a peanut and he was mine.

I watch them from the kitchen door, especially her. I can see her perfect profile from my vantage point. She's laughing, tickling my children, and I think about Monica. She looked a bit like Isabelle: the blonde hair, the wide smile, the blue eyes. He has a type, my husband, and ironically, I'm not that type. I find myself imagining that I'm watching another family. That Luis is married to someone else, someone like Monica, or Isabelle. That this is a regular Friday night dinner. They look beautiful, the four of them. Like a perfect family tableau and suddenly it's too much and I have to look away.

"Anyway, I don't know why we're talking about all that," I say when I return, even though no one's talking about all that. They're too busy laughing. I set down the cheesecake more abruptly than I'd meant to and everyone stops. Luis looks up at me, frowning.

"I'm just so glad we finally got to meet properly," I say to Isabelle, trying to reinsert myself back into my own family. Somehow Luis gets the message because he calms the kids down and cuts the cheesecake while Isabelle runs both hands through her gorgeous hair which got all messed up in all the fun they were having. She closes her eyes, slowly shakes her head and lets her hair fall perfectly back in place. It's like watching one of those slow-motion shampoo commercials.

Later, when the children have gone to their rooms and Luis is in the kitchen loading the dishwasher, Isabelle says, "You have a beautiful family, Anna. You're very lucky."

"Thank you." But I want to tell her it's not just luck, it's hard work. That a family is like a fortress you have to defend all the time. And you can't relax because there's always someone trying to get in, always someone looking for a breach. Someone pretty, someone pretending to be nice, someone just like her.

Luis returns and offers coffee and I flick my eyes up at him. I'm a bit annoyed he interrupted our conversation just when she was saying we were a beautiful family. I say no to coffee and pour myself another glass of wine.

"Hey, babe, maybe you should slow down." I look at him with narrowed eyes. I want to ask him to please not embarrass me, but I don't. I just smile tightly. "I'm okay."

"You said you wanted to prepare for your big talk. You asked me to—"

"Yes, all right, thank you Luis." I turn to Isabelle. "I'm delivering a lecture next week where I will present my proof of the Pentti-Stone, the conjecture I solved. It's organized by the Leo Forrester Foundation. They're the ones who award the prize that I won. It's kind of a big deal. A very big deal. No one solved it before. Which makes sense, right? Anyway, I'm the first. The only." I'm slurring my words, vaguely aware how childish I sound and that I should shut up now, but I can't.

"Yes, I know," she says. "And it's truly impressive. You must be very proud."

"Yes, I am. Thank you. And so is Luis. Aren't you, Luis?" And Luis says, "What?" and I say, "Proud of me?" and he says, "What for?" And I laugh and slap him playfully on the arm and say, "Never mind!" and turn back to face Isabelle. She's folding her napkin neatly, brushing it flat and folding it again and if I didn't hate her so much, that would earn her a point in my book.

"I really should go," she says.

We all get up, unsteadily in my case, and say goodbye. Luis helps Isabelle with her coat. It's funny, but he seems almost relieved that she's leaving, and she seems almost detached. Certainly not that friendly. They behave like colleagues, not like lovers, and I don't know anything anymore. Is it possible that I was wrong? I kick myself now, because I should have asked her when he was out of the room whether there's someone called Belle who works at the gallery. Maybe all this time I've been focused on the wrong person.

But when she turns to slip her arm into the sleeve of her coat, I catch a glint at her throat and I know. There is no other Belle. They're just playing it cool for my benefit. And I'm such an idiot that it's almost working.

"This is pretty," I say, reaching literally inside her collar for the delicate gold chain, trying not to scratch at her throat. It sits below the neckline of her woolen dress. I bet that's why she chose that dress, so she could wear it in secret. A secret between her and my husband. And the joke's on me.

She looks down. "This? Yes, isn't it?"

"Was it a gift?" I ask, my heart bouncing around my chest.

She has the gall to glance at Luis as she replies, "Yes, it was a gift." Then, after a beat, she adds: "From Patrick." And I have to walk away to stop myself from doing something I won't regret, like sticking a fork into her pretty neck.

Luis pops his head in through the kitchen door to say he will walk Isabelle back to her car. I nod, unable to speak, give a small cough to hide it.

"I'll finish in here," I say finally, clearing my throat. "Goodbye, Isabelle," I sort of shout out.

She too pops her head through the door. "Thank you for a wonderful evening, Anna."

"You're welcome!" I say, then under my breath I add, "*Not*," because I am a child. Then I wait until they're gone to sprint up the stairs so I can watch them.

It was supposed to be a guest bedroom, this room, but we use it as a storage space now, mostly for the children. It still has a bed, which is covered with god knows what: sports things they don't use anymore like hockey clubs and Carla's little tutus that I packed in crêpe paper and inside silk lined suitcases. I squeeze past Luis's old speakers and step over boxes of DVDs and guitar cases and hit my toe on a kettle bell. When I reach the window, I stand just off to the side of it, in the dark, and lift the edge of the drape with one finger.

It must have rained—the yellow hue of the streetlight across the road is reflected in pools of water on the asphalt. Her shiny silver Lexus is parked across the road. It lights up and beeps awake. Luis opens the door on the driver's side, they talk for a minute then he turns around and glances back at the house. When he turns back, she takes his face in her gloved hands—white, fur-lined at the edges to match the coat—and kisses him, eyes closed. It's a long, languid kiss, her mouth pressed hard on his, before the kiss turns strong, passionate and familiar, like they've done it before so many times they know each other's mouths by heart. I feel a sob crack in my chest. He takes hold of her wrists and brings her hands down. Then Isabelle lifts her face up to me and she looks right at me, like she knows I'm there, watching in the shadows.

And she smiles.

I jerk back quickly and the drape flutters down. She can't have seen me, it's dark and I was only looking through a sliver of glass, but she knows I'm here. She must have known I would be watching, because that kiss, it was for me.

I went to bed and pretended to fall asleep immediately so I wouldn't have to look at his treacherous face. He joins me not long after and within minutes he's snoring. I prop myself on my elbow and watch him. I picture myself throwing things, breaking things, throwing his stuff out into the rain and kicking him out along with it. How dare she—it's her fault, I'm just going to say that right now and never revisit that claim—do this to our family?

"Do you remember?" I whisper softly into his neck. He is lying with his back to me and I spoon him close, hold him tight. I breathe in the scent of him, sweaty and sweet. "Do you remember that time, we spent that entire week in your apartment? How we ended up living on brown rice because there was nothing else and we didn't want to leave? Old packets with long-gone sell-by dates that we found at the back of the kitchen cupboard. You joked the previous tenant must have left them there, you remember? But we didn't care. In the end we only came out into the light because we ran out of brown rice. You didn't want to let me go. 'I love you to the moon and back,' you'd say. Do you remember, Luis? You remember how obsessed with each other we were? That was your word: obsessed. 'You're obsessed with me,' you'd say, and I'd laugh. Am I? 'Yes. You are,' you'd say. 'You're obsessed with me. Tell me that you are.'

"'I am,' I'd whisper. 'I'm obsessed with you.' And you'd say, 'I would do anything to keep you forever.' And I'd laugh, because it was a strange idea—to have and to keep. But I liked it. So will you keep me forever, Luis? We could run away, all four of us. We could move to Martha's Vineyard and live in a gingerbread cottage. You could fall in love with me again. You could keep me again, forever. Just like you always wanted."

He doesn't reply. I want to bite the back of his neck. I want to break the skin and taste him. I'm so drunk I think I might just do it.

CHAPTER 24

I spend the weekend working on my presentation so I don't have to talk to Luis other than a few grunts here and here. He thinks I'm stressed because of the lecture and he makes sure the children stay out of my way.

The following Monday I arrive at work tired and moody. I've barely sat down when Geoff appears at my door.

"Do you have a moment, Anna?"

There's something about his demeanor I don't like. He appears overly relaxed and he's grinning, in a way that's just not good. "In my office? Now?"

I follow him because I don't think I have a choice, then immediately wonder if it's a trick just so he can get me alone in his office for a repeat performance of the other day. I grab my cell on the way out and when he invites me to sit down opposite him, I show him my phone.

"Mind if I record this?" I ask.

He shrugs. "Knock yourself out."

I expected him to sneer, to laugh at me. To say that I'm just a tease, that nothing good happens to women like me, but I suppose my recording the conversation is putting a stop to that. He taps the edge of a stack of pages on his desk and I begin to think we are going to be here all day, when he says, "I've just heard from Janette in HR. We've had a complaint. A formal complaint of sexual harassment."

I look up. He shoots me a pained look. Oh. My. God. So I am not the only one? Of course I'm not. How could I not think of that? He has assaulted other women—who? Mila? I don't think so, somehow, unless she really *is* having an affair with him. I think back to what I said to Ryan at the party all these weeks ago. *He's having sex with one of the math lecturers, so he gave her a full professorship.* I would laugh if the whole thing wasn't so horribly wrong.

I am so relieved I let out one long exhalation. I smile to myself because I know why I'm here now. He wants to know if I'll keep our dirty little secret.

"Who is it? Who put in the complaint?"

"It's confidential, I'm afraid."

"Is it bad?"

He glances at the top sheet in front of him. "It's pretty bad. Non-consensual sexual touching, forcing the complainant to comply under duress, that sort of thing."

This is going to be bad for the university, and at a time when we were just getting back on our feet.

"So, what do you want from me?" I ask.

He looks at me sideways. "I want you to listen and make your case, eventually."

"Make my case? Against you?"

He turns bright red then, moves his mouth like he's chewing on something before snatching my phone from the desk.

"Hey!" I lunge for it but it's too late. He has deleted the file.

"Don't ever say that again, are we clear?" He hisses. He throws my phone back at me. It lands on my lap. "The complaint is against *you*, Anna."

My mind goes blank. I wait, but he doesn't say anything else. "Me?"

"Yes."

"What? Who?"

He cocks his head. "You know I can't answer that."

I laugh, one short barking sound. "Wait a second. One of my students has accused *me* of sexual assault? Is this a joke?"

"I didn't say it was one of *your* students. Now, you know the protocol. We will conduct an investigation—"

I'm on my feet. "What the hell is going on? This is bullshit, Geoff. You can't seriously believe—"

"It doesn't matter what I believe."

"But it's a complete lie, I've never even touched a student! I am very aware of my responsibilities under our code of conduct. I would never—"

"Anna, please. I saw you, remember?"

I frown at him, my head shaking in confusion.

"The retirement party? You scuttled off with that guy." He leans forward across his desk. "I *saw* you."

I feel myself blush, remembering the moment when Geoff knocked on the door behind which I lay half-naked. I remember how he waited for me to answer but I never did. How minutes ticked by until he gave up. But he knew I was there, and that I wasn't alone.

I'm shaking uncontrollably and tap my foot against the leg of my chair as if that's going to help. Thoughts tumble in my mind and I can't make sense of anything. "He's not a student, he's an employee. He fixes computers or something. Or did. He's not even here anymore. He's also a stalker."

"I shouldn't even be discussing this with you." He takes his glasses off and puts them down on the desk. "He was a student then, Anna. He was in third year Law. And yes, he had a part-time job with the IT support desk, but that's irrelevant to the claim."

I feel lightheaded. "He was a student here? At Locke?"

"Yes. He didn't tell you?"

I shake my head quickly and he picks up his glasses again. "Maybe you can say that in your defense."

"So he's a mature student then. He must be in his thirties. Doesn't that mean something?"

"He's twenty-six."

I drop my head in my hands. "Oh my god."

"I'm supposed to read the rule book to you. So—"

"Nothing happened, Geoff."

He snorts with laughter. "Not according to him."

"Is that how you're going to approach this, Geoff? He's sick. He's doing all this to hurt me. And he's left, he's not here anymore."

"That's right. And he cited you as the reason he left."

"Bullshit."

He sits back, picks up his sheaf of paper and begins to read. "Now. On behalf of Locke Weidman, I assure you we will conduct a fair investigation. It is not in our interest to favor either one or the other party. You will be afforded the same respect as the person who filed the complaint. There will be a disciplinary meeting where you will have the opportunity to present any evidence or witnesses. However, no act of retaliation will be tolerated…"

But the blood rushing in my ears is drowning out his voice. Black dots dance in front of my eyes and I bend over, my head touching my knees.

"… no contact order in place. That means you can't contact him, directly or indirectly. Normally I'd have to ask you to stay away from certain sections of the university but I don't think that applies here."

I'm not listening anymore. I get to my feet.

"I have to go," I say.

"Okay. I understand. We can talk later. You want a piece of advice?"

"No."

"Get a lawyer, Anna. It doesn't look good. The timing isn't great either, what with the Forrester lecture coming up."

I return to my office and sit with my head in my hands. I just can't believe Ryan would do this. I don't understand why he hates me so much. What did I ever do to him? I don't even *know* him.

I have to find him. I have to talk to him. I can't let this happen; will they even let me have the prize if I'm found guilty of... what did he say again? Sexual harassment? That's ridiculous. Surely he will never prove that. My reputation is sterling. Is that the word? Thank god I got him to delete the photo. That's one thing I can be grateful for. It's his word against mine, except for Geoff that is, who will tell everyone. *I saw you, remember?*

An email alert pops up on my screen and I look up. It's from Jack Dawson at the Forrester Foundation and I click on it immediately.

> *Anna, we're so excited about tomorrow. Just one thing, if you could email me the scans of your proof notebooks. As you know, at the Foundation we appraise not just the proof but the creative process that led to it. I understand my colleague asked for this last week. Before tomorrow if possible, would be much appreciated.*
> *I look forward to it.*

I can't. I just can't. My brain is zapped. I vaguely remember some email about sending the notes and I just dismissed it. It's not my fault these people can't decipher an elegant proof unless it's pureed and spoon-fed to them.

I don't have time for this. My mouse hovers over the reply button but what am I going to say? I'll get back to you?

I shift the cursor over to the delete button and click.

CHAPTER 25

It is an honor to stand here and present, officially, my solution of the Pentti-Stone conjecture to the Forrester Foundation.

This is the opening sentence of my lecture and I repeat it to myself like a mantra—a trick that June taught me earlier—to keep myself focused.

"You only need to remember the first sentence," she said, "and the rest will come."

It is an honor... I am standing on the stage in the large auditorium. We only use this space for conferences, panels or public talks, like the one I'm about to give. Its raked seating is split into two tiers with a balustrade running along the middle. The walls are covered in beige cloth that, coupled with the comfortable grey seats—padded, no hard plastic here—gives the space an acoustic hush. Everything here was recently refurbished—thanks to a financial grant I secured two years ago—and it still has that smell of newness.

I'm a bit nervous, but in a good way. Frankly, it was a godsend to have June help me prepare earlier. It enabled me to put aside the Ryan situation, for one thing. I didn't tell her, although I will, but not today. Right now, I am focusing on the lecture and doing the breathing exercises she demonstrated earlier. I have my laptop, and a bottle of mineral water—again, June's orders, in case I start to cough. "Or even if you lose your train of thought, you can take a sip and get yourself back on track. No one will know." She also suggested I have my phone nearby—on silent of course—in case I need to access my notes.

"When did you become such an expert?" I asked her.

"I did a course on public speaking once. Never used it. I'm glad it's come in handy finally."

It certainly has. I feel calm, prepared, quietly confident. I've been mic-ed, we've tested everything, including the screen above me where my slides are projected. I look up at a sea of faces, hundreds of them, staring back at me. From my vantage point it looks like every single seat is filled, even the ones right up there at the back of the sloping seating. A deep, genuine sense of pride overcomes me, like a balloon slowly expanding in my chest and, in spite of everything, or maybe because of everything, I wish Luis was here.

To my left, on the edge of the stage, a technician fiddles with a camera on a tripod. He gives me a thumbs-up that we are ready to go. High above me the screen displays the first slide, which is just the title of my lecture: *The Pentti-Stone Conjecture, or Love among Prime Numbers.*

The Dean of the School of Science introduces me as needing no introduction, which provokes a ripple of laughter through the audience. Then a hush settles and I am ready to begin.

I click on my laptop and display the first slide. *What is it about prime numbers and their random affection for each other?*

I talk about *twin* primes, a pair of primes that are separated by two. I describe *solitary* numbers and how all prime numbers are solitary as far as we know. I tell them about *perfect* numbers and how together they form a *club*, to which *weird* numbers do not belong. I show them some *amicable* numbers, not to be confused with *friendly* numbers or, their relations, *sociable* numbers. I introduce *cousin* primes and *good* and *happy* primes and close this chapter with *betrothed* numbers, also known as *quasi-amicable* numbers.

"Whoever said mathematics wasn't sexy clearly never studied number theory."

They laugh. As an introduction, it was good. I can tell. People are quiet, they're taking notes, the ones I can see when I shield the light with one hand are smiling. Then I spot Geoff and Mila in the front row whispering to each other and it throws me. I wish I hadn't seen them. I take a sip of water and click the mouse. The next slide introduces the meat of my lecture and is titled, *What is the Pentti-Stone Conjecture?*

When my phone buzzes on the lectern in front of me I glance at it without thinking. It's a text with a thumbnail. I'm about to look away when I see the word. *WHORE.* I feel a sudden tightening of my chest as I swipe my thumb over it.

The room is silent. They're all waiting for me, but I can't move. I can't take my eyes off the picture which now fills the screen of my phone. I didn't recognize it at first. I didn't recognize *me.* But it is me, lying back on a dark grey carpet, my arm flung loosely over my eyes. I'm naked, although you can only see down to my waist, but my breasts are exposed, large, indecently filling up the screen. There's a murmur through the audience and I look up finally, and for a moment I forget why I'm standing here. Then my phone buzzes again.

Enjoy your next slide. I know I will!

I slap down the laptop screen and turn around, looking up. It's still the previous slide. *What is the Pentti-Stone Conjecture?* but I panic, lift my laptop and yank out the lead.

The screen above me is blue, with an error message in the center. *No signal.*

There's a rustle of activity offstage and the technician comes forward.

"What's going on?" he whispers. But I can barely breathe as I scan the faces looking for Ryan, except everything looks distorted, like I'm looking through thick, swirly glass. I hear murmuring.

"Let me help," the technician whispers. He picks up the lead and starts to plug the laptop back in.

"No!" I snatch it from him. "Just leave it," I hiss. It's like I'm in a nightmare; I'm in a scene from a horror movie. I'm almost surprised not to have pig's blood drop on top of my head.

In the front row the dean looks like he's having an apoplexy. The technician looks around, confused.

"I can fix it," he says quietly.

"I don't want you to," I reply, just as quietly. He looks up at the screen. By now I'm hyperventilating. "I'll keep going, leave it. Please go. Please."

He retreats offstage. Someone backstage asks him something and he opens his hands in a nothing-I-can-do gesture. I turn back to the audience. My gaze lands on Mila: she's waiting, like everyone else, a small smile on her lips.

"When Alex first pointed out the connection between…" I stop abruptly. Did I just say Alex's name? It's the photo, it's thrown me. I can't concentrate. The word pulses in my brain. *Whore.* The dean looks puzzled. They all do.

I close my eyes, picture my children. *Pretend they're here, in the audience.*

"You know what?" Miraculously, it works. "I don't need slides. I don't need prompts either. Because this solution doesn't need a lecture. This solution, it's a revelation. It's a story. And I'm going to tell it to you."

I take a breath. I've got them again, my audience. I can tell. I feel like I've been walking a tightrope and I lost my balance but I didn't fall. Now I am pumping with adrenaline and the other side is so close, I can almost touch it.

"I also want to begin this, um, second part of my talk by dedicating it to Alex Brooks. Alex was a talented student at Locke Weidman and he was an inspiration to many, myself included." I start to pace the length of the stage. "I'd like to say the solution came to me in an Archimedes-like moment, but unfortunately my flash of revelation was not so much a moment as an eternity.

You could say it snuck up on me over a decade or two. My work on prime numbers began with my mother, herself a scientist of some note…"

I get there in the end, one thought lurching into the next, and when the audience claps at the end they sound like they're on my side.

I get through the official prize-giving ceremony, the refreshments in the dean's office, the questions, the compliments, everyone politely ignoring my moment of panic. On the way out, I manage to catch the technician, whose name, I learn, is Steve, and I apologize to him. "I don't want your boss to think it had anything to do with you," I say. "I'll call tomorrow and explain."

"Thank you, I'd appreciate that," he says.

Then I'm in my car, feeling ill, reliving the moment when I received the text. I feel betrayed, even though Ryan is a stranger to me. He promised he'd deleted it. He even pretended to do it in front of me.

I pull out my cell, my stomach clenched in knots, and check the texts again. It's from a *private number*.

I put the cell away and open the laptop and load up PowerPoint to view my presentation. I scan through the slides, then I do it again.

There's no photo of me in them, naked or otherwise. I sit back against the seat and start to cry. I was so sure Ryan had found a way to insert that photo so that it would come up. Which makes no sense because it's my laptop, and I went through my entire presentation a number of times this morning. But then again, he's some kind of IT professional, isn't he? Who knows what tools he has at his disposal. And what else could the text have meant? *Enjoy your next slide. I know I will!* Did he simply want to throw me? Probably, and it worked.

I don't even understand what Ryan wants from me, but there's no doubt in my mind that he wants to hurt me. Why? Because I rejected him? Did he feel humiliated by me? I sit up. I wonder if he knows about the prize? Then a thought occurs to me: does he want a piece of it? Maybe he read about it on our website. Is that what this little exercise back there was all about? A taste of what he is capable of?

All this, because he's after my prize money?

CHAPTER 26

June and I had arranged to go to an early movie after work. It was me who suggested we go this evening because, at the time, I thought it would be a nice way to unwind after the Forrester lecture. Right now, the word *unwind* makes me want to punch someone, but I rally. I text her and say I'll meet her outside. And anyway, I don't want to go home. I can't bear the thought of Luis asking me how it went. The moment when I saw *that* text, thinking the photo was about to be projected on the screen for the viewing pleasure of the country's foremost scientists, is still burnt into my brain, making me smolder with humiliation.

On the way to the cinema June asks me about fifty times if I'm okay, and every time I say I'm fine.

"Is it because of your mother, that you're upset?"

"What about my mother?"

"That she didn't come to your talk? I assume she didn't come, am I right?"

I snort. "I would have been surprised if she had." Then I say I don't want to talk about it right now and keep walking. She pats me on the shoulder and gives a nod of understanding, and I'm grateful we leave it at that.

The movie is about a man who searches for his son but it's much deeper than that. It's about how relationships, no matter how solid, can turn on the smallest of events. Something you thought was strong and anchored and for ever can unravel in the blink of an eye. Which is when you realize that all along it was weak and unmoored and ephemeral and you were just a moron to believe otherwise.

There is nothing about this movie that reminds me of Isabelle, and yet I'm not thinking about my shame anymore; I'm not thinking about Geoff, either. All I can think of is her, smiling back at me as she kissed my husband. That's the moment my mind keeps lurching back to. It's the image that is imprinted on my retina: Isabelle, her hands on either side of his face, her lips on his. The feeling of time being suspended. The silence of my world breaking. She's all I can think about and now the movie makes no sense. June passes the bucket of popcorn over but I nudge it back towards her.

"Actually, June, I don't feel so good. I'm going to go home I think. Sorry." I'm sitting on my leather jacket and I move around, trying to wriggle it free.

"Oh, honey, sure! Let's go, some fresh air will do you good." She begins to gather her things but I put my hand on her arm.

"No, you stay, enjoy the movie."

"Don't worry about it. I'm not really into it, anyway."

Behind us a man makes an impatient click of the tongue and we scurry away, half bent in the darkness.

We end up at the Wonder Bar where we manage to score the window seat, a long padded bench nestled in a nook against the glass. I immediately order a Bourbon lemon tonic and lean back against the fake-fur pillows.

It only takes two sips before I tell her what happened during my lecture. She listens, her mouth agape, her eyes growing wider until she brings her hands against her face and groans.

"How horrible, Anna."

"Trust me, it could have been so much worse."

"But where did the photo come from? Who took it?"

The words tumble out of me, making me realize how tightly coiled they were inside me, like I've let a spring loose.

"I kind of screwed up." I say this with my teeth bared, like an emoji trying to be funny. "This was when I had my suspicions Luis was having an affair. I'd also just found out Mila had gotten the promotion instead of me. I'm not trying to make excuses here… or maybe I am." I wave a hand in the air. "Suffice to say, I felt like shit, and there he was, this nice man who made me laugh and who was interested in me. Somehow, we ended up in some empty office… Honestly, I didn't even know what he had in mind but when he started to kiss me… I went along with it. Let the god of perfect wives come down and strike me with thorns or something, but I was thinking about what Luis had done, and frankly I was in the mood for revenge. I was imagining myself telling him later, one day, a long away. *Guess what, Luis?*" I laugh. "Hey, now the joke's on me. And Luis will probably find out. One day, Ryan will strike." I press my fingers against my eyes. "I think he'll want money."

"Money? Like blackmail?"

I nod. "I should have tried to stop him long ago. I kept wishing he would go away."

"You weren't to know, Anna."

I look at her. "Oh, but I did. You remember the word on my car that day? I'm pretty sure *he* did that."

"But that was weeks ago! And, anyway, wasn't it just kids?" She looks doubtful.

"Will you help me find him, June? I don't know what else he's going to do but he's scaring me. He's stalked me in the past—"

"Stalked?"

"Yes. The day I found out about the prize, we went out for dinner to celebrate—"

"At the Confit d'Oie?"

"Yes! Wait. How do you know?"

"You told me!"

"Did I?"

"In Geoff's office. When we had those celebratory drinks."

I shudder when she says his name. Geoff. I'm yet to tell June what he did. I think I haven't because I want to banish the event from my mind. Pretend it never happened. But I don't think June would let me if she found out. She would tell someone, even if it meant she would lose her job.

I shrug. "Anyway, he showed up outside the restaurant. They've got those big bay windows, floor to ceiling. It was awful. He stood there for ages, watching me. Everyone saw him. Creepy doesn't even begin to describe it. I went to chase him up at work, of course, and that's when I found out he doesn't work there anymore."

"I'm so sorry, Anna. That's awful."

"I know. Then this… photo… what if he sends it to other people?"

She shakes her head for a moment, then she jerks her chin towards my bag. "Show me."

"No way. I don't even want to talk about it anymore." I knock back the rest of my drink. June motions to the waiter to get us another round.

"Okay. Tell me about the dinner with Isabelle, then," she says. "What happened?"

I hop from one bad experience to the next. I describe the whole evening, including the fact that Isabelle arrived so early that I wasn't even ready and I had to sit through dinner looking a hundred years old while she looked like she'd just stepped out of a fashion shoot.

June frowns. "How early?"

"More than half an hour."

She nods. "That's why."

"What do you mean?"

"She came early so you wouldn't be ready and she'd look fabulous. Compare the pair, sort of thing."

I think about this for a moment. "Seriously?"

She taps the side of her nose. "Old trick, my friend."

"Wow, that's nasty."

"That it is. What happened then?"

I backtrack, tell her about finding the receipt for the necklace, and then seeing it on her at the market that day, and again at my house.

"Maybe he gave it to her a long time ago," June suggests. "When they were still… you know…"

"Screwing behind my back? Except the date isn't very old. Last month."

"You're sure it's the same necklace?"

"I checked with the jewelry store."

"Ah. Five hundred dollars you said?"

"And ten."

"Huh. A gift like that? It's a commitment."

"Thanks, June, I really needed that!" I laugh quickly to take the sting out of my words. "Anyway, forget the necklace. It's the least of my worries." I tell her about the kiss, which is the crux of the matter. Anything else I could explain away, even her arriving too early, but not that.

But saying it out loud is a mistake. As long as it was small and wrapped tightly inside my mind, it was only a memory, and possibly a dream. I still had a chance then, but not now. Now Luis and Isabelle are out in the open; I've let them out of the box. Their kiss exists not just in my mind, but in June's, too. Isabelle belongs to Luis now. Extraordinary, beautiful, talented—or so he says—Isabelle. And then there's me. Sad, old, crazy.

It feels like hours later that we leave the bar. I feel regretful, like I talked too much. I'm vaguely annoyed with June for letting me.

I zip up my jacket and wrap my black scarf around my neck. June wants to call me an Uber. She probably thinks I'm too drunk to do it myself which makes me annoyed again. I hug her tightly and tell her I will walk, it's not far and the cold air will do me good. She gets into her ride and waves goodbye as I adjust my black beanie over my ears and slide my hands into my gloves.

I take a moment to get my bearings and I have to check maps on my phone to get it right. I start walking, turn right on West Huron, left on Detroit Avenue. There are still lots of people around, which is good I think, as it makes me less conspicuous. After about a mile I turn onto West 38th, then Franklin, and finally I'm outside her door.

The light is on inside. I stand in the shadows for a while, watching. She walks past the window. She's holding the phone next to her ear and I wonder if she's talking to Luis. She laughs, throwing back her pretty head, and rests the tips of her fingers on her throat.

Suddenly she turns around and looks right at me, and my heart skips a beat. She knows I'm here. I could go home. I should go home. There's still time.

But I don't.

She says something into the phone and hangs up slowly, her eyes not leaving mine. She walks out of the room and the front door opens, throwing a triangle of light onto the porch.

"What are you doing here?" she says. It's so rude, so devoid of any semblance of innocence that for a moment I am lost for words.

"I want you to stay away from my husband."

CHAPTER 27

My pillow feels damp against my cheek, and it's not just my pillow. The sheets around my chest also feel cold and wet, like I've sweated all the water from my body into the linen. I put a hand against my forehead. My hair is stuck against my skull. I'm so dehydrated I don't think I could swallow right now without tearing my throat. I press the palms of my hands against my eyes. The pain is like needles inside my brain, like having shingles behind my eyeballs. It's borderline unbearable.

This is a bad, bad hangover.

I open my eyes, squint at the daylight and feel as if I've rubbed salt into them. I pat the space next to me and find that Luis isn't there; the day feels half gone already, like ten or eleven in the morning. I try to remember how I got myself in this state but can only catch shreds of images as they flash past.

I'm running down the street, getting rained on.

I'm soaked, sitting at a bus stop with my arms around my torso and I don't think I'm waiting for a bus. My hands are cold and I don't know where my gloves are.

I'm inside a bar because I don't want to go home yet. The room is small and dark and on the walls are dim lights shaped like scallop shells and the mirrors behind the bar are etched and a man in a black suit plays jazz on the piano and is this what they call a *speakeasy*?

I drink a Scotch cocktail that tastes like smoke and I love it so much I get another and another and another. The bartender says he'll call me a taxi because I have to go home now. He hands me a paper napkin and I use it to blow my nose. I don't want to go home because I'm angry with Luis. I'm so angry with Luis I want to punch him.

My head hurts so much I can't think. I push the sheets off me and press my fingers against my temples. Something rattles in the kitchen, metal against metal. Luis must be down there. I'm trying to remember why I was so angry with him and when it comes to me it's like I've been punched in the chest. It propels me upright, gasping, eyes wide open, heart thumping behind my ears.

Isabelle is pregnant.

I remember now. I went to see her after June and I left the bar. I walked all the way to her house. She looked surprised to see me but then her face slowly morphed into something else and she turned triumphant.

I was shaking, my teeth chattering. "Come on in," she said. The house was warm. She was walking barefoot on the rug and I remember thinking, *That's a nice rug, gold and red and velvety, the kind of rug that would feel pleasant and soft under your toes. I must get one like that for the living room.* Then I told her again to stay away from Luis, stay away from my husband, and it didn't sound threatening at all. I sounded silly and hollow. Words that have been said so often they've become a joke. When did anyone ever stay away from the husband after being told to do so by a screeching fishwife?

She did what I might have done myself in her position.

She laughed at me. "You don't deserve him," she said. Then she too reverted to type by adding, "You don't understand him." And it was my turn to laugh.

I don't know exactly what happened after that. I know that I yelled until my voice was hoarse. I know that I cried and begged,

I think; yes, I'm pretty sure I begged. At one stage she left the room and I lifted the glass bubble vase of giant white daisies from the side table and dropped it on the floor. The flowers scattered at my feet and the water pooled onto the pretty rug, but the vase was still intact.

Then the memory melts, fragments go missing, like burn holes that start in the middle of a lit photograph and grow outward, leaving scorched misshaped rings in their wake until there's nothing left.

I close my eyes, press my fingers between them. I do my best to concentrate, will myself to remember, and slowly a memory comes into focus. I see Isabelle put the flowers back in the vase, hear her voice right next to my ear, like she's shouting at the side of my face.

He loves me, she's saying. *He adores me, he longs for me when he's with you, did you know that? He can't stand you. He says you're boring and dull, that you have nothing in common. I can give him the life he deserves, the life he should have had a long time ago. You have no idea how talented he is. He is wasting his life with you. He loves me, and I'm carrying his child.*

She put her hand on her belly then and stopped speaking, breathless.

Everything went still. Like there was no air left in the room.

"What did you say?" My voice was so soft, it was barely audible. I stared at her, my eyebrows knotted with shock, my mouth distorted in pain. I was begging her with my eyes. *No. Please no, say it isn't so.*

"I'm pregnant. We're happy. He's so happy, or haven't you noticed? Have you really not noticed how *fucking* happy he is?" Then she fiddled with the necklace at her throat and smirked.

And I lunged at her and yanked it off and she wasn't smirking anymore.

*

I gulp cold water from the bathroom tap, gallons and gallons of it. Then I wipe my chin with the back of my hand and lean with both hands on the vanity, staring at myself in the reflection. My eyes are bloodshot and the skin below them is bruised and papery. I glance at my hands and I don't understand why they look this way, why there are purple welts slashed across the soft pads of my palms. I open and close them into fists and wince with pain. My heart is hammering. I feel horribly sad, like someone has died.

I let the shower get as hot as possible and turn my face up to it, letting the water sting my skin. I stand there for a long time, crying, not crying, remembering, not remembering.

I see myself running, I'm bumping into people as I run past them. It's late, it's dark, it's raining. I'm out of breath and that's when I sit at the bus stop, breathless, and hug myself. I am standing in my kitchen in my wet clothes, in the dark. I look out to the backyard and the light is on in Luis's shed and I think it's late and he's in there. But he's not because I remember going into my bedroom and staring at Luis who was sleeping peacefully. I remember my whole body shaking and I couldn't make it stop. I took my clothes off and left them on the floor. I slipped between the sheets and pressed myself against his back, every square inch of our bodies skin to skin. I could feel the beat of his heart and wondered if it matched mine. If our hearts were beating in unison. Then I felt like I'd dropped down an inky black abyss and suddenly I am dreaming, and in my dream he has his lips close to my cheek, just next to my ear, and I could feel his breath, like a feather. And he whispered, *I would do anything to keep you.* And I was wishing so hard that it wasn't a dream, even though I knew it was.

As I turn the shower off, I remember something else, a vague memory of Isabelle leaving the room and I wonder if she went to call Luis. I can only imagine what she might have said if she did. *She knows. And by the way, she's certifiably crazy, she's insane, you don't know what she did to me. You need to come and muzzle your wife, Luis.*

I didn't go straight home after, I know that much. I went from bar to bar to bar, or maybe just the one bar. And I walked a long way. I remember that.

I enter the kitchen with a heavy heart. I am so not ready for what is about to happen and I'm already feeling the sting of tears behind my eyes.

"Well, hello you!" Luis says, laughing, and the first thing that pops into my head is not, *Hey, how strange, why isn't he upset?* It's, *How could you not notice how happy he is lately?*

Oh, but I did notice. I just thought it was because of me.

He stands there, one hand on the kitchen sink, the other on his waist, checking me out, trying not to laugh. Why is he amused? "That was quite a bender, babe! And what exactly did you two get up to last night?"

So he really *doesn't* know. She didn't call him after all. He didn't go running to save her from crazy old me.

I pull out a chair, sit down, rub both hands down my face. "Sorry I came home so late, I hope you weren't too worried."

He grabs the pot of coffee and pours a mug full. He hands it to me. "There you go. You don't look so good, if you don't mind me saying."

I try to smile, take a sip of the hot drink.

"You could have called you know? Didn't you get my texts?"

Texts? I try to remember the last time I looked at my cell but I can't. "Sorry. I didn't check my phone."

He raises a hand. "All good. Once I spoke to June I stopped worrying."

Oh god. That's right. June called me at one point. I only picked up because it was her. I was in a bar, she said Luis was wondering where I was and he'd called her. I asked her to say we were together, make up some story, tell him I'm in the bathroom.

"Sounds like you two were having a fine time. She promised to put you in a cab later. I went to bed after that. You got home okay, right? Obviously?"

"Yes, of course."

"I didn't tell the kids, just so you know."

I sit up. "Tell them what?"

"That their mother was out on the town, partying till all hours. I don't want to give them any ideas." Luis returns to the sink and that's when I notice the tools on the kitchen bench.

"You're fixing the tap?"

"Yep, I got inspired this morning." He organizes his tools and, without turning around, he says, "Was anyone else there?"

"What do you mean?" A drip of coffee rolls down my chin and I reach for the kitchen roll.

"Just that you were out so late, I thought maybe the whole team went out to celebrate after your big talk. You, Mila and the guys. How did it go?"

I close my eyes. My big talk indeed. I drop my forehead in my hands. "It was okay," I say, cringing at the memory. Should I tell him now, about Ryan? That would be the smart thing to do, tell him before he finds out. Before Ryan blackmails me or uploads his photo to the internet. Maybe he's emailed it to that nice journalist from the *New York Times* who's writing an article about me: *And what does Dr. Sanchez, Winner of the Forrester prize for the Pentti-Stone conjecture like to do in her spare time? See page 12 for photos.*

I can't believe I can't even win a prize without screwing it up. I cross my arms on the table and drop my forehead on them with a groan.

"What happened?" he asks. For a moment I think he's asking about Isabelle. I look up at him from under heavy eyelids. He's facing me now, leaning back against the sink. He refills his mug with coffee. He's asking about the talk. Of course. I can't tell him. I just can't. He'll want to know how the heck a photo of me naked almost ended up in my PowerPoint presentation. More to the point, he'll want to know how it came to be in existence.

"It was okay."

"You sure? You don't sound so sure."

"It could have been worse."

"So it was just you and June last night, then?"

"Yes, just me and June." I push my chair back. "I should go to work."

"Can't you take the day off? I can't imagine you're going to be much good over there!" He holds up one hand, shows me three fingers. "How many? Go on! Can you even count anymore, Ms. Math Teacher?"

"You're so funny, Luis, you should have been on the stage."

"That's what you always say."

Roxy gives a little bark at my feet.

"Did you walk her?" I ask. A reflex.

"Not yet. But I will. You go, babe."

I grab my leather jacket from the hook near the door. It's still slightly damp from last night and I vaguely consider getting another coat from the closet, but I don't. I slip the jacket on and grab my bag from the chair where I left it last night. I go to Luis; I want him to kiss me, to feel his lips on mine once more before he finds out and it all goes wrong.

"I love you," I say.

I already have one hand in my jacket pocket and my finger gets stuck in a hole in the lining. My fingertip brushes against something and I wriggle it out just as Luis grabs my face with both hands and kisses me on the lips. I raise my hand and glance sideways at it. It's a chain so thin it may as well be made of a spider's silk thread, with two thin diamond baguettes set a little off center.

CHAPTER 28

The young man who serves me in Starbucks does a double take. "Rough night?"

I give a rueful smile but don't reply. I pay for my coffee, grab my cup and walk out.

I'm late, obviously, but I didn't have a class this morning so I knew there was no need to rush. I did miss a couple of meetings, however.

As I walk down the corridor at work I think people stare at me, bringing their fingers over their mouths to contain the snigger. No, they're not. I'm being paranoid. Why would they do that? A group of students from my third year class, six or seven of them, walk up towards me and I'm convinced they're staring right at me with narrowed eyes and barely suppressed sneers. One of them bumps into my shoulder.

I don't feel well. I walk into my office and close the door. I take the necklace out of my pocket, hold it loosely, twirling it between my fingers. I can still feel the thumping of my heart as I realized what it was earlier, when I was kissing Luis goodbye. I immediately shoved it back in my pocket and put my other hand behind his neck. Just the thought that he might have seen it sends spasms of horror through me.

I don't remember how it got there but there's no mistaking the fact that it fit exactly in the red welts on the inside of my left hand. As if I'd grabbed it and pulled hard, so hard that it almost broke the skin.

"I thought this might help."

I snap my head up and in one quick motion I've opened my drawer, dropped the necklace into it and slammed it shut. June blinks in surprise.

"Sorry, you gave me a fright," I say, laughing. She's brought me the usual cookies and a cup of coffee. I glance at my own takeout cup. She follows my gaze.

"Oh, well, you look like you need two of those anyway." She smiles, puts down her offerings on my desk and takes her usual chair. "You okay?"

I rub my hand on my forehead. "I've had better days."

"I'm not surprised. You were on quite a mission last night."

"What does that mean?"

She laughs. "You were knocking them back, that's what it means."

"Oh, yeah, that sounds about right." I press my fingers against my eyes. "Thanks for covering up for me with Luis."

She waves a hand. "That's all right. It's what friends are for! What did you do, anyway?"

"Nothing, why would you ask that?"

I must have said it more abruptly than I'd intended because she recoils slightly. "No reason. I just thought you might have…" She shakes her head.

"Might have what?" I snap.

"Relax! I thought you might have been with some guy, that's all. You told me you were in a bar, you didn't know where exactly. You said you'd done something bad and you didn't want to go home yet." She laughs again, but I wince and my heart misses a beat or two.

"God, no. Just like you said, I got drunk, June, no big deal. I'm paying for it." I laugh. I could tell her, *I went to see Isabelle and we had a big fight.* But my old friend, the old feeling of doom, gives my stomach a sharp twist. I take a sip of the coffee, try to laugh but end up coughing and sending splatters all over my computer screen.

"So if it wasn't a guy, what was it? What did you do that was *really* bad?" She smiles, arms crossed over her chest.

"Nothing," I say, too quickly, wiping my monitor with the edge of my sleeve pulled over my hand. I laugh, a cackle of noise. "I just wanted a night out by myself! I'd had a pretty rough day. I was upset about Ryan, you know that. I can't tell Luis about Ryan. I just ended up... Okay, fine, I drank too much. What are you going to do, arrest me?"

She tilts her head at me. "Oh, okay. We don't have to keep talking about this if you don't want to. I should go, we both have work to do." She gets up.

"Thank you, June, for covering for me. I mean that. I owe you one."

"That's okay," she says. "It's what friends are for, right?"

It's the first of two final year math exams for freshmen. I walk down the middle of the room and pass out the papers, then I sit at the front desk and spend two hours trying not to think.

When it's over, I gather the tests and take them back to my office. June pops her head in asking if I want to go to lunch. I tell her I'm busy, but thank you. I point at the pile of exams and mutter something about having lunch at my desk. "Thank you very much, June," I say again, because I just don't have a lot of buffer right now. I can't afford to put anyone offside, June least of all. I didn't bring lunch, that goes without saying. I should go downstairs to the cafeteria later and grab a sandwich.

I spend the next two hours marking. It's easy work, if a little time-consuming, but it's what I need right now and I'm lost in it when my phone rings, making me jump.

And I know, I just know, my body knows, that finally this is the call I've been dreading all day and frankly by now it's almost a relief.

"Luis?" I try to sound normal and I can't remember what that sounds like so it comes out forced and overly cheery.

There's silence on the other end, and I'm about to ask if he's there, when I hear him take a ragged breath, the sound you make after you've been sobbing your heart out and it's finally over.

"What's wrong?" I ask. What I really want to say is, *I'm sorry, I'm so sorry.* No, I'm not sorry. I don't know what I want to say anymore but he speaks before me.

"She's dead. Isabelle is dead."

My heart leaps in my throat. I sit up. "Are you sure?" Then I realize the wrongness of my question and add, "We saw her only last Friday night, how could she be *dead*?"

"The police called me. She was found this morning. At her house."

"I can't believe it. Did they say what happened to her?"

"Not yet. Just that she was found dead this morning in her house."

"But I don't understand!" I'm on my feet now. I'm almost shouting. "How can she be dead?"

"I don't know!"

"When they did call?"

"An hour ago."

An hour ago. He has waited for an hour before telling me. There's the beep of another call in my ear but I ignore it.

He sighs, a beat of silence passes between us. I wait.

"The police are coming over, they want to ask me a few questions. That's what they said."

"What questions?"

"I don't know! Jesus, Anna! Are you listening to me? They're probably talking to everyone who knew her. Her colleagues. Other artists who worked with her. Her friends!"

Her lovers? "Oh my god, this is awful."

I sit down again. Do the police even know they were lovers? Then suddenly it occurs to me that maybe Luis didn't even know she was pregnant. I try to remember what Isabelle said to me last night. *I'm carrying his child...* But did she say she'd told Luis? Maybe she didn't. Maybe the police don't have to find out about any of that.

"I just don't understand." I have to calm down but I can't breathe properly. Thoughts are stumbling over each other and I can't think straight. Is this a panic attack? Is this how they start?

"Babe, I have to tell you something—"

The beep, again, intense and relentless. *Just go away, whoever you are.*

"No, you don't," I interrupt. "We can talk later."

"Anna, wait. I—"

"Please, Luis!" I don't want to do this, why doesn't he understand? "I have to go, I have to go to class."

Then he says something so low I can barely make out what it is. Barely, but it sounds like, "I'm scared."

I want to say, just tell them the truth and everything will be okay. But that's not true. Nothing can be possibly okay after this. And I don't want him to tell them the truth because then they'll know. And everybody will know, and I'll know for sure, that my husband didn't love me anymore. That he loved her instead, and that she was carrying his child. And now she's dead.

This is so bad. And yet I am numb. I have to pull myself together. People will be asking soon, *Did you know her?* I must say the right thing, think of her parents, her boyfriend, her colleagues, words of sorrow. But all I can think is, *Will they do some kind of DNA analysis on the unborn child? And what did I do with my gloves again?*

I have to think. There is no room for error now. "You still there?" he asks. I want to scream into the phone, *This is all your fault! Why did you have to do this, Luis? Why did you want to leave me? We could have worked it out. You could have talked to me.*

"I have to go, honey. I love you," I say instead.

"Anna, listen—"

Tell me you love me. Say the words, Luis, say, 'I love you too, I love you more than ever.' Because whatever I did, babe, I did it for you. And that's the whole truth.

But June walks in without knocking, and she's about to say something but she sees my face.

"It's going to be okay. I have to go." And I hang up.

She comes over, sits down. "Everything all right? What's happened?"

"I—just got really bad news." I don't say anymore, and she doesn't pry.

"Anything I can do?"

I shake my head, gnaw at a fingernail. "No, I don't think so. Did you want to talk to me about something?"

"I came to say a detective just called. He's been trying to reach you."

"A detective?"

"Yes, Detective Jones. He's going to be here in fifteen minutes to talk to you."

"Why?"

"I don't know, he didn't say."

"But he can't! I have a class in fifteen minutes!"

She checks her watch. "It's okay. I'll catch Rohan and get him to take it for you." She stands up but I grab her arm, making her wince.

"June, wait a second, please. I need to talk to you. I won't take long."

She sits down again, this time on the very edge of the seat. I drag over my own chair so our knees are almost touching. "What's up?"

"You know how you said to Luis that I was with you, around…"

I look up, try to think, still gnawing at my fingernail.

"Around eleven?" she says.

"Around then, yes, and after that too."

"Okay… What about it?"

"I was hoping… can you say that again if it came up? Say we were together? Like you said to Luis?"

The fingernail has broken off and now it's bleeding.

"What, that we were together?" she repeats.

"Please. Would you? Until maybe one? One thirty, maybe?"

"I don't understand."

"I mean you already said it to Luis, right? So I'm just asking that you don't contradict yourself, that's all. If it comes up. It's just that I went out drinking… God, did I go out drinking!" I laugh, rub my forehead. "It's not a good look right now, June. Especially after the presentation. So I'm just asking you this small favor. No biggie."

She thinks about this, her eyes never leaving mine.

"You want me to say we were together."

Frankly by now I thought that was obvious. "Yes."

"In a bar, drinking."

"Which we were."

"Until one thirty a.m."

"Yes, please." I wait, fingers in my mouth. "If anyone asks."

"But who's going to ask?"

"I don't know. Nobody probably." I laugh, but only for a nanosecond. "It would be too embarrassing for me, if I were to explain. Retrace my steps. You understand?"

She thinks about it, then nods, slowly. "Okay." And I feel such relief that I almost hug her. I get up and return the chair to its place. She gets up too, slowly, unsure, like she wants to ask me more.

"I'll get Rohan to cover your class," she says, one hand on the door.

"Oh, right, thanks," I reply, sounding like I've forgotten she was still here.

CHAPTER 29

I sit there, waiting for the detective, unable to concentrate, my stomach clenching a little more with each passing minute. I open the drawer and pull out the necklace from where I dropped it earlier and shove it in the other drawer, the one at the bottom, so that it sits inside the staff directory. Should I tell the detective that I heard about Isabelle before he says anything? Yes, I probably should. Unless he's here about something else, although that seems unlikely.

When he walks in at last, fifteen minutes late, I'm a mess of nerves.

"Detective Jones." He smiles, extends his hand to me. For a crazy moment I wonder if that's how they get people's fingerprints, if they have a thin film over their fingers like an invisible glove, and after they shake your hand they surreptitiously slip the film into an evidence bag hidden in their pocket.

A beyond stupid and paranoid idea, obviously.

Still, better safe than sorry. I raise my palms. "Probably not, I just peeled an orange." I grab a tissue and wipe my fingers. For a moment Detective Jones does not know what to do with his hand. He looks at it, and puts it in his jacket pocket. He glances at my desk, then at the almost full wastebasket on the floor. If he is thrown by the absence of orange peel, he doesn't say.

"Please, sit down, Detective."

"Thank you." He tugs at the crease of his blue pants as he does so. He's a big man, with a round face and a nice smile, and I tell myself it can't be so bad if he's smiling. Also there's only one of him. That's got to be a good sign too, surely.

He looks around, clearly impressed.

"This is nice."

"Thank you."

"I was expecting test tubes and Bunsen burners."

"You might find those in the chemistry department. Not in the mathematics faculty. We wouldn't know what to do with them."

"That makes two of us."

He pulls out a notepad, licks the tip of his finger and flicks it open.

I point at it with my chin. "I would have thought police would have gone full tech by now." That and invisible films over their hands to capture fingerprints.

"What, this?" He holds up the notepad. "I only trust my good old Moleskines. Not that it matters, as I can't imagine my department issuing us with iPads anytime soon, if that's what you meant." He flicks pages back and forth, finds the right spot, and looks up.

"Mrs. Sanchez, do you know Isabelle Wilcox?"

I sit very still. My immediate instinct is to apologize—nothing new there—to say how very sorry I am and I will *never* do it again. Suddenly, I don't know what to do with my hands. I feel like an amateur being asked to act on stage and I can't remember where they're supposed to go. I hook one arm over the back of my chair, then decide it's far too casual for the circumstances, so I bring my hands together in a steeple and rest my chin on my fingers, a pose I can safely say I have never held before.

"My husband just called me," I say, my chin bobbing over the tip of my index fingers. "I was very sad to hear the news."

"Was she a close friend of yours?"

"No. More like an acquaintance. She curated my husband's exhibition, at Perry Cube Gallery. Not that it needed much curating—I mean, he's just one artist with a limited body of work, not sure what's the curation part there, but you could say they got close, friendly I mean. How did she die?"

He stares at me for quite a while and my stomach clenches.

"She fell down the stairs," he says, watching me. "She hit her head. She was found too late."

I have to work harder to take a breath. It's as if the air has been sucked out of the room.

"An accident?" The stupidity of what I've just said makes me want to laugh. It's the anxiety. I rub both hands over my face to make it stop. I stand up and open the window a notch.

"When is the last time you saw her?" He ignores my question.

I look up to the ceiling, tap my fingers against my chin. Internally, I can barely breathe. I want to ask a million questions before I answer his. *Did anyone see me? Is that why you're here?*

"Lemeseee… we had Isabelle over for dinner last Friday, so that would be the last time I saw her."

It's funny, the power of words. I was at a fork in the road just now. I could have told the truth, or a version of it anyway. I could have said that I was there last night and we had a big, big fight, that I almost smashed her vase and snatched her stupid gold chain from her pretty neck and I'm sorry, but I'm not sorry. Then I'd just tell June not to worry about what we agreed to before. *Tell the truth!* I would have said. *I just did! It's liberating!*

But I panic. I lie. And when he asks if I've ever been to her house, I say, no. I don't even know where she lives, I say.

"What happened to your hand?"

I sit up and check my palm. The red welt goes all the way to the outer edge, around my little finger.

"Gardening. Pulling weeds."

He shakes his head. "Don't you hate that?"

"I sure do."

He checks his notes. "Last Friday night you said?"

"Yes."

"How did she seem?"

I think about this for a moment. "She seemed fine, friendly."

"Did she seem worried about anything?"

"Nope, not that I could see."

"Did she seem depressed?"

"Depressed? No, not at all."

"There was nothing unusual about her, then?"

"I don't understand the question."

"She didn't seem preoccupied? She wasn't acting in any way that seemed odd? She wasn't nervous?"

"No, no and no. She was perfectly relaxed."

"What about your husband? You said your husband and Ms. Wilcox were friends?"

"I said they worked together."

"You said they were close."

"Yes, I see, actually I think I said they *got* close, as friends, yes. They worked well together. He was friends with her fiancé, too. His name is Patrick. They called each other buddy, he and Luis, I mean. Like, 'Hi, buddy!' So he wasn't just friends with *her* is what I'm trying to say."

He was taking notes and now he looks up at me. It's the way I said 'her'. I couldn't help myself and it came out with the tiniest stress of scorn on the syllable. As soon as I said it I knew I'd screwed up. My cheeks feel hot and I wonder if I'm blushing. I get up again and open the window a little more.

"Have you spoken to my husband yet?" I ask.

"My colleague is doing that as we speak. Is there anything else you can tell me about her? About her relationship with Mr. Patrick Fowler?"

I shake my head. "No. I only met him once briefly. God!" I rearrange my pens in the holder. "This is really shocking news. I just can't believe it."

"What about your husband?"

"I thought we just went over that."

He checks his notes. "Not yet. How was their relationship?"

"It was normal. Professional." But my heart sinks. The police will know soon, if they don't already. It's not like there's no record of their affair. There are texts, for one thing. *I can't stop thinking about you.* There are probably lots more by now. I wonder what they say?

I'm pregnant. Are you happy?

Deliriously. I can't understand why Anna hasn't noticed.

That's because she's boring and dull. You two have nothing in common.

You're so right. I long for you. You're the only one who understands me.

Everyone will know. It will be plastered across the world wide web in one big fat masthead: *Beautiful Curator had Affair with Up And Coming Installation Artist. (More details on every single page of the internet.)*

Everybody will know he was unfaithful. They will ask, *Which one killed her, do you think? The wife? Probably the wife, it's always the wife. No, it's the husband. It's the husband who killed her.*

No, it's the wife. Because the lover was pregnant.

I taste blood and realize I am biting my bottom lip. I roll it out between two fingers. Pat at the tender spot.

"You okay, Mrs. Sanchez?"

I don't say, *It's Dr. Sanchez, actually.* I say, "Yes, thank you. It's just such a shock. Poor Isabelle. Yes, she and my husband were friends, friendly, as she must be—must have been, I should say—with a lot of her artists. It's the way they do things in that world, you see. I can't

imagine myself asking my husband to cook dinner for my colleagues—
I see them often enough as it is, truth be told." Chuckles. "But no,
I have nothing to add on that score. Nothing I can think of, sorry."

"Well, I won't keep you," he says, folding his notebook and
returning it to the inside pocket of his jacket. Then as we reach
the door, he turns around and smiles. "You don't remember me?"

"I'm sorry?"

"I spoke to you, although not in this office." He glances around
the room. "When your student died."

I raise my head slowly. "Yes. I remember now. I thought you
looked familiar," I lie.

"Alex, wasn't it?"

"Yes, that's right." I rarely ever think about Alex anymore. It all
seems like such a long time ago, much longer than the six weeks
or so since he died. I try to work out how I feel, hearing his name,
and I come up with nothing. I literally feel nothing.

"That's an odd case, too," he says.

My jaw tenses. "Is it?"

"Certainly. It's not every day you investigate someone who died
by jumping out of a window. Alex *Brooks*."

"That's right."

"You were rather close to him. That must have been a shock, too."

"Of course it was. All of us here in the mathematics department,
myself included, were rather close to him, as you put it. I'm pretty
sure we spoke at length to the police at the time. To you, I mean,
since it was you. I remember now."

"Just out of curiosity, did you and Alex Brooks ever have any
disagreements? Any difficulties working together?"

I have a headache. It's making my eyeballs wobble and I'm
having a hard time focusing. "Why on earth would you ask me
that now?" I finally manage to say.

"My apologies. I should have clarified. The examiner hasn't
ruled yet on whether his death was accidental or whether it was

suicide. It's taking some time. Since I happened to be here talking to you, and you and Alex Brooks worked closely together, I was taking the opportunity to ask about his state of mind. I know doctoral work can be very taxing on young people."

I shake my head. "Oh. Sorry, I thought… forget that. I wasn't thinking. Did you say suicide?"

"It's a possibility."

"I see." I think about this for a moment. Rub my hands over my arms, like I'm trying to warm myself up. "To answer your question, yes and no. I was his supervisor—"

"Which is why I was asking."

"Yes." I raise my hand. It's shaking. I cross my arms. "I understand that now. He was struggling, yes. He was late on his thesis—they all are, to be honest. Just once I'd like to see a student turn in a thesis on time!" I laugh, then catch myself. "I'm sorry. What I was going to say is, I hardly ever saw him because he stopped coming. He liked to work at home, on his own, in his own time. I was concerned he was using drugs, maybe some kind of amphetamines, stimulants of sort? I don't know if that helps."

"Thank you. It does."

"And I wish I'd said something sooner, about the drug use. If he was using I mean, I actually have no idea. Just an impression I got. I think I even mentioned it at the time."

Detective Jones watches me for a moment, then he nods abruptly, thanks me, and finally walks out.

I let out a breath as I sit there with my heart thumping and what's left of my fingernails between my teeth. Why did I have to say that? *I hardly ever saw him anymore but I was worried about his excessive drug use.* How would I know that if I never saw him? Did Detective Jones pick up on that? That I'm inconsistent? Of course he did. That's his job, catching people out when they lie. Also, did I say that the first time they came to ask about Alex? *I hardly ever saw him anymore.* I have no idea. I can't remember.

I call Luis. "Have they been yet?"

"Yes, a female detective. She's gone."

I release a breath. "A detective came to talk to me too, just now."

"What did he say?"

"Same as you, I suspect. Asked how she seemed when I saw her last. Which was last Friday. That's what I said." I wonder if he's going to contradict me, but he doesn't. "They said she died by falling down the stairs."

He doesn't reply.

We sit in silence for a moment. "You okay?" I ask.

"Yeah."

"Okay. Good. It'll be fine. Everything will be fine."

"I don't know what that means, Anna."

"I know. Just trust me, okay? Everything will be fine."

CHAPTER 30

Luis arrives back home and he stands in the kitchen, his shoulders bowed, his features distorted with sadness. I take him in my arms. I hold him, stroke his hair, and we stand there a while until he disengages himself and sits down heavily at the table. I sit opposite him and take his hand.

I tell him about Detective Jones's visit. We swap notes. Both our interviews—if that's what they were—were strikingly similar. When did you last see her? What was her state of mind? Did she seem upset? Preoccupied? Depressed? Was she afraid?

I drop his hand. "Did they ask that? If she was afraid?"

He nods, runs his fingertip over a spot on the table.

"They didn't ask me that. As far as I could tell, her fall was an accident. What did you say?"

He shrugs. "That she was great."

Great.

"Did she seem strange to you when you walked her back to her car?" I ask. I can't help it. It's because he said she was *great.*

He flinches, but there's tension in his jaw. "What do you mean?"

"I don't know, I'm just asking."

He doesn't reply. He scratches at the same spot but with more vigor now.

"Talk to me, Luis."

He remains silent and doesn't meet my eye. Then he gets up, grabs a knife from the cutlery drawer and returns to his chair. He uses the knife to scrape off something at the same spot.

"What are you doing?"

"There's a bit of wax or something. Or some gum. I'm removing it."

He's like a man obsessed. I put my hand on his. "Stop."

He raises his head and looks at me, and his features crumple with misery. I squeeze his hand. I check the clock behind me. "Pull yourself together, Luis. The kids will be home any minute." Just as I say that, Matti and Carla bounce through the front door into the kitchen. They leave traces of slush from their shoes on the clean floor and I don't care. I hug them tight, together and in turn. They complain, of course: "Mom! You're crushing me!"

"I don't care," I tell them. I just want to hug them forever. Luis just sits there scratching at the spot on the table but they don't seem to notice. I cut up some fruit for them, ask them about their day. For once I'm grateful for their trite responses. *Good. Fine. Okay.*

Matti grabs a chocolate milkshake from the fridge and drinks straight from the carton. Carla goes upstairs to do some coding for her school project. Matti takes his milkshake into the living room, mumbling something about playing with his Xbox. Normally that would be out of bounds at this time of the day—or so I hope, I'm not usually here now—but not this time. I am so overwhelmed with love for them that it makes my eyes swim. I will never stop striving to keep my family together. It's what courses through my veins, this craving to be everything that my mother wasn't, to keep my children safe, and happy. My kids will never grow up thinking they're unloved, or unwanted, or not enough for either of their parents. Anything I do to achieve that goal is, as far as I'm concerned, fair game.

My reverie is broken by the sudden sonorous tones of a news bulletin: *Homicide detectives are investigating after a woman was found dead in her home—*

Luis and I stare at each other, then rush to the living room. For a moment I'm confused, but it's only that Mateo has set up his Xbox game on the TV set. I snatch up the remote.

"Hey!"

"It's just for a second, Matti." I switch channels until I find it.

—this morning. The woman was found just after 9:30 a.m. by a cleaner.

Luis is next to me, eyes transfixed by the screen.

The medical examiner's office is yet to determine the cause of death. At this stage it's not clear whether the police are treating the death as suspicious. Investigators did not release any other information.

My cell rings and I look for my bag, which I find hooked on the back of the chair in the kitchen.

It's June.

"Hi."

"I saw the news—"

"I know. It's awful. We were just watching it as well."

"—and I'm not comfortable about lying, about whether we were together last night."

I walk out of the kitchen and through to the backyard. A gust of wind makes me shiver. I sit on a dry patch on the top step. "It's not really lying, June."

"Well, it is, actually. We weren't together. I don't want to make a big deal of it—"

"Why did you change your mind?"

"I don't know, Anna. I just don't feel comfortable with this. If you haven't done anything…"

I just can't speak. I sit there, my head shaking like a broken toy. "I haven't done anything," I manage to say. "Did the police contact you?"

"Of course not."

"Okay, so there's no problem then."

"But there will be a problem, Anna."

"Why do you say that?"

"Because the cops will want to know where you were last night. They're going to ask you for an alibi and you—"

"Why would they do that?"

"Oh, come on. Because your husband was having an affair with her! If she was killed—"

"Wow, back up a second. Nobody said she was killed. They think it was an accident, okay? I mean, I should know, I'm the one who spoke to the police earlier."

She waits a moment. "Look, I'm just not comfortable, that's all. Wherever you were last night—"

"I told you, I was drinking. I went to a bar. Bars."

"So you're covered, then. Just tell them where you went. You don't need me to lie for you."

I rub my forehead. I need to think. I'm so tired and my brain isn't working properly. Luis comes to the door, watches me.

"Can I come over? We could talk…" I ask.

"What, now?"

"Yes, please. Please, June."

It's raining again and I left my umbrella at home. By the time I arrive at June's house, water is dripping down my neck and into the collar of my jacket.

I take off my coat and lay it on the back of a chair while June makes room for me on the sofa by grabbing a pile of magazines and articles and putting them on a table near the window. She disappears and returns with two mugs of something warm and caramel-colored.

I take mine with both hands. "Thank you, it smells delicious. What is it?"

"It's a chai tea, with cinnamon. And a dash of bourbon."

"Thank you. That's exactly what I feel like." I take a sip of the hot drink. It's incredibly delicious. "Do you have a recipe for this?"

"Yes. I'll dig it out and give it to you."

"Thank you. I'd like that."

"Anna? What's going on? You didn't come to ask me for a recipe."

I sit back against the couch. "You know why I'm here."

"What happened last night?" she asks.

I look at her, right into her eyes. "I did something really bad."

"Oh god. What did you do?"

"It's not what you think," I say quickly. I tell her how I showed up at Isabelle's door. How we argued. The terrible things she said to me.

"She said she was pregnant."

Her eyes grow wide. "Luis's?"

"Yes. Or so she said."

"What happened then?"

I consider telling her about the necklace, how I snatched it off her, how it caused the thin welt on my hand, but I don't. I'll leave that for another day. I don't think June needs any more reasons *not* to help me.

"We argued. She said she loved him and… anyway, look. When I left her, she was perfectly fine, and that's the truth. I just walked out. She was laughing behind my back. I sure didn't kill her. And anyway, she fell down the stairs, according to the detective."

"Down the stairs?"

"That's what he said."

She shakes her head, like she's annoyed with me, like I'm not taking the situation seriously.

"But you see, June, if the police were to find out, it would probably get leaked to the press, don't you think?"

"Why would it get leaked?"

"Because she's… because I won the Pentti-Stone, because it's a lurid story… The usual reasons."

She thinks about this for a moment. "And you really, really didn't do anything to hurt her?"

"No, June, I promise you, she was perfectly healthy when I left her. She was in much better shape than I was, and that's the truth."

She takes the time to think about it some more, and I sit there, my heart in my mouth. Finally she says, "Okay, then I'll say we were together. I'll say we came back here if anyone asks."

"Oh god, thank you. Thank you. June, you have no idea what that means to me."

She shakes her head. "So what time did you get home?"

"Good question, I'm not sure, to be honest." I give a small, embarrassed laugh. By now I'm embarrassed about everything I've done, the way I behaved, how out of control I got. "About one a.m. I think. Maybe later."

"You really did go out on the town."

I sit back and sigh. 'I know."

"You hungry?" she asks.

I smile. "Why?"

"I have tons of yummy things in the kitchen. I'll bring something out."

I laugh. "Honestly, I've put on weight since I've met you." I follow her into the kitchen.

Her kitchen is nothing like mine. I've never seen a kitchen so messy. Jars with what looks like flour and sugar are left open haphazardly on the bench, which is already riddled with crumbs. I kind of wish I hadn't come in here. "Nothing too filling, please. I still have to make dinner for the children."

She pops off the top of a container and hands it to me. "Check this out."

I lean over to take a look. "Smells yummy, looks shocking. What it is?"

"Caramelized salted peanut toffee. I thought I could serve it with cocktails. Actually, I don't know what I was thinking. Anyway, I made a mess of it. I used honey instead of sugar and it's gone all hard and weird."

"You make it sound so tempting."

"I know."

"Why did you do that?"

"I was experimenting. Anyway, you're supposed to serve them with dry martinis or something."

"What are *they* like?"

"Disgustingly delicious."

"Can I have the martini without the salted caramel peanut disgusting thing?"

"No way. It's a job lot. All or nothing." She winks at me.

"Anyway, it's irrelevant," I say, my head throbbing again. "I don't know if I can ever drink anything ever again."

"Sure you can, just the one. It'll make you feel better, I swear."

I sigh. "If you say so."

She puts the crumbly, sticky mess on a plate, and hands it to me. "Take that with you, I'll bring the lemon and olives."

We're back in the living room when she asks abruptly. "Do you have a gun?"

"Me? No! Why would you ask that?"

"Don't you think if Isabelle had a gun, she probably wouldn't be dead now?"

"But that's ridiculous."

"No, it's not. If she was killed—"

"We don't know she was killed, June."

"But if she was… Well, this is why you don't want to be a woman living alone and not be able to protect yourself against an intruder. Trust me, I think about that all the time in this city."

"You're not making any sense. Do *you* have a gun?"

"Sure I do. I'd be stupid not to have one."

"Really? Where?"

"In my bedroom. It's a small one, a .380, but it'll do the job. You should get yourself one, honestly."

I think about Isabelle with a gun and suddenly, I am absolutely convinced that if she owned one, she would have used it on me. "I should go." I say. "I'll see you tomorrow?" I ask.

"You certainly will." She takes my glass and my plate and takes them into the kitchen. When she returns I have my jacket on.

"And don't worry," she says, hugging me at the door. "Your secret—*all* your secrets, I should say—are safe with me."

CHAPTER 31

The fact that Isabelle is dead makes me forgive Luis. That's how I think of it anyway, because what's the point of holding a grudge against a ghost? It's over. That's the thought that keeps popping into my head. *It's over.* And as far as the police are concerned, it was an accident. That's certainly the impression I got from speaking to Detective Jones.

God, just imagine it. Thinking you were so special, it was okay for you to rip another family apart, take a father away from his children, all in the name of *love*, and then poof! Neck broken. Game over.

There's poetry in that, I think.

Still, as we lie in bed together, me spooning Luis, I do want to whisper into his ear, *Don't do it again. Ever.* I can hear him sigh. Maybe he's even crying, I'm not sure. I put my arm around his torso and caress him, console him, just I like did all those years ago after Monica died.

Shh. There, there.

"I love you so much," I say softly. "Let's move away, you, me and the kids. Let's get away from this place. We could move to Martha's Vineyard." I talk to him like this, whispering softly. I looked it up, I say. You won't believe the amazing art community there, and there's a fencing club and a drama club and wait till you see the houses in Oak Bluffs and the Flying Horses carousel, the oldest carousel in the world, I say, although I'm not completely sure that's the case. It doesn't matter, anyway. Luis is asleep now, snoring softly in my arms.

The following morning I wake with a renewed sense of determination. I watch Luis sleep for a while, lay my hand against his cheek. He doesn't move. I slowly push the covers away and swing my legs out of bed, all in slow motion so as not to disturb him.

I wake the children, make breakfast, prepare lunches, check homework, sign a note to say Carla can go to the theatre with the class next Saturday morning to see *The Curious Incident of the Dog in the Night-Time*, which I first read as *The Curious Incident of the Curator in the Night-Time* and I almost laugh.

"Is Dad okay?" they ask.

"He's got a cold, that's all. He's fine." I ruffle their hair. "Have a great day at school. I love you. Go, now, or you'll miss the bus."

I feed Roxy, put everything in the dishwasher, wipe the surfaces and put on a load of laundry. I even find a tissue in the pocket of Carla's jeans *before* I turn on the machine. That's how good a day this is. It's the way my life should be. It's what makes me happy. I am happy when other people are happy. I was born for this role: wife, mother, homemaker.

When Luis walks into the kitchen, I wrap my arm around his neck.

"I thought you were going to sleep in. How are you feeling?"

"Okay." He runs his hand through his hair.

"You sure?"

"Yes, of course."

I rest my head against his shoulder.

"Thank you," he whispers.

"What for?" I reply. But what I'm saying, really, is, *It's fine. I love you. I would do anything for you. For us. I'm a rallier.*

I steered the ship through dark and choppy waters and I've brought us into the light. And I know it's crazy, but that's how I feel. Like the sunshine has returned to our lives and swept the shadows away and, with them, everything that is scary and dark.

The day couldn't be better. It's crisp, clear, luminous. Then I find that June has left a caramel cupcake on my desk. It sits on a piece of paper on which she's scribbled, *Enjoy!* I drop my bag on the floor, pick up the cupcake and devour it, licking my lips, catching every last crumb. It's unbelievably delicious.

Twenty minutes later she knocks on my door.

"That was the best thing I've ever tasted. Ever," I say, pointing to the empty yellow baking liner. "And hello, by the way."

She laughs. "I'm glad. All part of the service."

She sits down opposite me, her notepad at the ready. I have so much work for her to do, all the work I've been neglecting these last few weeks, in fact. Reports to send, applications to collate, class schedules to update and send to students.

"You can never work with anyone else but me, you know that, right? I couldn't bear it if you stopped baking me these divine treats."

"Well, I can't promise. I might just get a better offer, you know."

"Don't even try. Pretend this job is some kind of hostage situation. One hint you're considering another position and I'll blow the place up."

"You're in a good mood," she says, when she's finished cackling.

"I am!"

June gets to her feet, taps the notepad with a flick of her pen. "I'll go and get this done, shall I?"

"Thank you, June. You're the best, you really are." I glance at my watch. "Also, I have to leave early today, as I have to get

Mateo from soccer because Luis has a dentist appointment. Just so you know."

I teach my classes, sit on my meetings, do my job. At lunch I eat a Greek salad at my desk while scouring the internet for Christmas decorations. We've had the same ones for years, and I've decided it's time for a refresh. I want to get enough Christmas lights to outshine every other house in the neighborhood. The kids will be beside themselves.

And because this is a great day, the afternoon passes without me seeing Geoff at all. A record, I think. Which just goes to show the planets are aligned in my favor.

Until there's a knock at my door and, just like that, my happy mood disintegrates.

Because it's Geoff.

My stomach does a back flip. The complaint. Ryan. I've done nothing about it.

"What's going on?"

There's something odd about him. Something about the way he stands, overly relaxed.

"Do you have a moment?" He comes in without waiting for an answer. I dread whatever is coming next. It must be about the complaint. Some kind of follow-up maybe.

Then Mila shows up. "Hello, Anna, Geoff. Am I late?"

"What's going on?" I ask again, but no one answers. Mila closes the door and they settle themselves in the armchairs opposite my desk. Geoff hauls one leg over the other and takes hold of his ankle. I suspect he thinks this is cool and casual, but he's so out of shape it looks painful. Meanwhile, Mila just taps on her iPad.

No one says anything. "Did I forget a meeting?"

"No, no," Geoff says. "Sorry to intrude. This won't take long. Come and sit down." It's amazing, really, how perfectly civil he can be, like he didn't assault me, like he is a normal person and not a violent creep. Like he has nothing to reproach himself for because it was all *my* fault.

My cellphone buzzes. I reach for it and shut it off without looking to see who it is, then shove it in my bottom drawer.

Because they're occupying both armchairs, I have to bring my own office chair over. I'm now sitting higher than they are. It's awkward, seeing them so relaxed, with me perched on the very edge of my seat with my hands in my lap waiting to hear my fate.

"What's going on?" I ask again, desperate to get this over with, but also dreading what *this* is. *Please don't let it be about the complaint. Not in front of Mila.*

"Okay, so the situation is this." Geoff uncrosses his legs and leans forward, forearms on knees. "Jack Dawson from the Forrester Foundation got in touch this morning. They have some concerns."

"Excuse me?"

"I'm getting there. The upshot is, before transferring the prize money to you, they would like you to submit more information. The information you were supposed to— "

"I don't understand."

Geoff and Mila share a glance.

"The problem is, Anna, that while you wrote a paper about the solution, they feel you've never actually written about *how* you discovered the solution itself. I understand they've been asking but that you haven't been forthcoming."

"I haven't had time."

He raises a hand. "Sure, sure, but as you know"—he turns to Mila as he says this and I don't know if he's talking to her or me—"we, as well as the Forrester Foundation, have attempted a number of times to collect materials from you, unsuccessfully. The department is in a bit of a dilemma. We have put ourselves forward as your sponsors, if you will, as the university and specifically the department that facilitates your work. If the Forrester Foundation is not satisfied, then this puts us in a very bad light."

"How can they be not satisfied? The proof is there. Who cares how I went about it? I just don't have the time for this! What does it matter? It's my proof! It's perfect as it is!"

"They do care, Anna."

"Why?"

"Because it's their policy! It's in their rules, you know that."

"But why is it even in their rules?"

"You know why. Officially, anyway, it's because they consider the experiments, the vision, the inspiration, the creative process as worthy as the proof itself. Having said that, if I had to hazard a guess, I'd say they're covering their asses. They don't want, years from now, to be sued because someone else claims they did the work that led to—"

"Someone? Who?"

"A student, a colleague who might have shared some of their thinking process with you."

Mila politely raises a hand, although not very high. Still, it gets Geoff's attention. "Yes, Mila?"

"I believe one of the early innovation prizes awarded by the Forrester Foundation later led to accusations of plagiarism. Supplying preliminary work, drafts, notebooks, may be a way out to avoid the situation repeating itself."

It's the first time she's spoken. Then the door opens and June is standing there, looking from me to Geoff to Mila.

"June, please. We're in the middle of something."

"Anna, it's—"

"Can you take a message?"

"But I think it's important—"

"And whatever it is, I'll get to it. Can you take a message, please?"

I'm trying to contain my anxiety, but from the look on her face I don't think I'm doing it very well. She walks away and closes the door.

I turn back to them. "Where were we?" I say. "Ah, yes. Plagiarism. So, what you're saying—"

"No one is saying anything, Anna. Just that sometimes, work gets copied accidentally…"

"When's the last time you saw a case of plagiarism in mathematics, Geoff? Accidental or otherwise?" I cross my legs, hold my chin high.

"Well," he scoffs, "I don't have the exact cases before me—"

"Izanami Hindle," Mila pipes up.

Geoff clicks his fingers. "That's right! From Princeton, right?"

"Stanford. And Jeremiah Pell, who worked with German mathematician Fred Holze on the Poincare—"

"Exactly," Geoff says, turning to me. "Look. We understand how these things can happen… the pressure…"

I tilt my head at him, my expression naive and pure as a dove at a wedding. "Pressure?"

He turns to Mila. "Don't we, Mila?"

Her face goes through a number of iterations to show she's trying to understand how these things might happen, she really is.

"But not to me!" I say brightly. "There's no pressure on me! I didn't even make professor, for Christ's sake!" I laugh, although it comes out strangely high-pitched and deranged. Like that crazy parrot YouTube video Matti was forever showing me last year. "There's no pressure on me," I repeat, once I've recovered. "Other than to take good, clean minutes. And that's pressure, for sure, but I can handle it. I'm good under pressure."

Geoff waits a beat, then says, in a faux-sweet tone, "But that's the problem, don't you see? Anna?"

"No, Geoff, I don't. How is that the problem?"

He's on his feet, shouting. "Because you've never done anything like this before!"

Then Mila, ever helpful, leans forward and says, "You never even applied for a grant to undertake this research, Anna."

"Exactly!" Geoff says, turning around to look at her. "Unusual, right?"

I sit back and glare at them. "So, what you're saying is, I *stole* it." I feel my cheeks burn.

They both laugh. "No! Of course we're not saying that." Geoff sits back down. "We're just conveying what the Forrester Foundation said, which is—"

"Yes, all right. You've made your point. Repeatedly." I get up, go to the door. "I'll get you my notebooks first thing."

They follow my lead. I'm holding the door open and they leave. The moment they're out they're whispering to each other. I slam the door. I can't help myself.

I sit at my desk and start tidying up. I spray my computer screen and wipe it clean, organize paperclips by color, slide the corner of a tissue between the keys on the keyboard. I really should go home. I open the drawer and get my cell and glance at the staff directory. I can't believe how foolish I was to leave the necklace here. For all I know Geoff and Mila will be rummaging through my things looking for some scrap of evidence that I really have stolen the proof. Won't they wonder what it's doing there? They won't know its significance, but still, not exactly the world's best hiding place.

Can they really take the prize away from me? That's what they're saying, isn't it? That I have to prove my own proof? Now there's a laugh. I shove the necklace in my bag, turn my cell back on, and it pings. Then it pings again. I have seven missed calls all from the soccer club.

Matti.

CHAPTER 32

I'm running out the door, punching one arm in my jacket and hoisting my bag over my shoulder. I call Luis but he doesn't pick up. I leave a message, the phone wedged in the crook of my neck.

"Is Matti with you? Can you call me, please? I was supposed to…" I drop the phone and it clatters on the floor. I pick it up, dropping my bag in the process. I scramble to gather my things together and run to my car.

I drive to the sports field on Bainbridge Road like a mad woman. I can't stop thinking of my poor child, my baby, my Matti, who must be beside himself by now. I can picture him on the bench, wheezing through his panic attack. He has asthma and stressful situations make it worse. Did I pack his Ventolin? I can't remember. He must be so upset and the thought is making my stomach roil as I speed through at least one red light and almost run over a cat. I keep redialing Luis but it goes to voicemail every time.

When I get there, I park the car in a non-parking zone and run straight to the coaches' building. It's locked.

I look around. I'm so late there's no one here, no one clearing up after the kids, no lingering parents chatting, nobody. I try Luis again as I pull at my hair.

"Seriously, Luis, can you please call me? I'm getting really worried."

Maybe he went home with one of the other parents. Except he never does that, it's part of his anxiety. If Luis or I say we're coming, he'll wait. He just won't get into a car with anyone else, no matter how well he knows them.

I call my home number with my heart thumping in my chest. Carla answers.

"Honey, is Matti home?" I have one hand over my eyes as I pray silently.

"Yeah," she says, nonchalantly, and the relief that spreads through me makes my whole body wobble, like my bones are made of rubber.

"Oh thank god. Did Dad bring him home? Can I speak to him?"

"Dad's not here." I can hear her crunch through an apple. "When are you getting home?"

"So how did Matti get home?"

"Your friend brought him."

"What friend?"

"Um… June, I think that's her name."

"June?"

I've grown dizzy with relief and black dots dance in front of my eyes. I sit down on the bench, press the heel of my hand between my eyes.

"You want to speak to her?"

I sit up. "She's there?"

"She's upstairs with Matti. He was pretty upset, Mom."

"I know, honey. How is he now?"

"They're reading a book," she says.

"What book?"

"I don't know. Hang on."

I hear her run up the stairs and call out, "What are you reading? Mom wants to know."

I've returned to my car and I sit down in the driver seat, phone against my ear, feeling my breath return to normal.

"*Phantom Tollbooth*," she says finally.

"Oh, right! Well, that's good." *Phantom Tollbooth* is a good choice. One of his favorites, and the copy he has belonged to Luis when he was growing up. Which doesn't mean that much to Matti, actually. Still, a perfect pick when he's upset. "So he's all right?"

"He's hiccupping but he's okay. I think he likes June."

I just can't believe what I'm hearing. Matti never goes with strangers, ever. I don't know whether I should scold him or hug him when I get back. And the fact that he's not freaking out, let alone calmly reading a book... "Can you put June on please?"

"Okay, one sec."

Seconds later, June comes on. "Hi, we're all good here, did you get my messages?"

"Messages? No, I mean yes but I didn't listen, I was trying to reach Luis."

"I left a couple of messages, to let you know what was going on—hang on." She speaks away from the phone. "Yes, Matti? Oh sure, of course." She comes back on. "I'm being summoned back to reading. We were up to the part where Milo and Tock get arrested. It's a bit of a cliffhanger."

"He's already read it ten times, you know."

"I meant for me," she says, and I laugh. It's such a relief that tears start to roll down my cheeks and for a moment I can't speak. I wipe them with my sleeve.

"You're the best, June, you really are. I'm five minutes away. Can you wait till I get there?"

"Of course! I'll see you later."

I walk silently up the stairs to Matti's bedroom. Through the open door I see him sitting on the edge of his bed, right next to June, his head resting on her shoulder. He's holding an almost empty glass of milk on his lap and sucking on the corner of a plastic toy while she reads to him. When he looks up to me, his eyes are heavy and watery.

"Hey, sweetie." I kneel in front of him. "I'm sorry I was late."

"You didn't—*hiccup*—come for me."

"I'm sorry, Matti. I really am."

"You forgot me."

"No! I didn't forget you! I had to work, that's all. You all right, sweetie?"

He nods and gives a shuddering breath.

"Good." I turn to June and mouth, *Thank you*. She smiles.

"Matti, June and I will talk downstairs and I'll make you a hot chocolate, okay?"

June gets up and he tugs at her, and for a moment I think he won't let her go. She hands him the book and thanks him for his company.

"Can June stay?" he says to me.

"June has to go home soon, okay? Say thank you."

"Thank you," he says to June, and I hug him tight and kiss his head until he wriggles himself free.

Downstairs June sits at the kitchen table while I make a hot chocolate for Matti. She tells me how the soccer club had tried to call me on my cell but I wasn't picking up, so they called the department and got through to her, and as I was so tense in that meeting that I almost shouted at her to go away, she thought she was doing me a favor.

"Look, June, I'm very grateful. I really am, but next time probably best not to go and pick up my children without telling me first. I almost had a heart attack."

"I left you two messages and a text," she says, a tad defensively. I tilt my head at her. "One day…" I begin, then I stop.

"One day what?"

One day, you will have children of your own and you will think back on this moment and you'll understand how terrified you made me.

"One day, I'll find a way to thank you properly," I say instead.

I take Matti's hot chocolate up to him and when I return, June wants to know what the meeting was about.

"You all seemed so intense," she says.

I don't want to tell her. Not because I don't trust her, but why invite more questions about the whole thing, anyway?

"Before I get to that," I say, knowing I probably never will, "remember Ryan?"

"How could I forget? He was the reason you went AWOL the other night."

Oh right. I blamed my drinking binge on Ryan. Maybe I should start taking notes.

"Well…" I drop my head in my hands. "He's filed a complaint against me."

"What for?"

"Sexual harassment."

She laughs. A loud cackle. Then she realizes I'm serious and her eyes grow wide. I tell her about the other meeting I had with Geoff, the fact that he saw me disappear with Ryan that day. That I think Geoff could even be a witness for all I know. I almost add that he hates me enough to do it.

"I just can't believe it," she says.

"I know, especially considering he was the one who sent me the photo smack in the middle of my lecture. The creep."

"Well, that's good, right? You can give that to whoever investigates the case. It's not going to make him look good."

I hadn't thought of that. "You're right. The number was private, but he wouldn't deny he was the one who took the photo, would he? Or maybe he would. Maybe he'll claim he never took *that* photo. When I scrolled through his phone that day, I'm sure it wasn't there."

"He probably moved it to another device," she says.

I sit up abruptly. "Lakewood Park."

"What?"

"Oh my god, June! I remember now, the other photos on his cell. There were a number of them with a dog, a retriever."

I close my eyes. I can see the park, and I can see the dog, I can see the sunset.

I open them again. "I know how I can find him. I know where he walks his dog."

And just then Luis comes home. I introduce him to June, the kids come bouncing down the stairs to greet their dad. June says she has to go, and she puts on her coat while Carla ruffles through my bag for my purse because she needs money for new tights for her dance class tomorrow and before I have time to think, my hand has shot out towards her.

"Wait!"

I've shouted, and now they're all looking at me: Carla, Matti, June, Luis, their gestures snap frozen in the moment.

"Sorry!" I laugh. I take the bag from Carla and, as discreetly as I can, I feel for the necklace at the bottom of the bag, hide it in the palm of my hand, then hand the purse to Carla. "There you go, sweetie."

The necklace is still in my closed hand and Luis looks at it, and for a crazy moment I think he's noticed. I hug June goodbye, nudging the strap of her purse from her shoulder and it falls to the floor.

"Sorry! I don't know what's the matter with me!"

It's one of those bags with a million pockets and I'm on my knees, quickly shoving everything back into it and I manage to slip the necklace inside a small compartment on the side that closes with a press stud. I hand it back it to her.

"There you go, sorry about that."

'That's all right. Big day!" she says, with a wink.

I hug her goodbye, clock Luis looking at me oddly, his head tilted. I smile as I will my heart to stop hammering.

CHAPTER 33

I am sitting on a bench near the wooden platforms that I remember from the shots on Ryan's phone, watching the sunset. This is around the time he took those photos. I remember those distinct blue and pink hues hinting at the sky.

He might not come today, of course, and that's okay, because if that's the case, I will return tomorrow, and the day after, until I catch him. But dogs like routine, they like to go to the same places at the same times, so I think it won't take long. If he still comes here, that is.

Two dogs barrel down the path, pouncing after the tennis balls their owner has thrown for them. I watch a poodle dig a hole with two front paws, sending clods of wet earth all over the nearby swings. It starts to rain, big drops of water that stain the ground, and I think it won't be today. I'm about to give up when I see a retriever with a red scarf around his neck. My heart jumps into my throat even before I recognize Ryan, ten feet behind him, looking so ordinary, unhurried, so *normal* that it makes my jaw lock with rage. I watch him for a moment as he stares down at his cellphone, his thumbs sliding up and down.

He looks up at the sky and squints and before I have time to walk over to him, he has whistled for his dog and they've turned around in the direction of the gates, with me not far behind.

Fifteen minutes later, Ryan crosses Riverside Drive and walks up the short driveway of an elegant home. He uses his own key to open the door before disappearing inside, the dog running ahead.

This is good, I think. It's better than confronting him in the park. He can't run away from me if I'm in his house. I wonder if he lives alone. Surely not, such a big house. Is he married? Children? I'm pretty sure he said he wasn't but everything he says is a lie. I hope he's married. I want to tell his wife what kind of creep she's saddled with.

I walk up the steps to the porch, my pulse racing, my hands closed into tight fists, and ring the doorbell. The door opens almost immediately and I'm taken aback by the older woman in front of me. She smiles politely, pulling the edges of her powder-blue cardigan tighter around her.

"Can I help you?"

"I'm looking for my friend," I say, remembering not to choke on the word. "Ryan. Is he here?"

I'm absolutely expecting her to say something like, *There's no Ryan here, please go sell your wares somewhere else.* But no. She gives me a quick up and down appraisal and opens the door wider.

"Yes, he is. Come in."

She ushers me into the living room, a large space divided in the center by double doors that almost take up the entire width. The house is lovely inside, with arched doorways and eye-catching woodwork around the doors. A window looks out onto a backyard where the dog sniffs around a wrought-iron garden table.

This is absolutely not what I had in mind.

"Would you like to sit down?" she asks.

"That's all right, thank you. I've been driving. I like to stretch my legs."

"Of course. Did you come from far?"

"Not really," I say, thereby contradicting myself. I don't add anything else so after a moment or two, she smiles and says, "Well, I'll fetch Ryan. I won't be a minute."

I walk idly around the room, contemplate a framed poster of a Matisse exhibition at the Tate Gallery from 1953. In one corner of the room is a built-in cabinet, with shelves on top and cupboards below. I glance at the framed photos nestled among leafy plants. Ryan appears in a number of them, and they suggest that the woman who welcomed me is his mother.

Grown man Ryan lives with his mother.

Which goes some way to explaining things, I think. One photo, partly obscured by a split-leaf philodendron, catches my eye. I reach for it, and a rush of something like anger, or fear, erupts inside me. I have to pick it up, to look closer, to make sure I'm not mistaken. Blood is pulsing in my ears as I study the group photo, close to twenty people maybe, all gathered around Ryan's mother, who is seated in the center. Most people are standing, some of the younger children are sitting crossed-legged on the floor. Ryan is standing next to his mother, his hand loosely resting on the back of her chair. I peer even closer but there's no mistake. In the next row, to the left, plainly visible…

"Here we are," she says behind me. I'm still holding the photo when I turn around. Ryan is standing next to her, staring at me, an astonished look on his face. His gaze drops to the photo in my hand, and a patch of crimson grows up his neck and spreads across his cheeks.

"What's this?" I ask him, holding the photo, my mouth trembling.

His mother frowns, looks from me to him. "It's from my birthday," she replies. "If you must know." She tilts her head slightly, one hand tapping lightly on her sternum. "What was your name again?"

"Anna. Ryan, can I have a word?" I can feel my nostrils flaring.

"Is everything all right?" his mother asks.

My eyes won't leave his face and without answering her, he says, "Yeah, sure, it's this way."

I put the photo back on the shelf and follow him down to the back of the house.

Ryan has the run of the basement, a large room divided loosely into sections.

"How did you find me?" he asks. I close the door of his room and he looks nervous suddenly. Good. I think back to the day I met him at the party. I can still see him pointing to Geoff on the opposite side of the room. *Is he your boyfriend? Your husband, then?*

"You want to tell me what's going on here, Ryan?"

He sits down on a beanbag, doesn't offer me a seat—not that I want one. I'm standing, my fists on my hips, so angry I'm vibrating.

"How do you know Geoff?"

He looks down at his hands. "He's my uncle."

"Oh my god!" I have to sit down after all. I pull out the chair from the front of his desk. "Your uncle?" I have a headache. It's knocking at the back of my skull. "So why did you pretend not to know him when I met you that day?"

"Because he asked me to."

"Why?"

"He wanted me to take a photo of you."

"He wanted a photo of me? You're going to have to do better than that, Ryan. What the hell is going on?"

He looks at me, cheeks burning with embarrassment. "He wanted a naked selfie of you."

I could tell him, technically, if he takes the photo it's not a selfie, but I don't. I listen, my head in my hands, while Ryan explains our almost-tryst was a set-up. He was supposed to approach me as soon as Geoff left me alone, and lure me into that empty office and somehow get a photo of me naked.

"I was amazed you went along with it," he says, watching me from under hooded eyelids, but there's a trace of manly pride dancing on his lips and I am nanoseconds away from smashing something into that face.

I take a breath. "That makes two of us," I say. But a wave of shame ripples through me as I remember how jealous I felt that day. How I suspected Geoff was turning his charms towards Mila, and how hurt I was that he had asked me to the party, and immediately left me alone, like he had more interesting people to talk to. And in the end, it was because of Geoff that I went along with Ryan's attentions. I wanted him to *watch*.

See? I've still got it. You might be losing interest, but just watch. He's younger than you too, and much, much more attractive.

"And that's it? He wanted a photo of me naked?"

He nods. "He says one time in Chicago on a trip you led him on and then rejected him. He wanted to get you back. I don't know what he was going to do with it exactly, he never said."

Oh, but I know. He was biding his time. Sending it to me during the lecture was just a taste of things to come. He was going to tease me with it occasionally, keep me on tenterhooks with fear and shame, probably wait until I'd officially received the prize and only when the release of the photo could most humiliate me would it find its way into some public forum on the internet.

All because I almost had sex with him one night, but saw sense at the last minute.

"What about my car, did you do that too? Scratch it?"

"He did that. He told me."

"Really? Wow." I let out a laugh, a bitter one. "I hope you realize it's illegal, what you did. It's a criminal offense. You could go to jail. All I need to do is report you. You sent me the photo, I'm sure the cops can trace your phone from that." Although I'm not sure about that last part.

"I didn't send it to you," he says quickly. "He did."

"Geoff?"

"Yes. He gave me his cell that night."

"*His* cell?"

"Yeah, to take the photo with."

Which is why I didn't see it when I returned the next day and I scrolled through Ryan's phone. It was never there in the first place.

I'm going to be sick. I sit there, fingernails digging into my palms. It's amazing how you can go for years with an idea of someone. You might not know what they think of you exactly, but you have a firm idea of what kind of relationship you have, then one day you wake up and find out it's completely different. Before Geoff cornered me in the storage cupboard the other day, I really, really thought he liked me—professionally, and yes, perhaps with a little, understood-not-to-be-acted-on flirting involved too. Realistic between colleagues who got on so well, I always thought.

Turns out he really, *really* hates me.

"Did he send you to the restaurant, too? That day you stood outside watching me?"

"No! I just happened to walk past and I saw you, with your kids and your husband, and I felt bad. I thought about going in to tell you what was really going on."

I give a startled laugh. "You filed a sexual harassment complaint against me, Ryan. You can't be feeling that bad."

He looks puzzled. "I didn't file a complaint. Why would I do that?"

"For the same reason you did everything else, because he asked you to."

"No, no. He didn't ask me to do that and I wouldn't have done it if he had. He knows I'm out."

I think about this for a moment. Suddenly, I wonder if Geoff made it up, and the more I think about it, the more I suspect that's right. Surely complaints like that are handled by HR, not by another professor, even if he's the chair. God. I'm such an idiot. I almost reach for my phone but realize it's too late to call them now.

I think back through the weeks of torment he's put me through. The scratch on my car, the text he sent me in the middle of my lecture. *WHORE*. Geoff thinks I'm a whore not because I had sex with him, but because I didn't.

I lift my bag from the floor.

"What are you going to do?" Ryan says, and I'm thrilled to detect a note of panic in his voice.

"I don't know yet."

Halfway to the door I turn back to face him. "Do not say a word to Geoff, you understand? As far as he's concerned, I know nothing. If I find out you've told him that I know, or that we even spoke, I swear to God I will turn you over to the police. Am I clear?" My mouth is so tight I can barely speak.

Then a voice rings out from behind the door: "Everything all right in there?"

I lean close and point a finger so close to his face I could almost stab him in the eye. "I can't imagine you'd want your mother to know you're involved in some sordid blackmail scam, either. So don't test me, Ryan."

I sit in my car and I cry, because I'm so stupid and I'm humiliated and I think of my mother, because I always think of my mother when I get this overwhelming certitude that deep down, I'm a bad person and I deserved this. I think of that day when Geoff undid the top button of my shirt and I was *flattered*. I thought it was *sexy*. So what did I expect? I give myself a pass and look what happens: bad things, that's what. Just like Geoff said. *Bad things happen to women like you.*

CHAPTER 34

I get home, and Luis is instantly at me, itching for a fight.

"Where were you? What happened with Matti this afternoon? I got all these calls from the soccer club, from you... what the hell? Where were you? Did you forget? Did you have your phone off?"

He waves his phone at me then drops it on the table.

"I'm sorry!" I repeat, for the umpteenth time. I reach for a bottle of red and check it against the light. I grab a tumbler from the shelf and set it on the table.

"You're drinking too much."

"Oh, be quiet."

"Honestly, Anna. You look exhausted."

"I am." I rub my hands over my eyes. They feel tender and swollen. He pulls out a chair and sits down heavily.

"Where are the kids?" I ask.

"In their rooms." He scrubs a hand over his face. "The police wanted to see me this afternoon."

I set the glass down with a bang. "What?"

"They wanted to ask me about you."

"About *me*?"

After a pause he says, "I need to tell you something."

He takes my hand, holds it, and I watch his face slowly become distorted with sadness. "Babe, I'm so sorry. I'm so very sorry."

I am on feet so fast I almost knock my chair over. "Don't say it," I urge. *Don't say it, Luis, if you do it will be real, please, Luis. Don't say things we can't come back from. It's me, only me, remember?*

Remember how you would do anything to keep me forever? Remember? You love me so much, and I'm still here, baby. It's you and me, against the world.

But I'm too slow. He says it.

"I've been having an affair."

And there it is. The confession, in all its pathetic, self-serving glory. I reach for another bottle of wine, having finished the first one. When I sit back down I'm shaking and I spill some on the table. Luis pretends not to notice. I think he's grateful for the distraction as he tells me that *it* started, months ago, around April. I don't tell him, yes, I know all about *it*, you can stop now. Spare me the sorry details. I already have them anyway. I've been chewing on them relentlessly for some time now. And what did she do to deserve such a pretty necklace? Was it a gift in celebration of the happy news, perhaps? A baby! Everybody loves a baby!

No. I don't tell him any of that. I just listen to his story, from which all the sharp edges have been smoothed down and rounded. So it's not so bad, really.

He was working on the show with Isabelle, he says, planning the pieces; they worked late one night, had a drink, one thing led to another.

"Well, that's original," I quip.

"I don't want to make excuses," he says, before proceeding to make excuses. "She was so... she loved my work, Anna... She looked up to me. I know it's stupid but it felt good! To be wanted like that."

I try not to smash my glass into his face as I say all the predictable things. *I love your work, too. I look up to you. I want you like that. So what's wrong with me, why am I not enough?*

I'm staring down into my wine when I ask the question that's been burning my throat all this time. "Were you going to leave us?"

He stops talking then and stares at me, his face aflame.

"Oh my god! You were?" Suddenly I'm standing.

"No! Okay, yes, fine. I was tempted, yes—I had a moment there where for a second I thought I could have another kind of life. One when I wasn't at your beck and call all the time."

I blink, raise a hand, palm out. I've managed to keep it together so far, but even I have my limits.

"My beck and call?" I say, still blinking.

"Anna! Come on!"

"This is *my* fault?"

"I didn't say—"

"I'm sorry, but I'm missing something here. Are you saying *I* drove you to have an affair? Because of what, exactly? I ask that you walk the dog occasionally? Is that it?"

"Don't—"

"Is that it?" I shout. I'm trembling with fury. Behind me are two mugs drying in the rack. I spin around and grab one and throw it at him. Roxy barks at my feet, spinning around, tail wagging.

Carla thumps downstairs. "What's going on?"

I straighten myself, run a hand over my hair. "Nothing, sweetie. Dad and I are just talking."

"We're good, Carla. Go back upstairs. Mom's over-reacting. Go back upstairs, Carla!"

After she's gone I turn back to him. "*Mom's over-reacting*? You think that was over-reacting?" I open a cupboard and grab a pile of plates, four, five of them.

"Anna, don't," he whines.

"You want over-reacting?" I ask, dropping them on the floor. "I haven't even started yet."

Carla reappears, this time with Matti by her side. "What's going on? Dad?"

"Carla, can you please not ask your father anything? He doesn't want to be at your beck and call. Also, if you could look up to him that would be great. And make him feel good about his art, otherwise—"

But Luis has taken hold of my wrist and twists it. "Shut up," he hisses. "Don't do this here. Let's go outside."

He releases my wrist and I shake my shoulders. He goes to the children and puts his arms around them. "I'm sorry, my darlings. We were having a fight. We're fine now."

But I'm breathing through my nose so hard it's making my nostrils flare. I don't think anyone would believe I'm fine. The children glare at me over his shoulder. He speaks to them in a low voice and after a while Matti picks up Roxy in his arms and the three of them go back up the stairs.

I sit back down, exhausted and deflated. I'm still there when Luis returns.

"I was trying to end it," he says, "and that's the truth."

"You were?"

He reaches for the other tumbler, fills it with wine and knocks it back in one swill.

"That's why I didn't want her to come to dinner that night." He wipes his mouth with the back of his hand.

I raise my chin, stare at him. *Liar. I saw you. You kissed her. That wasn't the kiss of someone trying to end things. And what about the baby?*

Then, suddenly, I understand why he's telling me this now. "Do the police know?"

He nods. I notice how gaunt his face is then, how crumpled his clothes are. How sad and thin he looks. Like the life has been drained out of him.

"Yes."

My eyes begin to swim. "What did they say?"

He looks at me, his eyebrows knotted together, and he tilts his head slightly but sweetly, like a puppy. "They wanted to know about you."

CHAPTER 35

I didn't sleep at all last night. My brain did its zapping thing, *Zap! Zap!* Like there was a lion tamer venting his rage with a bullwhip. Next to me Luis looks as peaceful as a lamb. But then that's Luis. Always. Can sleep through an earthquake, he'd say proudly. Unless I wake him up.

In between zaps I kept going over what Luis had said.

"They wanted to know about you."

"What about me?"

"Where you were the other night?"

"But why me?"

"Because they know about me and Isabelle," he said finally. And it's just as I thought. There were texts and emails that would have left little to the imagination.

"What else did they ask about me?"

"Where you were, what time you came home."

"What did you say?"

"Babe, what could I say? I told them the truth! But it's okay, it's okay because you were with June so there's no problem, they won't even suspect you."

"Suspect me of what?"

"I don't know, they didn't tell me anything, they just asked questions."

I nodded, feeling lost.

"But you were with June, so it's good, isn't it?"

"Yes, it's good." I said. *No, it's not good. Not good at all.*

*

On the way to work, I confirmed with HR that there are no claims against me, so that's something, I guess. There never was, they said. Just as I thought, it was a hoax. Geoff must lie awake at night thinking up new ways to torture me, turn the screws that little bit tighter, just so he can watch me suffer.

I stand outside his office. The door is ajar and I can see him staring at his computer. He types slowly, looking at the keyboard, then at the screen then back at the keyboard. He types the next letter or two then he pushes his glasses further up his nose and does it again. I stand there, my eyes burning. I could walk in right now and tell him I know everything. That his career is over and he is going to die in a rat-infested jail where the only way to tell the difference between rice and maggots is whether it moves or not.

No wait, that's me.

"What are you doing?"

I spin around. "June! Hi, I was day-dreaming."

She looks toward the office.

"About Geoff?"

"You could say that."

"Takes all sorts, I guess." Then she leans closer. "What happened last night? Did you find him?"

I grab her arm and pull her into my office, closing the door behind us.

I sit her down and tell her everything. I have to go back to that day in the store cupboard for it to make any sense. I have to go back further than that, to Chicago. The conference Geoff and I attended together.

"You know, I really don't want to make excuses here, I really don't, but the next day Geoff kept joking about how drunk I was, how much I knocked them back. But I don't remember doing that. Maybe I was tired. Maybe that's why the alcohol went to my head. Not that it's any excuse."

She actually wipes a quick tear. "I can't believe it. I mean, I can. He's such a creep. He's always trying to get me to go out drinking with him in a suggestive way that makes my skin crawl. And I hate the way he's always standing too close when I'm in his office."

"No! You never said!"

She shrugs. "What's there to say? That's what he's like." We're both silent for a moment. "So what will you do?"

"I don't know. What do you think I should do?"

"Will you report them to the police?"

"I don't think much will happen if I do. It's Ryan's word against mine whether I was aware of him taking the photo or not."

"But you can't let him get away with it!"

"I'm trying, June. I'm just not sure how. The only way for him to be prosecuted is if he does something like this again. And then we'd still have to prove it."

"What do you mean?"

"Say he and I were in a compromising position"—I make air quotes as I say this—"and he was taking a photo unbeknown to me. How could I prove I wasn't aware of it? Or even that I wasn't doing it willingly? I just don't know the finer points of the law. I suppose we could find out."

"You said Ryan used Geoff's phone, right?"

I nod.

"So he must have the passcode."

"True."

"Ask him what it is. Then you can get rid of the photo."

"He'll have copies saved on the cloud, probably on a computer as well." We're both silent for a moment. "We should get to work," I say. "But thank you for listening. It means a lot."

She leans forward and blurts out, "He set you up."

It's like I haven't spoken just now. "I know! I just—"

"You can't let it go, Anna."

"I know that! But what do you want me to do?"

"I don't know! But you can't let him get away with this! I mean, what happens when he becomes the dean? What if he does this to other women?"

I tilt my head at her. "What do you mean, becomes the dean?"

"He's got his panel interview this afternoon. He must be in the running, especially with you and the prize. It might have been your work but you're in his department. He'll take credit for it, Anna. You watch."

"He's applying for Dean of School?"

"You didn't know?"

"No."

She shrugs. "They'll give it to him, Anna."

"They can't."

"They will." After a moment she says, "I could get his cellphone. We could take it to the panel, tell them what he did."

"What time is the interview?"

"Two o'clock."

I think about this. I know what these interviews are like. They take place in the executive office of the administration building, in a large room, with state-of-the-art audio visual equipment.

I check my watch. "Let me make a phone call."

Twenty minutes later, I call June back into my office.

"Is Geoff going out for lunch today?" I ask.

"He always does. Twelve thirty on the dot, returns between one and one thirty."

"Okay, that's good. In case he doesn't for some reason, you think you can get him out of the office anyway?"

"I'll try, why? What's going on?"

I don't reply, I have to think this through. "And his interview is at two, you said?"

"That's right."

"Can you go to him at say, quarter to two, and tell him they've asked to postpone it by thirty minutes? Tell him the other candidates are taking longer than expected, something like that."

She chuckles. "He won't like that."

"Good. Even better."

"And if he's not in his office at quarter to two?"

I sigh. "I don't know. I'll think of something else."

I tell her of my plan. She listens, one eyebrow raised. When I finish, she grins. "Genius. I love it. You think it will work?"

"No idea, but it's all I have right now."

I spend the rest of the morning distracted, but I feel good. Better, at any rate. It's what I need, this feeling of doing something. Of taking control, of being in charge of my own destiny.

As June predicted, at twelve twenty-five, Geoff exits his office, shrugging his jacket on, and locks his door. June pretends to do the same. She pops into my office with her coat on and her handbag looped over her shoulder. She removes both as soon as she enters.

I call Steve, my new best friend. Steve, who looked so despondent the day of my Forrester lecture when I wouldn't let him fix the connection. I wrote an email the following day to his boss explaining that I'd decided at the last minute not to use slides, and I apologized for putting Steve in that position. He called me to thank me. It's the little things.

"Coast is clear," I say.

"Roger that," he replies, which makes me chuckle.

I don't see the next part, but I know that June will unlock the office and let Steve inside, ostensibly to do something about phone line repair, should anyone ask. He works in the audiovisual department, but I don't think Geoff would know any different if he happened to return.

CHAPTER 36

At one fifteen, June texts me to say Geoff has returned from lunch. At a quarter to two, I stand in the corridor outside his office. June is inside explaining that there's been a delay, and the panel has requested Geoff attend at two thirty instead.

My heart is thumping in my ears while I wait, chewing on a fingernail. Finally, June walks out.

"Hi, Anna!" she says, sounding convincingly surprised to see me there.

"Is he in?" I ask.

"Yes, you're in luck. Go on in," she replies.

I almost laugh at how ridiculous we sound. As we pass each other she whispers, "Good luck."

"What are you doing here?" Geoff snaps without looking up, as I close the door. "I hope—"

I raise a hand. "Save it," I say. I know he was about to bring up the Pentti-Stone notebooks, and I don't want him to.

"Something strange happened. I thought you might be able to shed some light on it. I called Janette from HR."

He looks up then. "Did you? And?"

"There's no sexual harassment complaint against me. There never was."

He leans back against his chair. "There isn't? Well, fancy that."

"You made up the whole thing!"

He laughs. "I was going to tell you it had been dropped. I just wanted to see you squirm a little longer. My bad. Should have done it sooner. Oh, well. Now if that's all, I have things to do…"

"It's not all. I have decided to report you. To the police."

He gets up then, and in two strides he's at the door. My heart is in my throat. He's going to tell me to get out. I can argue all I like but he can easily have me thrown out.

He opens the door a crack and checks outside. Then he steps out and yells: "I'm in a meeting, June. I'm not to be disturbed."

"All right," she sings out.

I'm so relieved I close my eyes for a moment and let a long breath out.

"The police? And why would that be, Anna?" he says now. He has closed the door and returned to his desk.

"You assaulted me, Geoff. Why do you think?"

He cocks his head at me. "You're sure you want to go there? Firstly, I don't think I assaulted you. I only did what I thought you wanted me to do."

"I never wanted to have sex with you, and you know it."

He laughs. "Really? What about Chicago?"

"You know, I'm glad you brought that up. I've thought a lot about Chicago lately. And it occurred to me that I didn't drink *that* much that night. I just had some wine and one nightcap with you at the bar. Certainly not enough to explain waking up in your room, disoriented and confused."

He pushes against the back of his chair, and rocks back and forth. "You must have, since that's exactly what happened. I'm not responsible for how much you drink, Anna."

"I think you spiked my drink."

"You can't prove that."

I smile. *Wrong answer.* "I'm right, aren't I?"

"Hey, I just made it easier for you. That's all."

"How was that easier for me?"

I've been standing this whole time but it's hard to keep up the bravado when my legs are about to give way. I reach for a chair and sit down.

"I know your type," he says. "You want to play but you don't want the guilt. So, I gave you a little nudge, that's all. Made it easier for you to say you didn't know what you were doing." He winks. "I should have upped the dose."

I feel sick. I'm back there for a second, in that hotel room in Chicago. I can't believe I came so close… I have an urge to lunge at him, scratch that smirk off his face, but I don't. I'm not done yet.

From the way he tidies up papers in front of him, I can tell he thinks our little chat is over. He starts to get up when I say, "I had an interesting visit with Ryan."

He sits back down, slowly. Up till now, he was smirking. Supremely confident that he could talk his way out of anything I put to him, but not anymore. His jaw locks and his mouth is so tight, his lips are almost white.

"You coerced your own nephew into setting me up, so he could take a nude picture of me. On *your* cellphone. Then you used that photo to rattle me. You wanted me to feel paranoid and frightened. All the while pretending it was your nephew who was doing that. Do you have any idea how sick you are, Geoff?"

He throws his pen on the desk. It bounces off and onto the floor.

"You only have yourself to blame. You come on to me—"

"What are you? Some kind of incel? You can't accept that a woman doesn't want to sleep with you?"

He's leaning on his desk now, arms crossed, a fierce look on his face. "There are consequences for women like you."

"And there are consequences for men like you," I reply. "You scratch vile words on my car—"

He laughs. "If you don't like it, then resign, Anna. I'm not stopping you."

"You make an imaginary sexual complaint against me—"

"Prove it. It's your word against mine." He leans back again, crosses his hands behind his head. "All of it is your word against mine."

Then suddenly the door opens, and I'm thinking, *Finally. Thank God.* For a moment there, I was seriously concerned it wasn't working. That it really would all end up being his word against mine.

Geoff is on his feet. "June, I said—"

"I think we've heard enough!" the dean bellows. Behind him are the four committee members, and Steve too. He gives me a thumbs-up.

"You're fired, Geoffrey," the dean yells. His face is red with anger. "Effective immediately. Get out. Now."

"Me? No! Roy! Come on, man! Why?" Geoff is looking from one person to the other like he's going to cry, and I start to laugh. I can't help it. I think it's my nerves, the tension uncoiling.

"They've heard everything, Geoff!" I say finally. "No, wait, they *watched* everything."

"We'll refer the matter to the police immediately," the dean adds.

"That's right! I set you up!" I raise my hand. "Sorry, probably not fair to complain of you doing it to me, then to do it right back at you, but there you go. I told the panel—actually, June did—that you had a video for them to watch before the formal interview."

I give a little bow in Steve's direction. "My cellphone is positioned on the shelf to your right, see? It's streaming everything directly to that giant video screen mounted on the wall in the admin building. You know the one. I don't think your interview is going too well, Geoff, by the way. Just saying. Oh my god! You should see your face!"

I'm still laughing when I realize everyone is looking at me now. Even the dean. "Would you like a glass of water, Anna?" he asks.

I cough, tap my chest. "No, thank you. Sorry." I quickly wipe tears off my face.

Geoff is closing and opening his fists and for a moment I think he's going to spit at my feet. Then June pops her head in and says.

"The police are here."

"Already?" I turn back to Geoff. "Wow, impressive. That was *very* fast. I told you it was against the law. Or maybe I didn't, I can't remember. Anyway." I check off my fingers one by one. "Assault. Taking an intimate photo without the person's consent, *and* distributing it. Spiking your colleague's drink for nefarious purpose. Vandalizing private property—that's my car by the way. Am I missing anything? Well, off you go, Geoff, what are you waiting for? Go on, hands in front of you for the handcuffs. You know the drill." My voice is rising with every word, sounding increasingly hysterical. I'm about to shout, "Come on in! He's all yours!" when June tugs at my sleeve.

"They're here for you." Then, eyebrows knotted, she mouths, *Sorry*.

I freeze, turn around slowly and come face to face with Detective Jones.

CHAPTER 37

They just wanted to talk to me, they said. Detective Jones and the other one, Detective Dalloway, a woman with short black hair and a scar over her top lip. I wonder if it's the same one who interviewed Luis the other day. I let myself be led away, head bowed, cheeks flushed with humiliation. I followed, obedient and meek and so frightened it made my legs feel like rubber, and was put into the back of a black sedan that stank of stale cigarettes.

They have brought me to a small room with white walls and a plastic table. They both introduce themselves even though I know who they are already. It's for the camera, Jones says. He asks me to do the same.

"My name is Anna Sanchez," I say, my voice shaky. "Am I under arrest?" I ask finally, staring at the manila folder on the table.

"No," Jones says. "We just have a few questions. Just a few things to clear up and you'll be out of here in no time. Would you like a lawyer present?"

A lawyer? I feel faint. I ask for a glass of water. There's a water fountain in the corner of the room and Dalloway fills up a white plastic cup for me. I drink it and some of it dribbles on my chin, like my mouth can't function properly.

They wait, patiently, while I try and think if I want a lawyer. Everybody says you should have one, no matter what, but I don't know where to get one. I consider asking to call Luis, but I desperately want to know what this is about first, and didn't Jones just say I'll be out of here in no time? That doesn't sound like I'm in any trouble. It sounds like they need my help. I just need to remember that's why I'm here. To help. I'm fabulous at helping. I'm a team player.

"No, I don't need a lawyer. What did you want to ask me?" I say, my voice stronger now that I'm on familiar territory, rallying to the cause.

"I should tell you first that we're now conducting a murder investigation around the death of Ms. Wilcox."

My heart skips a beat. I wonder how many I have left, how many more I can skip before my heart gives up completely. I stare at him, replaying the words in my mind. "You think she was murdered?"

"Mrs. Sanchez, you said the last time you saw Isabelle Wilcox was on the Friday when you and your husband hosted a small dinner party."

I think of June's sad face as I walked out. *Sorry.*

"I did, didn't I." It's not a question. "I made a mistake."

He writes something down. "What mistake would that be, Mrs. Sanchez?"

"I saw Isabelle the night she died." I say this quickly, on the out breath.

"I see. That's quite a mistake. Did you forget about that?" He sits back in his seat and chews on the top of his pen. *That is a bad habit,* I want to say. *I've been trying to get Carla to stop doing that and it's really hard. Do you know how many trillions of bacteria you're ingesting right now? Where has that pen been? In your unwashed pocket? Have you dropped it on this filthy floor lately? Of course you have.*

"Mrs. Sanchez?"

I blurt it out. "I told you before, I went out with someone from work, June. I said we were together until I went home, but we weren't together all night. We went our separate ways around eight p.m. I think. After that I went to Isabelle's house, to talk to her, that's all, just to talk. And before you ask what it was about... it was nothing. It was about my husband, actually. She was home, she let me in. I... my memory of that night is a bit fuzzy, so please bear with me."

"Sure. Take your time."

I pick at the skin around my thumbnail.

"I asked her to leave him alone. I suppose you know that she and Luis..."

I look at him, for help almost, for confirmation. But he just waits for me to continue.

"Well, I suppose you know that they had some kind of fling. Very brief, and he had ended it by then. Except I didn't know that. Anyway, she wasn't going to leave him alone, that's what she said. Because they were in love. I may as well tell you, since you probably already know, that she was pregnant, and that it was Luis's... but I don't know if that's true. I called her names, told her to stay away from my family, then I left."

"What time was that?"

"Um... ten? Eleven maybe? Then I went out to a bar, I don't remember where exactly."

"Okay. So why didn't you tell us this the first time?"

"I was embarrassed. I didn't want you know about Luis and Isabelle. The fewer people who knew..."

Detective Dalloway, who is sitting on a flimsy plastic chair in a corner taking notes, turns to Jones. "I understand that," she says. Then to me she adds, "If my husband was cheating on me, I wouldn't want anybody to know about it."

"Right?" I say, relieved. "Exactly."

Jones makes a face. "We've all been there, Mrs. Sanchez. Having a partner cheat on you is a nasty feeling. Especially when there are children involved. I don't blame you for wanting to have it out with her."

I flinch. "I wouldn't say 'have it out'. More like a frank and honest discussion."

"Right," he says. "So that frank and honest discussion took place over... three hours?"

"No! God, no, I don't remember what time I left but it couldn't have been that long."

"That's all right, we have CCTV that places you in the neighborhood, walking away from Ms. Wilcox's home at... eight minutes past ten. So let's call it two hours, then. And just so I understand clearly here, you went to Ms. Wilcox's house, you told her to stay away from your husband, you called her names... Then what did you do for the other hour and fifty minutes?"

"We argued! She told me she was pregnant, I cried, we shouted at each other!"

"Did you assault her?"

"No!" I rub my hand across my forehead. "I knocked over a vase. That's all." I think of the pool of water on the carpet, her crouching and putting the flowers back in the vase. How incongruous it all seems now. "She was perfectly fine when I left her."

"Did she agree to"—he licks a fingertip and flicks over a page—"leave him alone?"

I take a moment to reply. "No. But it didn't matter. Luis had already broken it off."

"Had he?" Jones says, eyes wide, as if this is the first he's heard of it. I tilt my head at him.

"He must have told you."

He turns to Dalloway. "Did Mr. Sanchez say he'd broken it off?"

She raises her hands in a *Search me* gesture. They exchange a knowing glance, then Jones turns back to me. "Let's accept that your husband *had* broken off the relationship."

I wince at the word 'relationship'. Such a happy and committed word, utterly inappropriate in this instance. But I let it pass.

"Then why did you feel the need to go and see her?"

I rub my finger again on the same spot on my forehead. The skin is starting to peel there. "Because I didn't actually know at that point in time."

He leans forward. "See, if that was me, Mrs. Sanchez, and I went to see my wife's lover—for the sake of argument—and I was *politely* asking him to stay away from my wife, and he said no, I don't know what I'd do. I'm being honest here, I really don't. But you accepted her response and walked away, is that right?"

"I wouldn't say I just walked away."

"Because you said, you called her names, and you left. You'd gone all that way to save your marriage, then you just took it on the chin and left?" He lets the question dangle between us.

"How did you get that mark on your hand, Mrs. Sanchez?"

I look at the welt. It's almost gone now. "I told you. Gardening."

"Did you know your husband had gifted Ms. Wilcox a necklace? She was very fond of it. She wore it all the time. In fact, she told her colleague that she never took it off." He opens the folder and pulls out a clear plastic envelope. Inside is a photo of Isabelle and another man at what looks like an art opening. They're standing close together smiling at the camera, a glass of champagne in one hand. Clearly visible around her neck is the necklace.

I can't stop staring at her. I can't stop thinking how beautiful she is, and a flash of outrage bolts through me. How could Luis possibly resist? She's like one of those plants that are beautiful on the outside but carnivorous on the inside, all bright colors and pearls of dew, but get too close and they'll entrap their prey and won't let go until they're completely suffocated.

"Mrs. Sanchez?"

I raise my head. "She never took it off?" They exchange a glance, and I know it was the wrong answer.

I sit back. "I didn't know that he had given this to her, no."

"Not even when you visited the jewelry store on November 12th with the receipt from your husband's purchase, claiming your husband had in fact given the necklace to you?"

For a moment I feel like I'm falling, the ground rushing towards me and I'm scrambling to hold onto something. "I knew," I say, feeling the corners of my mouth pull down.

"So that was another mistake then, you not telling us just now?"

I don't know what to say. My eyes well up, and a fat tear rolls out onto my cheek. I brush it off.

"Why didn't you say so, Mrs. Sanchez?"

"Do you know why she didn't have the necklace on her that night?" Dalloway asks. "She had it on her during the day. She didn't have it on her when she died. We searched her house. We didn't find it."

"Because I took it from her," I say. "She was playing with it as we spoke, taunting me. I–I grabbed it and pulled it off her." I rub the side of my hand. "It was fastened more tightly than I'd expected."

"I see. So you did assault her."

"No!"

"Come on, Mrs. Sanchez. You said so yourself, she taunted you. She was pregnant. She wasn't going to end the relationship with your husband—"

"It was already over! He'd already ended it!"

"So you keep saying, but you also admitted you didn't know this at the time. You don't think grabbing someone's throat qualifies as assault? How did you get her upstairs?"

"What?"

"She fell from the top of the steps leading to the main bedroom. She was pushed. Did you follow her up the stairs?"

"Was that when you pulled the necklace off her? Is that what happened?" Dalloway says.

"Was it an accident?" Jones says.

Their voices are drowned by the blood roaring in my ears. I press my fingers against my throbbing temples.

"Tell us what happened, Mrs. Sanchez."

I close my eyes. I can see her face, her eyes wide in shock.

"Why did you lie about being there, Mrs. Sanchez?"

"Did you push her down the stairs, Mrs. Sanchez?" "

"No!" I'm on my feet now, shaking and confused. I stare at Jones, then Dalloway. "I'd like to leave now," I say. I bend down to retrieve my bag at my feet. I fully expect them to stop me, to tell me that I'm under arrest after all, and all I can think about are my kids and I imagine their faces when they find out and my heart snaps in two.

Jones says the interview is terminated at four thirty-two and closes his folder.

"Dalloway will accompany you outside. We'll be in touch. Don't go too far, and if you need to leave the state, we'd appreciate you letting us know."

I called Luis. I didn't think I could get back home by myself. I am numb and confused, the way you might feel when you wake up after fainting and you're not sure what happened or where you are or why you're here. "Will you come and get me?" I asked. Pleaded, really.

"Anna?"

I was looking at my hands and I didn't see him approach. I look up and there he is, looking broken, and I don't know if it's for me or her anymore, and when he says, "What did you do, Anna?" I think he's going to cry.

He helps me to the car, one hand on my elbow.

"I asked my dad to take the kids tonight."

I nod. "That's good." I wipe my tears with my sleeve. "It's better for them to be there. They love being with him. I'm glad he could take them. It's nice of him."

"Yeah." We don't talk after that. When we get home I go upstairs and lie down on the bed. I can't even describe to Luis how frightened I am right now. He comes upstairs and hands me an Ambien and a glass of water. I take it wordlessly and fall into the abyss.

It is dark and silent when I wake, and I already miss my kids more than I can say. Luis is lying next to me, watching me. I turn to face him.

"Luis?"

"Yes, babe."

"I'm really scared."

He takes my hand. "I know."

We go downstairs and he makes ham and cheese sandwiches for us but I can't eat anything.

"I didn't do it," I tell him. "She was fine when I left." But I also tell him we have to make plans, because it's not looking good for me.

"I'm so confused," I say, my mouth trembling. "I'm so scared, Luis. They're going to put me in jail."

"No, they won't, we'll get the best lawyers—we can afford it, right? We can use your prize money. We'll get the very best."

I don't tell him the prize money is a mirage right now. "Yes," I say. "You're right. We'll be fine. But if we're not—"

"You have to think positive, Anna."

"Luis, please. Listen to me. I want us to talk about the children, if something happens to me."

He sits down at the table next to me, runs a hand through his hair.

"Will you promise me that you will look after them, that you will keep them safe? Matti spends too much time on his Xbox and we need to do something about that. And try to keep Carla off social media for as long as possible? They love you so much, Luis. You're a wonderful, incredible father. But you'll have to be strong."

He's crying. "I can't do it without you, Anna."

I reach for his hand. "Sure you can. You're the best father, the best parent. Do you remember when Mateo fell off his bike that time?" I laugh through my tears. "Do you know how jealous I was that he called out to you instead of me? They adore you, Luis. You're their whole world."

He squeezes my hand. "I have to tell you something."

I can't. I just can't deal with anything else right now. I press my fingers against my temples. "What?" I say, without looking up.

"I asked Matti to fall off his bike that day and call out for me."

I wait, feeling a smile on my lips. "You didn't."

"I did. I paid him five bucks, too. I wanted to show you I was doing a really good job bringing up our children. You were flying, Anna. You were so smart, so successful, you were like a shining star and I wanted you to see what a good job *I* was doing at home. Five bucks was a bargain, I think."

"The ninja turtle plasters?"

"All part of the plan."

"Seriously?"

"Cross my heart."

"Wow."

"I know."

"He fell quite hard."

"He's a great little actor."

"He could have cracked his head."

"True, true."

"And Matti went along with this?"

"Five bucks."

I'm laughing now. I brush off my tears and rest my head on his shoulder. "I can't believe you did that just to impress me."

He caresses my hair. "I'll look after them, I give you my word."

But that's not what I wanted to hear after all. I wanted him to keep saying how it was all going to be okay, and we didn't even need to have this conversation.

Because if Luis doesn't believe in me, then nobody will.

CHAPTER 38

I lie in bed most of the morning. Luis brings me cups of tea and watches me, his eyebrows knotted together. "Can I get you anything?" he asks. He makes it sound like I'm ill and I need tending. He sits on the bed next to me. "I think the kids should stay with my dad another night."

"Yes," I reply. "Yes, you're right. They all right? They got to school okay?"

"It's Saturday," he says.

"Of course."

"They're good, they're with their friends. They don't know anything."

"Okay, good. That's good," I say, then wait till he leaves the room to bury my face into the pillow and bawl my eyes out.

At one point I think there's a knock on the door and my heart lurches because I think it's them, they've come to arrest me, and I sit up, but it's next door. I should get up and get dressed, though, because they will come, won't they? I don't want them to find me like this. I reach for my phone to call June. She must be worried sick. I want to tell her I understand she had to tell them that my alibi was a lie. She must feel terrible. She doesn't answer and I leave a message. "Hi, it's me." My voice breaks. "I'm home," I say, in case she thought I was arrested. "God, that was scary. Call me soon."

I take a shower, get dressed in practical clothes, flat shoes, pants that don't require a belt—you never know, what if they take it away from me? I think about these things.

I expected to hear back from June but there's no message. Luis made some calls and has found me a lawyer. "He's the best," he says. I promise him that I'll call this afternoon. I don't tell him there's no money, there probably never will be.

"Go to the studio if you have to work," I say. "There's nothing you can do here."

He takes my hand. "You sure?"

"Of course. I want to visit June anyway." I don't add, *While I still can.*

I leave another message then drive over to June's house. I'm actually getting worried about her. It's not like her to not return my calls. Also, I desperately want to apologize. I should never have asked her to lie for me. Maybe she's angry about that, that I got her mixed up in this whole mess. I'll explain that I just panicked. I thought if the police knew I was there that they would come for me. In the end they did anyway.

I am thinking all this as I walk up to her porch, hugging a potted purple hyacinth because I read somewhere they signify *Please forgive me.* I ring the doorbell and after a moment I see her outline drawing near through the frosted glass pane. I quickly stand to the side with my arm extended so she'll see the plant before she sees me.

"I'm sorry," I blurt out as she opens the door, my head tilted, my eyebrows raised. "Please forgive me?"

"God!" She slaps her hand on her chest. "You scared the bejesus out me!"

I recoil in surprise. "I did? I'm sorry. I left you a bunch of messages. Well, three, anyway."

I wait, holding my pot plant against my chest, but she doesn't move.

"I've come bearing gifts—one gift anyway. And to say I'm sorry that I asked you to lie for me. That was wrong. You okay? They didn't give you a hard time, I hope? I told them it was my fault."

She stands there, a little shakily, and takes the plant from me. "Thank you. It's very nice." She's smiling but it looks forced and makes her lips twitch.

I put one hand on my hip and tilt my head at her. "What's wrong?"

"Nothing. I'm kinda busy, that's all."

I blink. I imagined myself coming here, moving piles of baking magazines from her couch and sitting down with a cup of that chai tea she makes, holding onto one of her flowery cushions. It never occurred to me she wouldn't want to see me.

"Can I come in?"

She glances over her shoulder.

"Oh? Sorry. You have guests?" Then it dawns on me, and I look around, try to pry through her front window. I lean forward and whisper. "Is it the police? They're here?"

"No. The police aren't here. Nobody's here. I'm just tired, that's all."

I nod. "Of course. I should go. Oh god, June! I don't want to go! I'm so sorry! I can't say it enough. I'm probably going to be arrested, unless a miracle happens and I can't imagine what that might be, so I might not see you again after this." I pull out a used Kleenex from my coat pocket and wipe my nose.

She tilts her head and she looks so sad suddenly. We both are. She sighs and moves out of the way.

"Thank you," I say in a small voice. "I won't stay long."

She sets down the hyacinth plant on the small table and makes no move to unwrap it.

"What happened, June? Is it because I asked you to lie for me? About the alibi? I'll say anything you want me to say. I'll tell them again, of course, that it's my fault."

I want her to say something, to make it better, offer solutions, do the June thing, but she just stands there, her arms crossed over her chest. We've moved into the living room but she hasn't invited me to sit down yet. I glance around the room. As always, her coffee table is messy, covered with homemaking magazines, opened recipe books, empty cups and glasses and small plates with a scattering of crumbs. June still hasn't moved. And then it dawns on me.

She's afraid of me.

"What's going on?" I ask.

"I found the necklace, in my bag."

Both hands fly to my mouth. "Oh, no. Oh, please, let me explain."

"Did you plant it on me?"

"No! I swear to god! On my children, never, ever." I move to touch her but she jerks away. "You remember when Carla was riffling through my bag for my purse, the night you were looking after Matti? I had it in there, and I panicked, remember? I knocked the bag from your shoulder, and I put it in one of the pockets because I didn't want Carla to find it. I didn't want Luis to find it, either. I did it on the spur of the moment. I was going to tell you but with Ryan and Geoff I… I'm so sorry June, I just forgot."

"Then why did *you* have it?" she asks.

"Listen to me. When I went to see her, she had the necklace around her neck and I was so upset, I yanked it off her. That's how I got this, see?" I show her my hand, the light pink line only barely visible. "That's all. I put it in my pocket and I left."

She shakes her head slowly, her fingers on her lips.

"You have to believe me. I didn't put it in your bag to hurt you, I just needed a hiding place and I was going to tell you."

We stare at each other in silence for a moment. She looks like she's going to cry.

"I should go," I say. She nods. As I pass the hyacinth, on impulse, I start to unwrap the cellophane.

"I'm telling you the truth," I say, my back to her.

"Don't," she says quickly. I turn around. She has one hand up, reaching toward the table.

"What?" I follow her gaze. Half sticking out from under the pot is a small square of paper on which she has scribbled something. I shift the plant and pick it up.

"Give it to me," she snaps.

FlowersDirect, Purple lisianthus and daisies. Next to that is the address of the university and a date.

"What's this?" I'm still staring at it when she lunges, tries to grab it from me. I hold it up in the air. "What is it?" I ask again, more firmly this time, because *Purple lisianthus and daisies* are the flowers that my mother always sends me. Always the same.

"Give it to me, Anna."

"This is the bouquet my mother sent me." I tap the note with one finger. "And this is the online florist who delivered them, isn't it? On the day of the dinner in the hall. What's this about, June?"

She's silent for a long time, biting the inside of her cheek, rubbing her hands over her arms like there's a draft in here.

"June?"

"I know you sent them to yourself."

"What?"

She's shaking all over now. "I was trying to help you. I really, really wanted to help you, because I liked you, Anna!" Her voice breaks and tears roll down her cheeks. She wipes them off with shaking fingers. "When they took you away yesterday, I wanted to find your mother," she says.

"What? Why?"

"Because I thought you needed her, I thought it would be good for you, and she owed you and she should be here for you right now, and I didn't know her last name or where she lived, but I remembered the flowers she sent because I was the one who took delivery and I remembered the name of the store."

"Oh, June…"

"But it wasn't her who sent them," she says.

Her eyes grow wild suddenly, like she's realized I'm standing here, barring her way, and she's looking for an escape.

"Of course she sent them," I say gently.

"No, she didn't! You did."

I shake my head vigorously. "No, that's not true, don't say that!"

"They told me who sent them, and it was you, Anna! And you've done it before! You're a regular customer there, always the same bunch of flowers! You're sending them to *yourself*!"

"June, stop, please, you know how crazy you sound right now? Obviously there's some mistake! The store got it wrong, they got it mixed up and gave you the recipient details, which is me! Don't you see? Think about it, June! Why would I do that? It makes no sense! Why would I send myself flowers and pretend to everyone they're from my mother?"

"Because she's dead!"

"Luis?" I'm crying. Sobbing, really. Big wet sobs that bubble up and explode in a series of snotty eruptions.

"What's wrong, babe? Where are you?"

"I'm in my car," I say. I managed to drive away because I didn't want to sit outside June's house but I only made it two blocks and I had to get off the road before I caused an accident.

"You have to help me, Luis," I whisper.

"Baby, I can't hear you. I don't understand what you're saying. Have you been in an accident?"

"No, it's June. She said…"

"She said what?"

"Oh Luis… I did some bad things…"

"What things, babe?"

I put my hand over my mouth so that no one hears me, even though I'm alone in the car. "I killed my mother," I whisper.

His silence is long and distant and slices at my heart. I think he's hung up. Out of the blue a thought pops into my head: *Did he already know?*

What did you do?

"Am I crazy?" I bring my hand over my eyes. I'm so frightened I can't bear it.

"Oh, Anna. Honey."

"I killed my mother!" I can barely speak after that. Every word comes out chopped, lurching into the next. It's like I'm speaking in morse code—everything has to be interpreted, linked into a sentence. "My mother has been dead for sixteen years. I've been sending myself flowers."

"No, Anna, no."

"Luis, I'm so sorry…" Again I drop my voice so low, so low that maybe even I can't hear it.

"Listen to me, Anna." His tone makes me snap to attention. "I don't know what June thinks she's doing, but you did *not* kill your mother, do you hear me? That's insane! Don't you think we would know if your mother was dead?"

"I don't know," I wail. "Would we?"

"Yes! Of course! Don't listen to June, Anna. Come home now. We'll call your mother together, and then we'll go and talk to June, okay?"

"I haven't spoken… to my mother… in such a long time, Luis."

He is silent for a moment. When he speaks again, his tone is different. Softer, but heavier. Weighted with pity. "It's going to be okay, Anna. No matter what you did, baby, I love you. I will always love you. I'm here for you. No matter what."

A man with a dark beard knocks on my window. *You all right?* he mouths.

I nod, raise my hand. *Thank you*, I wave. *Please go, I'm all right*. The man hesitates, then tips his hat and walks away. But I'm not all right, I'll never be all right, and what is going to happen to my kids when I die? Because I'm going to die. People like me don't get second chances. They're going to put me in prison for a very long time for all the bad things I did.

"Where are you?" I ask.

"At the studio. But I'll come home as soon as I can. I'll see you there, okay, babe? We'll call your mom together. And everything will be fine, you'll see. No matter what happens, Anna, we'll get you some help, I promise. No matter what. But it will be okay. You'll see."

"How long… will you be?"

"One hour max. Okay? Don't go back to June's on your own please, babe. Wait for me. We'll find out exactly what's going on together, you and me, then we'll go back and tell June. Together. It's going to be okay. I promise."

"Thank you, Luis. I'm sorry."

"I love you, Anna. No matter what, okay?"

"I love you too. I'm so sorry."

CHAPTER 39

I start the engine, then I sit there, letting it idle. I don't know what to do. I can't bear to go home and be on my own, so I drive to the studio because all I want right now is Luis. I desperately want him to hold me, to help me make it right even though I know nothing can ever be right again. The police will come for me soon. Hey, maybe they're at the house already. I have so little time and all I want is to curl up on the sofa and maybe watch him work, just to pretend for a little while that none of this is happening.

I let myself into the building and up the goods lift. I knock on the heavy door but he doesn't hear me. I rest my forehead against the cold metal. I can faintly hear music inside. I pry the key loose from its trusted place and let myself in.

"Luis?"

His large sculpture, *The Nest*, is back. It's bigger than I remembered. More somber, too, somehow. I walk around it and to the other end of the studio, and turn off the sound system.

"Luis?"

I check my cell but there's no message.

I stare at the sculpture. *The Nest*. His apogee. I think how much I wanted him to succeed, how much I supported him, loved him, trusted him, admired him. And that work? His grand masterpiece? It should have been about us. *The Nest*. It should have been for *me*. And I can't stop crying as I think back to that night at the opening: *Isabelle might have a shot at selling* The Nest *to the contemporary art museum for their permanent collection.* I think of him crossing his fingers, his eyes closed, his face turned to the ceiling, and I remember the words that floated in my mind then, like a whisper. *He's in love.*

I don't know what happens after that. I just feel all the pent-up pain and fury roar through me and before I can stop myself my hands have gripped the long metal rod that seconds ago was leaning by the window and I'm screaming as I raise the rod over my head and strike the sculpture as hard as I can. But the hook gets caught on something and I pull the rod up and blindly thrash into it again, and again and again until the cables snap and the whole structure falls with a loud crash and the creatures in their eggs roll out and I smash them too, I smash their faces and their eyes and the delicate shell around them and I'm screaming because they should have represented our children, shouldn't they? This should have been *our* nest, shouldn't it, Luis? Didn't we deserve this homage to your genius, Luis? Weren't we enough for you that you had to fall in love *her*?

And I can't see anything anymore and it's all his fault and everything I did, I did for us, and all there is now is noise and dust and splinters flying and bouncing against the walls and I'm still screaming and I can't breathe but I don't want to stop until it's gone, until that *thing* that sits there like a monument to all that went wrong is *gone*.

I am on my knees. I drop the rod with a clank. I can't breathe. I don't know how long I sit like that, in the middle of the wreckage, my arms wrapped tightly around my sides. I open my eyes and see the creatures at my feet, broken, eyes smashed, no longer pleading, like they were real and now they're dead, and suddenly I have this overwhelming urge to put them back together. I scramble around the floor to find the right pieces and grab a chunk of the shell, then another, and I want to put them back together but they don't fit.

I stare at them in my hands, sobbing. Something catches my eye: Letters. Words. The shells were made of paper, glued together and shaped. I pull it apart gently and smooth the creases out as much I can, and I see now, what caught my eye. It's my name, on an official document, or what's left of it. It's stained with dark spots, like it was kept somewhere damp for a long time.

It's a residential purchase agreement for the house I grew up in, in Youngstown. What I think of as my mother's house, after my father died, before she moved to California. I know that my mother sold that house and moved years ago, but I don't understand why Luis would have a copy of this purchase agreement. I look closer, and I know then that something isn't right with me. That I'm doing things I have no memory of doing, because the seller on that document is not my mother, it's me. It says it right there. In 2006, I owned, and sold, my mother's house to a complete stranger.

I gather the other pieces I can find, carefully separate layers of paper and smooth them out as much as I can, and now I'm wailing like an animal, because Luis said my mother was alive and of course she wasn't dead, he said. Wouldn't we know? But he must have known, because this, in my hand, is a piece of her death certificate. And when I look at it again it's as if the light dims around me and the walls are closing in and I throw it to the floor and push myself away from it as far as I can, and I hit the wall with my back and I'm stuck there, shaking, crying, calling his name and I'm so scared, I'm losing my mind, because the manner of death is *Accidental fall on stairs*.

The floor is littered with debris and as I scurry around on my hands and knees, blood roaring in my ears, I catch sight of something long and strange and out of place. I pick it up. It's some kind of tube, partly transparent, with a yellow and white sticker, and at first I think it's a tube of solder wire, and it's only when I read the label that I realize what it is.

Epipen.

I haven't seen this exact type before. It's different from the ones that you would see today, but that's what it is, and my heart knocks around in my chest because I know, without a shadow of a doubt, that this belonged to Monica. It falls out of my hand and disappears under the couch. I'm on my knees and I peer underneath. It's been stopped by something small and shiny, like a button, and I have to extend my arm as far as I can to reach it. I feel it with my fingertips but accidentally nudge it away. I have to use the rod to drag it out, and it slides out, along with the shiny button. Except it's not a button. It's a ring. Silver, oddly shaped.

He's a very interesting metal artist. French.

CHAPTER 40

My chest feels so tight, even drawing in a breath feels like a burn. I have to calm down. I make myself breathe but it hurts, like a stitch. I close my eyes, my forehead against the steering wheel, the phone pressed hard against my ear and I notice my hand is bleeding.

I press my fingers between my eyes as the call goes to voicemail.

"Luis?" My voice cracks and for a moment I think I can't do it. I can't summon the will to pretend that everything is as before, that nothing's changed. I have discovered nothing. Then I think of my kids and I bend down at the waist, a hand over my mouth covering a silent wail. When I take a breath again, it's like I've come out from under water.

"Luis, it's me. Are you home yet? I need to talk to you. Will you call me as soon as you get this?"

I hang up, and call June.

Pick up! Pickuppickuppickup...

"Hi! I'm sorry I can't take your call right now, but please leave a message!"

"June." My voice is high-pitched with panic. "It's me. Listen to me very carefully. If Luis comes over to your house, do not answer the door, do you understand? Pretend you're not there. If you're home, go out now, as soon as you get this. Go anywhere, go to the mall. Stay out. But under no circumstances should you let him inside your house."

I hang up and dial again. I do it twice more. I tell myself it doesn't mean anything that she's not picking up. June doesn't know what to think of me right now. I bet she hates me. She's convinced I killed Isabelle, and maybe even tried to pin it on her. She believes I'm insane and I'm dangerous. Of course she's not taking my call.

I call Luis's dad. He answers on the first ring, his voice raspy by decades of smoking.

"Anna, you okay? I heard—"

"Rob. Is Luis there?"

"Luis? No, why? Should he be? I thought Carla and Matti were staying till tomorrow."

"Listen, Rob. If Luis comes over, don't let him leave till I get there, all right? Tell him to wait for me. I'll be there shortly."

"Is everything all right?"

"Yes. Everything is fine. I'll see you soon. Call me if Luis gets there before me."

But I will go to June's house first, and if she's not home I'm going to leave her a note. That's what I'll do. I'll tell her in writing. And if she is there but won't let me in, I'll scream it in the window.

Then I'll go and get my kids. That's what I'll do.

I drive so fast I almost have an accident, twice. At June's, I abandon the car across the road and run to her house. I slam on the door with both hands. *Open the door!* But she's not there. I turn to rush back to my car, find a piece of paper to write on, when I catch something in the window. It's the blinds. They've moved, I'm sure of it. Just an inch, like someone is peering through the slats. I slap the glass with the palm of my hand. "June! I know you're in there! I have to talk to you!"

I'm frantically searching for a rock at my feet, something to throw, when the blinds suddenly fly up in one quick rush, and I scream.

Luis's face stares back at me.

*

"You shouldn't have come, babe."

He has opened the front door and pulled me inside.

"Oh my god." June is tied up in the corner, a scarf tied around her mouth. Her eyes are red, wild with terror. I rush to help her but Luis has wrapped an arm around my shoulders and he's pulling me back.

"You shouldn't have come. I told you not to come here, Anna. Didn't I say? Don't go to June? Wait for me at home? Didn't I say that?"

"You have to let her go! She has nothing to do with anything!"

"She shouldn't have tried to track down your mother!" he shouts, pointing at her. "And that's on her, okay?" He turns around and grabs his hair with his fists, pacing the room. "I have to take care of it now. I'm taking care of it."

I'm crying so much I can barely speak. "Who are you? What did you do, Luis? Did you really do all those things? Did you really hurt all these people?"

He looks into my eyes for a long time, then his face slowly crumbles with misery. "Don't look at me like that. Of all people, Anna, you're the only one who would understand."

He drops to his knees and holds on to my jacket, his face upturned, pleading.

"What are you doing here, Luis?"

"I've come to take care of June," he says quietly. "You have to trust me, Anna. Everything will be fine. I promise."

"No. Please don't hurt her. I'm begging you! You have to let her go."

He pulls me down so that we're both on our knees. He takes my hands in his. "Come on, babe. You understand, don't you? Of course you do. Because you're dark, like me. We're the same, you and me."

"No, Luis, we're not."

"We're going to be okay. I'll take care of this, then we'll get the kids and we'll go away. The four of us, okay? We'll go wherever you like."

"What did you do to Isabelle, Luis?"

"I made a mistake. I told you that. I should never have done it. I could never be with someone like Isabelle. Women like that, they're too bright, too shiny, too perfect. It was just a fling, that's all, but she wanted more—she wanted to have a baby and how could I leave you?"

"We have to go to the police, now."

"No! We don't have to do that! I'll take care of everything, I promise. You understand, don't you?" He grips my hands tightly and pulls me closer to him. "You're made of dark waters, like me." And he says it again: "We're the same, you and me."

"No, Luis, we're not. We're not the same."

"No one loves me like you do," he says. "You're obsessed with me, see? And I'm obsessed with you." And I think back to all the times he said it. *You're obsessed with me.* And I thought it was pure, true love, and all the time it was something so much darker than that.

"You and me, we would do anything for each other. We'd kill for each other. I've always known that about you. But Isabelle, she wanted to break us. I made a mistake, I admit that. But I couldn't let her do that to us. You see that, babe, don't you?"

"Why did you go there that night?" I ask.

"Because she called me after you left. And she said she told you about the baby, and I was free now, to be with her. But I didn't want to be with her, Anna! I didn't want the baby. So I turned on the light in my shed and put some music on and locked the door so that when you came home, you'd think I was in there. Then I went to her house and I tried to talk to her, I really did, but she wouldn't listen. And she was going to tell Patrick, and Perry at the gallery, and everyone she knew that she was having my baby, and I couldn't do that to us, babe. You see that, don't you?"

I dislodge one hand and wipe my cheeks. He grabs it again.

"Did you push her down the stairs?"

"She was so mad, she threw the ring I gave her at my face and she was going to tell everybody, and I pretended I was sorry, I pretended to kiss her and I said, 'Let's go upstairs, let's go to bed,' and then…" He raises his shoulder slightly. "She fell," he says, simply.

"Luis, no. Oh God." I feel sick. And I don't want to ask my next question—I don't want to, but I know I have to. "What about Monica?"

"That was an accident. I swear to god. I wanted to go with you to that party, remember that party?"

"Of course I remember that party."

"I knew she'd taken back a piece of cake from the cafeteria that day," he continues. "She always did that. Remember how she always did that? She'd keep it in a tin, with flowers on it, remember that? And pick at it while she finished her assignment."

"Yes, I remember," I say.

"I crushed some peanuts together into crumbs then I told her to meet me somewhere, that I had a present for her, so she'd be out of the room. I went in there and sprinkled it over the piece of cake and took her Epipen. I rushed back to where she was waiting, and gave her a drawing pad, remember how she used to draw all the time? She thought we were going to meet later at the party, but I'd already fallen in love with you, you see? I just wanted it to be you and me. I thought she would be sick and go to bed. I didn't know she would *die*, I swear to god I didn't know."

I drop my head in my hands but he grabs them again, holds on to them so tightly he's crushing them. "You understand, don't you?" June makes a sound in the corner, like a moan.

"And—and my m-mother?"

He lets go of my hands and grabs a fistful of his hair. "Your mother, she was nasty, you know that. She said to me there was something not right about me, and she found out some things about me, some things I did that landed me in detention when I was a kid, but I wasn't like that anymore, not since I met you, and I told her that, but she wanted to tell you, she wanted to break us up, Anna. And I…"

He doesn't say anymore, just looks around wildly, rubbing his face, pulling at his hair.

"After she died, I panicked. I didn't know how to tell you. I pretended she was still alive. The police said it was an accident anyway, and you two weren't speaking at the time. And you never liked her, she was horrible. But then when Carla was born you wanted to reconcile and I… I just kept pretending! I pretended she'd moved away, I picked a place as far away from us as I could, and I bought a PO box in her name, and I really thought you'd give up, but you didn't, and you invited her to Christmas and birthdays and I'd send flowers and send emails and you'd call her and leave messages but she'd never call back, just send you emails, and it just got out of hand."

"But you sent the flowers in *my* name, not yours." I cry. "Why? Did you rent the box in my name too?"

He takes my face in his hands.

"I thought if anyone found out, it would be easier to explain that way, see?" He looks at me, pleading. "I'd had enough of all the lies, of sending flowers, of pretending your mother was alive. I was going to send you a letter, from her, to say she never wanted anything to do with us, that she was moving away and not to contact her again. I made *The Nest* for us, Anna! I put all that stuff in it, your mother's things, the Epipen, some other things you wouldn't know about… I wanted to get rid of these things and start again. But I couldn't just burn them, I had to do something more, something transformative, a new beginning. That's why I had to make something big out of it, something for *us*. That's why I took Isabelle's ring and put it in. And then I was going to sell it, it would sit somewhere, in a gallery, and only I'd know, and it would be like a song, to us. Do you see?"

I'm shaking my head, crying so much I can't speak.

"We don't need to tell anyone anything, Anna. No one needs to know. Not about your mother, not about Isabelle, not about Monica."

"Oh god, Luis. Yes, they do." I wipe my nose with the back of my hand. "They will know about Isabelle, they'll figure it out, and there's June…"

"Don't worry about June, babe. I'll take care of June."

"You have to let her go! I'll tell everyone what you did if you hurt her—you have to let her go, Luis!" I've turned around and I'm on my knees, scrambling to get to my feet but he grabs my ankle and I fall, hitting my head against the corner of the coffee table. He's yelling for me to stop. He's shouting: *Where are you going? What are you doing?* He wants me to listen, but I can't listen anymore, and I'm screaming and kicking him and there's a second when he lets go and yelps in pain and there's a door next to the fireplace and I've lunged through it and slammed it shut after me and I lean against it, panting.

It's June's bedroom.

"What are you doing? Babe? Don't make me do this! Anna?"

He's kicking the door and I'm screaming for him to stop and suddenly he's on top of me and he pulls my hair and slams the side of my head on the floor and I'm clawing for something, anything and with one hand I've grabbed the leg of the bedside table and I've pulled it so hard the lamp has come crashing down and Luis is swearing, and I can't reach the lamp and I claw at the drawer of the table, grappling blindly, and then I feel it.

Small, hard, metallic.

June's gun.

I've kicked him hard in the face and he holds his nose, his face scrunched up in pain and I'm on my feet, my arms outstretched, my hands shaking so hard I don't know how long I can hold it.

Luis drops his arms to his sides. His nose is bleeding. He shakes his head slowly. "No. Don't." Then suddenly his hands are on my face and there's a noise, so fast, so sharp, it rips through the air and, just as quickly, silence. Except for a high-pitched sound, like a whistle.

Luis smiles so sweetly and his eyes fill with tears and when he mouths the words, *I love you*, it's pure and real and he looks down at the blood on his chest and I scream but I can't hear myself, just the high-pitched noise, and when he falls I fall with him and hold him tight, and I say it to him, over and over, *I'm obsessed with you.*

CHAPTER 41

I stand at the window gazing at the trees filled with brilliant white blooms. They're all over campus, blossoming in unison, tall and dense, wide and round at the bottom and pointy at the top, which has always struck me as poetic, since they're ornamental pears, and they really are shaped a bit like the fruit they bear.

"Hey."

I turn around. June has walked in with a plate of cookies. I laugh.

"A selection of your favorites," she says, setting it down on the desk. We hug even though I saw her this morning. I stay with her in her new place whenever I've needed to return for the investigation.

I grab a cookie and sit down at my desk. Which is not really my desk anymore, although no one has filled this office yet.

"It's so quiet around here," I say.

"I know, spring break, no students. Don't you love it?"

"I sure do." It's the first time I've been back to Locke Weidman since Luis died, so I'm grateful there are very few students around. I don't think I could handle the stares, although I'm getting a lot better at that.

"How is Roberto?" she asks. I smile. She's the only who calls him that and I think he secretly loves it.

I smile. "Rob's wonderful. He's been taking the kids fishing a lot."

"They'll love that," she says.

I will never forget—and I've said this so much lately—the day Luis's father, Rob, came to get me outside the court house. We had just found out so many things about Luis. That he had been forging my signature for years. That he signed for my inheritance, that he forged a power of attorney to act on my behalf so he could sell my mother's house once enough years had passed, and he kept the money, too. He never spent it. All this time it's been sitting in a term deposit account which he had opened, also in my name.

But there was one thing I never knew, which was that when Luis was young he set fire to a man, and killed him. No one knows the circumstances exactly, and he was charged with involuntary manslaughter. Because of his age, he went to juvenile detention for eight months. Somehow, my mother found out and tried to tell me. But everything I believed about that still stands: it may have been the truth, but the only reason she wanted me to know was to hurt me. To push me to end the relationship because she just didn't like to see me happy. It would have made no difference if she'd told me. I would have believed with all my heart whatever Luis did back then had been *involuntary*.

But that day on the lawn outside the court house, Rob broke down and sobbed on my shoulder because he'd never told me about it. *But we both thought he was good and kind*, I said. *You didn't know either, what he was capable of. You thought he'd made a mistake, you didn't want it to tarnish the rest of his life. I would have done the same for my kids.*

But he put a hand over his eyes, and asked if I was going to forbid him from seeing his grandchildren now. "They all I have left," he said.

"So come and live with us," I replied. "They adore you. You're on your own now. Apart from me, you're the only family they have left. You're the only family *I* have left."

And he sobbed again on my shoulder, for a long time, but with relief, and some joy too, I think.

*

I've resigned from Locke Weidman, sold our house, and we've moved to Martha's Vineyard, to a small but charming rented house. The money I got from the sale of our house is not enough to buy something over here and, until earlier this week, I didn't know if I'd ever get the money in the term deposit account. I'm not sure I want it, anyway. And I certainly won't be receiving the prize money. The Forrester Foundation has kindly allowed me more time to give them my notebooks, but I'd already decided to refuse the prize. I wanted to wait until the district attorney concluded his investigation to tell them formally, and explain that it was Alex who solved it, with a little help from me, and that the prize should be awarded to him posthumously. Maybe his parents will use it to create a scholarship in his memory, especially now that the medical examiner has officially ruled his death was suicide.

This came about because of his ex-girlfriend, a young woman called Lauren who used to go out with him when they were together at NYU. She'd broken it off but he had refused to accept it. After two years of behavior that bordered on stalking, he had emailed her to say he wanted to show her something, and after that, he promised he would no longer harass her. It was the last thing he was asking of her.

I don't know the exact details of all this but, suffice to say, she flew over to visit him—without telling her parents, who would have forbidden it. When she arrived at the apartment, the door was not quite closed. He wasn't there. She walked in, waited, and she left. The consensus was that he had hoped she would understand he had killed himself because of her, and he wanted her to know.

Did I leave the door open? I must have. Because when I saw her picture I knew she was the young woman I'd passed on the stairs that day. Not because of her face—I never looked at her—but because of her ring. A class ring in the colors of NYU, silver and purple.

I don't know what he wanted to show her and I don't think he was going to kill himself. But some days I think maybe he was, and other days I think he was not well and he didn't know what he was doing.

But even without all that, it's a big letter to write, and my head just wasn't in it so I waited until the district attorney's decision, which has been made, as of last Monday. The DA decided on the evidence that there was no need to take the case to the grand jury, so, I'm free. I will write that letter today, make things right, and after I've packed the rest of my things from this office, I'm going home to my kids.

I point at a package on the desk. A UPS midsize box.

"What's this?" I ask June.

"I don't know. It came for you last week. How long are you staying, by the way?"

I pick it up, turn it around. "I'm going back tonight. You want to join us for your break? We'd love to have you."

"Yes, please!" June beams. "I've been brushing up on my chess skills. I can't wait to try them on Matti."

I laugh. Rob has taught Matti to play and now Matti's obsessed. And he's very good. He played all the time with June over Christmas and again when she came over last month, and she only beat him once.

"How are they?" she asks, as I retrieve a pair of scissors from the drawer and cut through the tape.

I stop, tilt my head at her. "You know, last time you were there, I heard Matti laugh for the first time. He sounded the way he used to. It was the most beautiful sound." She nods, and her eyes water. "And Carla has made some friends and there's a light returning in her eyes." I take a breath. "I think they're going to be okay."

"And you?" she asks. But it's a joke between us, because I reply, "I'm okay, and you?" And she'll say, "I'm okay, and you?" until we laugh. It's stupid, but it's *our* stupid. It's all part of our way of coping.

It's taken a lot of therapy for June to be where she is now. She's only just returned to work, and she's been promoted to senior administrator in the English department, but she doesn't know how long she'll stay. Not very long, is my bet.

It's taken a lot of therapy for me, too, but I have my kids, and Rob. And I never say this to anyone, but I miss Luis. I miss him so much some nights I cry myself to sleep.

June gets to her feet and brushes her hands. "I should get back to it. Lunch?"

"Yes please."

"Okay. I'll come get you around one."

After she's gone I finally open the UPS box. Inside is an envelope with my name on it, and below it is another, smaller, cardboard box, but this one is different. It's old and battered, like something you might have kept in an attic for the last fifty years. It isn't sealed and I lift the flaps.

It's the smell that hits me. An image of my old school flashes into my mind and for a surreal moment I am transported to another place and another time.

I pick up the letter and slide my finger inside its flap.

Dear Dr. Sanchez,

You wouldn't remember me but we met once. My name is Vernon and I used to share Alex's condo in Tremont. In the chaos of moving out I accidentally packed some of Alex's things, and everything has been in storage until now, which is why I haven't returned these to you before. These notebooks belonged to Alex but as they bear your name I am returning them to you.

Sincerely,
Vernon Tuckey

I open the box again. Inside are plain, wire-bound notebooks of varying colors. I know the style well—I used the same when I was at school. But these are old and musty, discolored in places.

I pull out the first notebook from the pile and open the page and there's a moment when it feels like the room tilts as I read my own name, in my own childish handwriting, on the first page: *Anna Miller*

I snatch Vernon's letter from the table and read it again. ...*but as they bear your name...*

This makes no sense. And how would Vernon know my maiden name? I pull all the notebooks out, more frantic now. Twelve of them in total.

The Pentti-Stone conjecture, a solution, by Anna Miller

It's like reading another girl's old schoolwork. Pages and pages of mathematical equations in small, dense handwriting that starts neat in the early pages but seems to trip over itself by the last ones. Lines and lines of calculations framed by doodles of flowers, round petals floating over the margins, sometimes Hope's name with a little heart to it, my mother's diagonal flick of the pen across the page.

I did this? Yes, I did. I know it, but I don't. I recognize the sequences, the logic, the rationality, the inferences, but I recognize them from Alex's notebooks, and I am shocked that, at the time, I didn't recognize my own work.

Then I see why Vernon returned them to me. Inside the cover page of a number of them is written: *Dr. Anna Sanchez, senior lecturer, mathematics department, Locke Weidman University.*

I know that handwriting and it's not mine, it's Alex's. I flick through every notebook, every page, more frantic now. They are riddled with his notes, exclamation marks, excited markings. *So close! Yes! No! Why?*

I lift the old cardboard box and study it, looking for a clue. On its side, in blue marker, is written: *$2 the lot.*

I vaguely remember when I moved out of home to go to college, my mother had a yard sale of all the things I was leaving behind, including my textbooks. She could've written this. This could well be her handwriting. This box would have contained my math books too; she would have packed the whole lot together. How it came to be in Alex's possession, I don't think I'll ever know.

I go through each notebook again, one by one, and I am shocked at how far I had come to solve the Pentti-Stone. But I remember distinctly showing these to my mother, my heart quickening with anticipation and her shaking her head: "No, Anna. That's not right. Try again."

But it *was* right. How could she not see it? Did she deny it on purpose, because she didn't want to live up to her end of the bargain? *If you solve the Pentti-Stone then you can go and play.* She never believed I could solve it. She never bothered to check my work. She just slashed the pen across the page with barely a glance. *No, that's not right, try harder.*

And how could I not remember these? Is this what trauma does? Makes you block things out? I remember nothing that is in these notebooks other than the pain and the frustration they still evoke now. The moment my mother released me from working on the Pentti-Stone conjecture, I banished the content from my mind but I could not forget the anger, the sadness, and I never wanted to think of it again, until Alex brought it up, and then I had to.

I'd come so close. As close as Alex was when he showed me his own drafts. Which makes sense, since they were mine. I remember him coming to the university—because of me, he'd said. He'd read a paper I'd published, a perfectly ordinary paper on Brownian motion, a topic completely unrelated to the Pentti-Stone.

"I must do my thesis here! With you!" he'd said. Of course he had. He already knew he was going to tackle the Pentti-Stone when he came to Locke Weidman. He was smart enough to know what these notebooks contained: the solution, except for one missing piece. He must have come to the conclusion he couldn't finish it alone, so he tracked me down. And irony of ironies, I finished it for him. I came up with the last piece of the puzzle. I called him in the middle of the night. *What if…?* Then I let him take all the credit because I'd only contributed that tiny morsel, believing he'd done everything else.

He hadn't. I had. And after that, I was no longer needed.

I've changed my mind…

I go through them again, slowly this time. Then I open the last notebook to the last page of equations. There are still blank pages, untouched, at the back of that notebook, and I grab a biro from the holder and without having to look it up, I proceed to write down the last piece of the proof.

The letter I write to the Forrester Foundation, two hours later, is not the one I thought I'd write. It's a lot shorter, for one thing, and it makes my heart sing, for another.

Dear Jack,

I trust the enclosed twelve notebooks comply with your requirement for supporting documentation detailing my process to arrive at the solution.

With gratitude and kind regards,
Dr. Anna Sanchez, née Miller

A LETTER FROM NATALIE

Dear reader,

Firstly, a heartfelt thank-you from me for choosing to read *Unfaithful*. If you would like to keep up to date with my new releases, please sign up to my newsletter. Your email address will never be shared and you can unsubscribe at any time.

www.bookouture.com/natalie-barelli

Some books are easier to write than others. Some of them come almost fully formed in the writer's imagination before putting pen to paper or finger to the keyboard.

In writing *Unfaithful*, I chose to begin with this idea: Can our childhood experiences inform our adult choices to the point where we would break the law? Commit fraud, for example? Can Anna's actions, in taking credit for work that wasn't hers, be forgiven once we understand that being the best, being brilliant, winning prizes, was the only way she could get her mother to love her?

This novel was far from fully formed by the time I put finger to keyboard and after that initial idea, the story took many twists and turns. If you've come this far, you'll know that idea made up only one small part of the plot. But it was the germ of the story for me. After that, I let the characters tell me the rest. I hope they entertained you (and surprised you!) as much as they did me.

Reviews, as you probably know, are the best way for readers to discover our books, and if you enjoyed *Unfaithful* I would be hugely grateful if you would leave a review. It makes a massive difference, so thank you.

Until next time,
Natalie

ACKNOWLEDGMENTS

It takes one person to write a book, but it takes a lot of people to write a better book, and I'm massively lucky to have some brilliant people helping me along the way. This is where I get to thank them properly.

My favorite mathematician, Laura De Carli: I can't thank you enough for sharing your insight into the world of university mathematics, for your detailed answers to my many questions and for all your great suggestions.

The very kind and always patient Mark Freyberg, for answering all my law-related questions. This is the fourth time you are in these pages, Mark, and I am hugely grateful to you.

Jessie Botterill, editor extraordinaire, thank you so much for your patience, your enthusiasm, for fixing up all the bad bits and coming up with all the good bits. I can't wait for us to do it again.

My writing buddy, Debra Lynch: thank you for being such a great support and for making me laugh! (A lot!)

My family and my friends, for being such a generous cheering squad, especially my husband for supporting me above and beyond in every way.

And to you, dear reader, for reading this book. It means the world.